Marigold Armitage, elder daughter of Sir Arthur ('Bomber') Harris, was born on an RAF station in Lincolnshire. During World War II she was an ambulance driver and a despatch rider. After her marriage she went to live in Ireland (Tipperary and Limerick); whilst in Ireland she wrote the novels *A Long Way to Go* and *A Motley to the View*. Returning to Yorkshire she wrote the play *Angels on Horseback*. After many years of hunting, racing, breeding chasers and whippets she now lives in the West Country.

A Motley to the View

by

Marigold Armitage

Alas, 'tis true I have gone here and there,
And made myself a motley to the view,
Gored mine own thoughts, sold cheap what is most
dear . . .

Sonnet CX

Robin Clark
London

First published in paperback by Robin Clark Ltd in 1990
27/29 Goodge Street
London W1P 1FD

First published by Faber & Faber Ltd in 1961
© 1961 Marigold Armitage

British Library Cataloguing in Publication Data
Armitage, Marigold
A motley to the view.
I. Title
823'.914[F]

ISBN 0-86072-128-0

Printed and bound in Great Britain by
Cox & Wyman Ltd., Reading, Berks.

To
RUPERT and PETER
with love

The previous experiences referred to by some of the characters in this book have been related in *A Long Way to Go*.

Chapter One

"It will end in tears," said Gillian. "That's for sure, admit?"

Benny was looking tough, and loving it. Wearing a fantastically and quite unnecessarily dirty T-shirt, and a pair of corduroy trousers belonging to me, which really had washed white under the slow hands of Nature and Nanny, he stared ahead into the setting sun, his eyes narrowed dramatically, his dark, mad face glistening with spray. The wind was coming in sudden, forceful gusts off the mountains, sending catspaws, like strips of velvet stroked the wrong way, across the bay. Every time these reached the dinghy she heeled sharply, the sea hissed creamily over her lee strakes, and Gillian—steering rather tentatively and humming "Night and Day" under her breath; always a sure sign of strain with Gillian—let her come up into the wind. After this had happened a time or two Benny said restively, "You shouldn't keep luffing in a small boat like this, baby."

"I'm not," said Gillian sharply. "I don't think it's in the least funny—I'm actually quite frightened, but I'm so brave I don't show it. What's more, I'm almost certain I'm feeling sick."

"Gee, you poor kid, you. Let me take her."

"Certainly not. You're not in the least sympathetic, you just want to show off. Ah, there!" She luffed again.

"Honey," Benny said, "I just want to show you what you should do, instead of luffing this way."

9

"But I'm *not* doing anything of the kind—I'm what they call grim-faced."

"*Luffing*, kid, not laughing, is what you keep doing."

"Well, that's what I was taught to do—and do stop talking, you have such a lovely, virile voice."

"You shouldn't do it, all the same, honey, in a small boat like this," said Benny, whose voice, I reflected now, was indeed almost aggressively lovely and virile—French-Canadian in origin and now speaking American with a wildly rolled r and the faint, lilting remains of a tonic accent—it seemed unfair that Benny should have that voice, as well as so much else that was so effortlessly dramatic.

"I was taught in *big* boats," said Gillian provocatively, "tremendous, rich numbers at Cowes."

"O.K., honey, O.K." Benny was not subdued. "Just hand this bucket over to me, then, and you can get sick in comfort and learn about how the poor live."

The wind came again, in a puff forceful enough to raise a faint howl as it came. Gillian luffed up into it automatically, and Benny groaned.

"Don't you see, baby, how you keep stopping her? This boat has so little shoot in her she stops dead at once—and a boat with no way on her in a wind is a dangerous boat, see?"

"Lend an ear to the old sea dog, darling," I said. Benny, to my certain knowledge, had never been in a sailing boat until the last two weeks. I watched and waited, in admiration and irritation, hoping that neither of them would actually capsize the dinghy and then expect me to set matters in train again.

"What do you want me to do, captain, sir?" Gillian now asked Benny, rather hufflly. "Press on all canvas and drive her under, I suppose? Always the one for sensation. . . ."

"You get me wrong, kid, dead wrong—I'm just a perfectionist."

"Well, that's a great thing to be if you don't weaken."

"Sure it is—it's the *only* thing to be."

"So what should I do?"

"Why, just slack off the mainsheet, honey, when the wind hits you, and haul it in again when it eases off."

"Do you see my tiny, white hands?"

"Sure," said Benny, drawling reverently, speaking silently of love and lust and longing, creating suddenly in the little cold, creaking, salty boat a quite other, boundless world of darkness, warmth and tactility. He smiled slowly at Gillian, with his infinite, intimate charm, his strange face full of the tenderness and sympathy that never quite reached his empty, restless eyes. The voice is unfair, I thought again, idly.

"I do so agree, darling," said Gillian, answering Benny, not my thoughts. "And just think how they'd look if I hauled in and slacked off on this great rope for an hour or two."

"Give her to the he-man, little woman," I said. "Let him show off his muscles."

"I have some good ones, at that," said Benny, unmoved. "Any time the little woman wants". He took the boat confidently from Gillian, and, hunching his shambling length over the tiller began a recitative about a girl from Venezuela who wore a blue sash ("Why blue?" asked Gillian, restively) which she had been awarded for all the things she could do. He sang the chorus very loudly in his lovely, virile voice, and appeared to be completely oblivious of our presence.

"He ought to be in the zoo," said Gillian, peering fondly out at him from the shelter she had taken on my lee side.

"He is," I said. "We all are, of course, but he's the one people come to see."

"They ask where he is as soon as they get through the turnstiles."

"They buy bags of very special tit-bits for him."

"Then they're disappointed when they find they're not allowed to feed him."

Benny sang on.

His thin T-shirt was soaked. I was wearing a flannel shirt and a thick sweater, and was regretting having had to part with my coat to Gillian, whose tiny hands were very frozen, and whose teeth chattered suddenly from time to time when she forgot to keep her face stiff. A late September evening in a small boat homing after a long day in the sun can be astonishingly chilly, even off the Mediterranean coast of Spain—but Benny had no small human weaknesses like feeling the cold. His were all tremendous, impressive Hemingway ones, like women and bulls and brandy.

"It will end in tears," said Gillian. Benny looked languidly sideways at her along the sparkling white sand, dropping cigarette ash on to his naked, black-haired chest. "You mind that, honey?" he inquired, gently surprised.

"Of *course* I mind it. I'm not a sadist like you. I'm just a normal, healthy girl—I hope."

Benny made the thick, choking sound that meant he was amused.

"You tell me what normal is, what healthy is, huh?"

"I do not, darling. Maybe *you're* healthy and normal but, if so, God send me three legs and a frightening disease."

"Anthony might not like that, baby."

"Well, if he's a polymorphous pervert. . . ."

"Honey—you been reading a book?"

"That's what you said last night."

"Last night! Last night I was drunk. Last night doesn't

count any more. Last night never counts. Last night is last night."

"Not for the head waiter it isn't, darling, I bet you, nor for that female with the wig, nor, I'm *quite certain*, for that blonde."

"Yeah, the wig . . . the wig was something . . . really something." Benny scratched himself reflectively and yawned, stretched, rubbed his feet in the sand, curled and uncurled his toes, coughed and spat, grinning, unself-conscious as an animal. "The wig . . ." he murmured happily, closing his eyes.

Gillian watched him with fascination. "I don't think he's actually got to the zoo yet—he's still in the jungle, wouldn't you say? He drops on his prey from trees."

"Very likely."

Benny appeared to be asleep. With his mouth half-open, his too long hair, gluey with salt water, falling across his eyes, he looked pretty horrible, and rather ill into the bargain—as well he might, I reflected. He snored faintly. A look of delighted anticipation came into Gillian's face suddenly. She pointed silently over my shoulder, and I looked round. Last night's blonde, undressed for battle, and looking appallingly luscious in that sparkling air, was heading for us with determination.

"Some people *like* being dropped on from trees, that's all," said Gillian. With one accord we slithered shiftily away through the burning, creaking, white sand—away from Benny, away from the disasters, the misbehaviours, the fireworks, the incredible brouhaha that surrounded him like some strange personal miasma, and in which he knew so well how to embroil his oddly faithful, appalled, despairing friends.

Much later on, back in the London fog, Gillian said to me again, "It will end in tears."

13

We were sitting in a plushy place listening to a smoothly finished girl with a gin-husky voice singing old Jean Sablon songs and looking as if she couldn't wait to go to bed with the microphone.

"Very probably," I said. "Everything that happens to Benny, or that Benny causes to happen, ends in tears—for other people."

"Then *why*——"

"Big money, darling."

"But what about Your Art?"

"Anybody who uses capital letters in a voice like that ought to be spanked."

"All right, but what about it?"

"To hell with it," I said, feeling noble and badly-used and barely able even to laugh at myself for feeling it. A few months before, my contract to write plays for that meretricious mummer Richmond Kerr had come to the end of its term, and I had decided not to take up the option on its renewal because I was deathly tired of the type of drawing-room-comedy-laced-with-bitter-sweet-undertones that it required me to write for him. I had written instead a play that I had wanted to write for years —put my heart's blood into it, toiled and sweated and despaired over it, attempted—possibly a feeble attempt—a certain amount of intellectual honesty.

The result had been that no management would touch it. If I had been a small boy I should now have been kicking stones gloomily, with my hands in my pockets—a healthy reaction, and not one likely to have repercussions on innocent bystanders, unless they determinedly place themselves in the path of the stones—but I was supposed to be an adult person, so instead I was going to make dollars by writing a screen play for Benny, and thus show that curious, amorphous hierarchy known as Them, that somebody thought I was brilliant, somebody, in fact, wanted me.

14

As I sat, now, sulking, kicking my stones, Benny and Phillippa appeared, and there was a stirring along the smoky-grey silken banquettes; a smoothing of sables; a shifting sideways of male eyes and a narrowing of female ones. For Benny was famous. His dark, mad, simian face, wearing a confused expression of pleased reproach to those who had this curious wish to photograph him, was at this time scarcely ever out of the papers, and Phillippa's heart-halting beauty had been celebrated in a sonnet sequence—very inadequately, I had always thought—by an archbishop of a poet who was more famous than Benny, though not nearly as often photographed. I had known Phillippa, on and off, for ever, but never in that long time, meeting her again after absence, had I failed to be astonished and moved by the morning star quality of her beauty, which—rare, rare though it be—yet exists, and enables its owner to look even more beautiful when tired or recovering from 'flu.

Phillippa looked tired now; but that only made the faintly violet shadows of her temples lie more tenderly on her white skin, and the honey hair droop a little darkly, in touching tendrils, behind her enchanting ears.

"Her clear shining is never laid to sleep," I said, mistakenly, out loud.

"What?" said Gillian, letting me down: and, to Phillippa, "Darling, you look so tired. But, oh my goodness, how I wish I could look like that when I'm *not* tired."

Phillippa grinned, and became a witty Madonna, faintly blasphemous, and quite entrancing. "Do you hear the nice lady?" she asked Benny.

"Yeah, I hear her," said Benny, glumly. I became uneasily aware that he was in one of his worst moods. He was slouching far more than was necessary, and turning his lowered head angrily from side to side, like a bull making up its mind about its charge.

"Only this morning," said Phillippa cheerfully to us, "he told me I had a face like a lump of china clay."

"I do so hate husbands, don't you?" said Gillian. "But fear nothing, we have delicious drinks ordered."

Before the drinks arrived, however, Benny suddenly made up his mind about the direction of his charge.

Dissociating himself from us, he picked up his chair, carried it across the crowded and surprised room, and set it down very cosily beside the sultry singer's piano.

"Well, for heaven's sake. . . ." we heard him say.

"Someone he knows?" asked Gillian.

"Someone's he's going to know," said Phillippa, resignedly.

The diseuse, obviously a girl who knew how to live, began without hesitation to sing the theme song from Benny's latest film, and somebody's over-enthusiastic cousin (we must take poor Helen along—after all, she's only up for two nights, and she never gets any fun) began to clap, and was sternly hushed by her more sophisticated relatives.

"Isn't he hell?" said Phillippa, faintly and fondly.

"Darling," said Gillian, pressing a delicious drink on her, "it's no good saying *how could you*—because one does so see how you could."

And that was just it, of course. The first reaction of anyone seeing Benny and Phillippa as husband and wife would always be how *could* she?—followed, very swiftly, as his shocking charm began its subtle, amoral work, by how could she—or, indeed, any woman—not?

"Do we get him back tonight, do you suppose?" asked Gillian.

"I wouldn't know," said Phillippa.

"Anthony can try trapping him when we've finished these delicious drinks." She had already finished her own and she now picked up the one waiting for Benny, and smiled at me over it with her dark, entrancingly tired eyes. I saw what she meant. He had been quite drunk enough when he came in. "I'd rather try trapping a gorilla," I said.

"That would be child's play," said Phillippa.

"It will end in tears," said Gillian again, solemnly.

"When I say a thing three times it's true?"

"Whatever number of times I say it it's true, and you know it. It's madness for us to go to Ireland again, and it's peculiar, deliberate madness to go to Ireland with Benny, bless his heart. You know I couldn't love him more, don't you darling?" she added, belatedly, to Phillippa, in whose flat we were dining, "Where is he, by the way?"

"So far as I know," said Phillippa, with delightful deliberation, "he's what they call shacked up with Rose Hillchester."

"That bitch!" said Gillian, after a short, reverent silence. "Well, we all go through it, darling. But the last time I saw her, which was about a week ago, she said she had a slipped disc, and was in plaster up to the neck."

"Poor old sweet," I said. "Shall we ring up and see how she's making out?"

I was prevented from indulging in this not very kind act by the sudden arrival in the doorway of a small, disapproving blond bulldog clad in a rather disgusting nightshirt with rabbits all over it, and on the verge of tears—Phillippa and Benny's son, aged four. "I'm wet," he announced, defiantly, glowering, rocking with sleep, his lower lip thrust ominously forward, his fine angel's hair standing peakily on end, damp with sleep.

"O, *darling*," Phillippa scooped him up cosily into her lap. "So you are, you terror."

He lolled his tender head confidently and triumphantly against her and asked, "Can I smell your Martini?"

17

"Why aren't you in bed?" Phillippa countered rather weakly.

He thought very deeply for a moment, and then said "I were", like somebody successfully answering an awkward question in the House.

"He has all his father's skill in sliding out of difficult situations," said Phillippa proudly, and gave him her Martini to smell. He buried his convex button nose in it, sniffed dramatically, and looked at me challengingly.

"I *like* it," he said.

"So do I," I told him.

This clearly disappointed him. He had hoped that I might be immensely shocked, and then he would have been able to tell me again how much he liked it. He looked around for a more sensitive audience, and his glowing blue eye fell on Gillian. "I sipped," he said to her.

"So did I," said Gillian.

He looked at her rather strictly.

"Once, Panda sipped."

"All right—I'm shocked."

"Panda loves Martinis—will I show you Panda?"

"Yes, please," said Gillian.

"I'm afraid his Panda is Wet, Madam," said a repressive voice. Phillippa's nurse had arrived. She was a cheerful square girl with a bad skin and, luckily, a great pure passion for Phillippa, whose sufferings she liked to fancy were shared. She advanced upon her charge, who immediately began to burrow hysterically into Phillippa's bosom, with short, sharp howls of rage and despair.

"He's not really crying," said Phillippa in a voice of unconvincing firmness, trying not very hard to disengage herself.

"Not a bit of it," said Nurse Simmons comfortingly. "Just see, he can't squeeze a tear. Don't let him worry you, Madam."

She plucked him skilfully off, as if he had been a leech, and shook him with a gaiety to which he did not respond. "Out of bed the minute my back is turned, and Wet into the bargain! What do you suppose the lady and gentleman will think?"

She hurried him off, shrieking, bent defiantly backwards into a purple-faced bow in her arms.

"O, dear," said Phillippa, twitchily. "I always long to go and comfort him, but nurse won't let me."

"She's so right," said Gillian. "Couldn't you get one like that for Benny?"

"I don't think even a College Trained Nanny (that's what she's called) could deal with Benny while he's an Existentialist, poor sweet."

"Poor sweet Benny, or Nanny?"

Phillippa smiled. "Whose side do you think I'm on?" She rose, with her unique, gentle grace. "I'll just go and kiss him good night and look into the Panda situation."

"It's weak," said Gillian.

"I know. Give yourselves a drink." She blew us a mocking kiss, and went.

"Well," I said. "Some chaps are lucky. Imagine having a mother like Phillippa to kiss one good night."

"How disloyal."

"You know you're not the maternal type, my love."

"No, I suppose not . . . though I always long to be. . . . O, dear, I do wish Phillippa had married almost anyone else—Guy Hillchester, even."

"Der solide Mensch?"

"Exactly."

"Such a waste of Phillippa—she'd have nothing to work on at all."

"She might find that a relief."

"Come, come, my love. You know she adores Benny."

"Explain being an Existentialist to me?" said Gillian, chasing a bit of lemon peel round the bottom of her glass.

"Not in so many words, I couldn't."

"Try. Does it mean you exist?"

"Roughly."

"It sounds dreadfully dreary, doesn't it? Like an old donkey in a wet field in November."

"An old donkey in a wet field in November is a mad whirl of gaiety compared to an existentialist boîte on the left bank at *any* time of year."

"But you couldn't say Benny isn't gay. He's relentlessly gay."

"He's just skimming the cream. Any minute now he'll turn into a Zen Buddhist, mark my words."

"Darling, you haven't told me a thing."

"No. Well—the idea is that you must never not do whatever it is you happen to feel like doing at any given moment—that if you fancy giving your dear old white-haired Mom a dose of rat-poison you mustn't feel bound by any preconceived code of ethics, morals, religions, or what have you, as to whether you do it or not."

"How quaint and old-fashioned."

"Old-fashioned?"

"Well, it's straight back to whatever Piltdown Man wasn't, isn't it?"

"Darling, I love you dearly."

"So do I. . . . Wouldn't Rose be maddened if she knew that the great director is shacked up with her because he mustn't feel bound not to? I can't wait to explain it to her."

"If I know Benny he's already explained it to her, and if I know Rose she thinks it's wonderfully original of him. He has to realize himself, he's told her, by choosing freely without referring to any code of conduct outside himself."

"The silly kipper," said Gillian indulgently. "Isn't he referring like mad to existentialism? Doesn't he feel terribly bound not to feel bound, because whoever made up the new rules told him he mustn't?"

"Say that again, if you can?"

But Phillippa came back then, wearing that fatuous and touching expression of inner content and outward self-depreciation worn by all good mothers who are yet not without a sense of the effect their cherished young may have upon their friends.

"If we do go to Ireland," said Gillian, "don't let's go back to Knockmoree, for Godsakes."

"We couldn't, anyway, it wouldn't be big enough to hold us all."

"*Because*, darling, you do realize, don't you, that I'm still not absolutely safe about Roger?"

"What do you mean?" I asked, knowing perfectly well what she meant.

"Sometimes I feel I could be madly sensible about him, and don't think about him at all, quite honestly, for months at a time, and then suddenly something happens —like last week, I was looking at a *Queen* while my angel Bruno was combing me out, and there he was—Roger, I mean—at some opening meet or other—looking, I must say, quite hideous and half-witted, and goodness, he has put on weight—absolutely nothing there to inspire a girl at all you would think—but suddenly all my guts went into one tremendous cold knot, and I couldn't breathe properly."

"That's a sure sign of true love," I said, unkindly. "Indistinguishable from having eaten a doubtful oyster."

"I could slap you," said Gillian, without heat.

But I saw that she looked suddenly woebegone and

rather strained, and I wondered quite seriously for a moment if the whole curious, slightly bogus, project really would end in more genuine tears that we had bargained for, and if so, by whom and for whom the tears would be shed.

Chapter Two

We had just run across Benny, without surprise, on the Spanish Mediterranean coast, where he was lurking with a dark, dramatic and, I thought, rather dirty, girl who had tremendously intense views on cinematic art—but had abandoned them and him after the episode of the blonde and had returned, bravely holding back the tears, to the flat in Kensington Court which she shared with My Friend, and from which she should never have departed. When I asked Benny why he had bothered thus to upset the poor girl he had looked surprised, and had said that she seemed to want to come—which appeared, when Benny said it, to be quite sufficient reason, explanation, and apology—if apology were necessary at all—for the whole hideous episode.

Gillian, who had known Phillippa since they had squeakingly gone cub-hunting together on wise, self-sufficient ponies, had said to Benny rather coldly, "How can you be so messy, darling?" and Benny had grinned and poured himself some more Fundador and held his hand out to her lovingly and invited her to go to Athens with him—and, she told me, she had very nearly done so at once.

"Do stick closer than a brother, Anto—*much* closer—while he's around. He fascinates me—I feel just like a poor frail, willing rabbit in front of a quite irresistible stoat."

In this fashion Charles Benoit, French-Canadian by birth, English by adoption, international by reputation Hollywood by tendencies of taste, and at heart perhaps nothing at all—for anyone who aspires to be all things to all men takes the slow but irrevocable journey towards becoming no man—had romped disastrously through his forty-five years, bringing tremendous bother to his friends; ulcers to his business associates; romance to the one or two nice, foolish women who were too silly not to believe what he told them; a sensation of helpless fury to countless nasty, clever women, and something close to heartbreak to Phillippa, who unfortunately happened to love him.

Phillippa's first husband, tall, blond, simple, sunburnt even in the winter, and as honourable and lovable as a golden retriever, had died gallantly at Salerno, his honour and simplicity intact, in a manner which had earned him a posthumous M.C., and Phillippa, who had become engaged to him in her first season—never doubting for an instant that here was her true love—was left with a golden retriever puppy of a son and a good deal of money; both of which she took back to her old home in Gloucestershire, where they were received with open arms by her father, who was very fond of children and money. With Phillippa's willing co-operation he greatly enlarged the home farm, built a palace, neat but not gaudy, for his Guernseys, laid down a tremendous amount of port and madeira that didn't need laying down ("for the boy"), increased his subscription to the hunt, and at the same time organized bigger and better fox-shoots amongst his willing farming neighbours. He was a much detested figure at local meets, when he would stand four-square amongst hounds, maddeningly knowledgeable ("What was the bitch? Vanity? Ah, yes, Belvoir Weaver, of course . . . great nose . . . great nose. . . .") and announcing that the new huntsman couldn't kill foxes, he wasn't a real foxy feller.

"He really was heaven," said Gillian, who had stayed there a lot during this period, while resting from her own first husband. "Such a bluff, stupid member of the county, you know—a backwoods baronet trying to do his duty by King and Country, and baffled by the knaves in office who made the milk accounting so difficult and *such* a thorough-going old knave himself at heart. I've never forgotten the goings-on when Phillippa announced she was going to marry Benny—tremendous stumpings-about, and 'I will not have a daughter of mine marryin' a film-actin' feller' but, of course, feelers out like anything in the States to find out exactly how favourable the dollar situation would be if she did."

"You might have thought", I had said, "that Phillippa, tucked up in the depths of the country with lovable papa and little son and the Guernseys, would have been fairly safe from Benny."

"Nobody is *ever* safe from Benny. He had one of his spaniel-women on his hands at that time, and he had suddenly decided—you know Benny—that an old fishing inn would be romantic. When he found it wasn't, he began to look around for something that would at least be comfortable—Phillippa and her papa happened to come into the pub for a drink, and that was that."

"Don't tell me that Sir John deserted his rôle sufficiently to welcome into his house a completely strange film-actin' feller and his spaniel-woman?"

"No, not quite. Phillippa told me that he and Benny hypnotized each other from the start. Benny got under his guard with some informed chat about sporting prints —I expect he'd found a book lying about and read it out of boredom—and it ended with papa asking Benny to luncheon on Sunday, and totally ignoring the spaniel—if only it had been a *real* spaniel, poor sweet, it could have gone along."

"And Benny went to luncheon on Sunday?"

"Naturally."

"Alone?"

"Naturally. I can just see it all, can't you? He would have rung up some side-kick in London, and told it to ring him back with some startling information about something breaking wide open in Paris and needing his immediate attention. There would have been great chat about chartering a plane from Bristol. Then he would have patted the spaniel, given it its fare, and popped it into the next train, saying he would call it as soon as he got back, and leaving it terrifically impressed—can't you just see?"

"Yes, easily. Was Benny ever taken in by lovable papa, do you suppose?"

"I don't really know. He would rather fancy a hale old aristocrat, of course. But Phillippa told me once that she thought papa had gone a tiny bit too far at that very first Sunday luncheon, when he told Benny he was just readin' a very interestin' book about an extraordinary feller called Pan—poor chap never grew up—you ought to make a film of it—can't you hear him saying so?"

Phillippa herself had never been in the least taken in by her lovable papa, and had never ceased to find him lovable; being herself capable of an amused, tolerant, and compassionate love—a rare capacity, which, having been entirely wasted on the golden lad now come to dust, was now being strained to its uttermost by Benny, so often too busy being a legend to remember that he was supposed to be a man.

"Do let's go to Ireland, Anto, darling," Phillippa said to me. "Why are you being so fearfully stuffy and unresponsive about it? It will be so restful, and we can hunt all the time. Do encourage Benny like mad?"

"He doesn't need any encouragement," I said, gloomily. "He already sees himself as the Surtees of the film industry, salting sport with social satire."

"Too many s's," said Phillippa. "Let's go, anyway."

"What makes you think that it will be so damned restful? If it was so restful last time that Benny wants to make a film about what happened, what do you suppose will happen this time?"

"I can't think," said Phillippa. "But I'm mad for an uncomfortable eighteenth-century house, with bad, willing servants and lots of dust and hound puppies and young horses—O, the heaven, after Beverley Hills! *Please*, Anto?"

"Hell," I said, "Benny will go, anyway, whether I do or not."

"No, he *won't*, darling—I know he won't—he's got it into his mind that you are the only person who could write the screenplay for it. He's dead right, of course. So please, Anto? Otherwise it will be that film about gauchos—and that will mean Mar del Plata."

"Many poor girls would give their all to go to Mar del Plata for the winter."

"Can't you imagine how boring glamour can get? Endless, endless glamour . . . I want stable smells and turf fires and cabbage and dirty paws on the sofa. . . ."

"Whose?"

"Don't be disgusting, you know perfectly well I meant dogs, and *please* don't let me have to go to Mar del Plata. Darling, I mean it, please don't?"

She looked quite wild with misery, so I said, to cheer her, "We could live with Peter, I suppose."

She cheered at once.

"Would he like that?"

27

"He'd love it. He's always penniless and mad for lodgers—lodgers with dollars would be a dream."

"Peter who?"

"Peter Dungarvan."

"Oh, *Peter*—why didn't you say so? Yes, do let's do that. He was about when I was debbing, but I haven't seen him practically since then—goodness, how old we all are—I remember he was rather a dashing jockey before the war."

"He's had a tough time since," I said.

"Has he? Poor Peter—I know the *on dit*, of course."

"Which is?"

"Peter Dungarvan's gone completely native, he drinks like a fish, and he's damn near as crazy as his child." Phillippa wrinkled her gentle brow. "*I'm* not saying that, I'm just answering your question."

"He's the most remarkable man I know."

"Remarkable?"

"Yes. He's good."

"Oh," said Phillippa doubtfully.

"It's not half as disappointing as it sounds." Gillian encouraged her. "Anto has different ideas about goodness."

"Different from what?"

"If we ever get there, you'll see."

In the end we got there quite quickly. Benny could always make anything difficult that he wanted to do appear astoundingly simple and easy, just as he could make anything that he didn't want to do appear astonishingly and impossibly difficult.

He was bored with Sartre, and of being *l'homme libre* with Rose Hillchester, and he now spent hours glued to a telephone persuading somebody in California called, I think, Louie, that an Irish story would have tremendously much more appeal in every way than an Argentinian one, as well as a much better tax angle.

"Do I know it, kid?" I heard him ask, hoarse with emotion, at one moment. "*Do I know it!* Listen, has that country got something—and I'll deliver up the heart of it to you on a plate."

I listened, myself, with unashamed fascination, knowing the extent of Benny's acquaintance with the country the heart of whose mystery he was so ready to pluck out. He had once stayed with—or rather, in the castle of—a dissolute peer who at that moment was finding it wiser to stay in Jamaica, and who had rented the castle to a chum of his, a rich, renegade bookmaker who, conveniently, was himself finding it best to stay out of England for a bit. Besides the bookmaker, Benny's companions had been: his third wife, a charming, foolish, cheerful girl who enjoyed everything that came her way and didn't bother about anything else; a sweet and slender male artist, who had frightened the bookmaker badly by making passes at him; the chargé d'affaires in Paris of a South American republic and his newest, richest, and most newsworthy wife; a rude, successful jockey; and a minor African prince, who had madly enjoyed every moment of this simple Anglo-Irish country life.

I had an illegible letter from Peter, smudgily and irregularly typed, signed with an inky blot which might or might not have reminded a psychiatrist's patient of something. The only part I could read at first was the letter-heading, and it was some time before my eye became sufficiently accustomed to his highly individualistic style to enable me to decipher the rest.

". . . do come, I'd love to see you and Gillian again, only thing is, will you find it too uncomfortable? The draughts are hell. I remember Phillippa debbing—doesn't she lead a very dashing international existence with film stars these days? Won't she find this place very dull?"

("O, I *do* pray so," said Phillippa.)

I also had a letter from my mamma.

". . . *so* lovely, darling, to see you both again quite soon, I only wish you could come here, Nanny will be dreadfully disappointed, but if there are so many of whatever you say in your letter (it looks exactly like side-kicks—I thought that was something in football?) I daresay Hesther might make difficulties, although the servants would love it, of course, particularly if Mr. Benoit kept ringing up America, which is what they do, I believe. I saw a photograph of him in the *Sunday Express*—he looked untidy but very charming—Rose Hillchester knows him, but I expect you know that.

"Hubert is being a little tiresome at the moment—I daresay he gets tired managing the place, poor dear—and seems to want Roger to go and plant tea in Assam, so unsuitable, I believe the gin is quite dreadfully cheap there. Roger is delighted you are both coming over again, it will be such fun for him."

("O, I *do* pray not," said Gillian.)

Another letter from Peter ended up:

". . . Shall I quickly get out a tasty brochure, or just charge you all through the nose anyway? Are you well insured? The roof may fall in while you're here."

"Isn't he a love?" said Gillian to Phillippa. "And he really has a desperate time—hasn't got a tosser to keep the place up and works like a black, and looks after his perfectly heavenly child—she really *is* crazy—and can't ever get away."

She then drew a deep breath, and it appeared not unlikely that both she and Phillippa would burst into tears.

"He hunts four days a week," I said, bracingly. "And I don't think he particularly wants to get away."

"Don't be so bloody, darling," said Gillian, brushing

me off. "*And*—" she went on "—that perfectly heavenly French girl he married (he only just scraped out of Rose, mind you, the idiot) was killed by a flying bomb when she came over to see Peter in London, and he'd been in various hospitals for ages, because he got fearfully knocked about at Anzio and lost all his eyes and arms and legs and things——"

"Not all," I said, automatically, but hopelessly.

"Well, no, but bad enough, poor Peter, goodness knows, *and*. . . ."

The warm and glowing delight of being sorry for Peter was kindling in her eyes and in Phillippa's, and the next step, I knew, would be to produce a suitable wife for him. I knew, also, that there was nothing he would hate more. I went quietly away.

Peter Dungarvan has gone completely native, of course, he's really a hopeless chap, he drinks like a fish, and he's damn near as crazy as that child of his—so said the restless, throbbing drums of the bush telegraph, it seemed. They did not add, Peter Dungarvan is unselfish, unsuccessful, unlucky, and unselfpitying. The bush telegraph is always inclined to the limited view, beating out its swift, dramatic conclusions with no indecisive playing around with cause and effect. Somebody[1] once pointed out that one of the hardest things to face up to in life is the fact that to behave well may in the end make one a worse or weaker character. O, hell, I thought, I hope he can cope with us all—perhaps we ought to leave him in peace, he's really much too nice a chap for this sort of a circus.

When I said something of this kind to Gillian she replied, with a lack of logic so splendid and assured as to seem absolutely logical, "He managed not to marry Rose, so he must be fairly smart. I shouldn't worry, darling."

[1] I think it was Desmond McCarthy.

Chapter Three

Slowly, the curious caravan assembled, hounded on by Benny, nipping at its flanks like a sheepdog. One morning he appeared in a rich car and a dinner jacket, woke us up, and demanded that we should go with him to the airport to meet Jake Hogan, who was flying in from the States. Gillian squinnied sleepily up at Benny and then went grumblingly under the bedclothes, murmuring that it was too early to dress. I felt fairly disorientated myself.

"Why, for Chrissakes?"

"We-e-ll," Benny drawled consideringly, sitting at Gillian's dressing-table, and studying with care the remarkable circles under his bloodshot eyes, "We-e-ll, now, Jake's kind of a jumpy guy."

"All the more reason for us not to meet him at the airport—but I always thought he was desperate tough."

"Yeah—that's what makes him jumpy—people misunderstand Jake—he's a real nice warm-hearted guy, Jake."

"Then he certainly won't want us to meet him at the airport at this hour—not if he's that warm-hearted."

"Come on, kid, get dressed," said Benny reprovingly, "Don't fool around, there."

He leant forward and stared earnestly at himself in the looking-glass, then took up Gillian's comb and ran it slowly through his hair. It did no good. I got up as far as one elbow, lit a cigarette, and tried to assemble the will-power which I felt slowly and inexorably ebbing away from me.

"Listen, Benny—come clean. Jake Hogan is the tough guy darling of the teen-agers—why do you want him for a plotless genre story set in Ireland?"

"I don't want him, kid. I get him. But if I get him, I'll use him." He looked directly at me and said softly, like a hypnotist, "He could be a very good actor."

I uttered a four-letter word, and he lolled back and began to file his nails. The gentle menace in his attitude and in his next words was startling.

"Listen, your business is writing, ain't that so?"

"Maybe," I said, "when I get paid for it."

Gillian twitched beneath the bedclothes, apparently electrified by the atmosphere, even in sleep.

Benny stood up, yawning, and slouched over to the windows, where he stood with his hands in his pockets, looking out.

"City waking up . . ." he said. "It's always magic, any place. . . . You want to call it off, then?"

Gillian shot up suddenly, tousled, wan, and cross, and glared at him.

"*Yes*," she announced. "Yes, yes, *yes*, you great ape."

Benny looked round, smiling, full of warmth and charm. He came slowly over and knelt down by the bed and put his arms around Gillian and kissed her tenderly on the forehead.

"Then we won't, baby."

So we went to the airport to meet Jake Hogan—and his wife and his secretary and his publicity agent and his two boxers. (This had been an idea of the agent's—they were such masculine dogs—but he had forgotten about quarantine, and only the secretary knew their names.) Jake Hogan stood, looking sullen, half-way down the aircraft steps, and gave the photographers, who bounced and crouched indefatigably beneath him, his famous deadpan face—while beside him his wife achieved the not

33

inconsiderable feat of scintillating while standing still. Then Benny was photographed, looking ill and remarkable, but composed, in his dinner jacket. (The captions in the evening press said "Director Benoit had come straight from a late supper party.") Then I was photographed.

"You look so thin and surprised, darling," Gillian said later, studying the result.

"I was," I told her.

I had yet another letter from Peter saying that now he had Rupert Chichester staying with him—would we mind?

"Peter has Rupert Chichester staying with him, and wants to know if we mind."

"*Mind?* Why, I adore Rupert, he's so shameless, the old beast."

Rupert Chichester was the chap of whom all well-behaved and decently established people said "Of course, I simply will not have Rupert Chichester in my house." Nevertheless—if they were not too dull for Rupert to deign to visit them—they were secretly flattered to have him, and always allowed him into their houses at once, after giving the butler confidential orders about the silver, and sending the youngest housemaid to stay with her aunt.

Rupert was heir to his extremely grand and old and pompous uncle, whose only weakness lay in the almost panicky haste with which he was prepared to supply his nephew with remittance money. "Don't come anywhere near me, damn you," he would bawl down the telephone, "my solicitors will send you a cheque tomorrow." He always greatly pleased Rupert, who was fifty, by referring to him as "Poor John's boy".

The clubs and countries that were barred to Rupert had multiplied since he had been sacked from Eton at a tender age—"for being too good-looking", he held. "That's always been my trouble. People are jealous, just beastly jealous, that's all."

At one moment in his full life they had been so jealous that he had been forced to become a librarian for six months—a position in which it was highly doubtful he ever gave His Majesty any pleasure—at other times they had shot at him, and been shot by him. He had seduced their wives, played hot poker with them, issued them with false prospectuses, lamed their best hunters and sold them ruinous animals in exchange, poached their birds and salmon, corrupted their children, and generally abused their hospitality. Small wonder that people were, indeed, jealous. Rupert had been in and under all the most distinguished beds and out of all the best windows. He owed money all the time to all butlers, most brothels, any bookmaker who would take him on, the only two bootmakers to whom it was worth owing money, and Rosa Lewis. He had accepted as his due the two rich women who had been married by him and who had attempted to reform him; he had whizzed joyfully through their money even as they attempted it, and gone happily on his unreformed way; while they, not really very much wiser, but far less rich, had gone sorrowfully to work in flower and hat shops run by sympathetic but triumphant friends.

He had been hammered on the Stock Exchange. He had pleaded the Gaming Act. He had been asked to resign from his regiment (he had stayed in) and to go home while hunting with the Pytchley (he had stayed out). He had been posted in Tattersalls—and also as missing in the war. He had been missing, but only in a very curious quarter of Cairo, much to his uncle's disappointment and fury.

"I may be a ruin," Rupert would say, holding forth complacently in whatever club he had been allowed into for the moment, "but I'm an interesting ruin."

He was in fact more interesting than he knew to any-one who looked a little beneath the surface. A youthful hedonist—given the good looks, the health, and the money which are essential to success in hedonism—is a natural and joyful and charming thing; but an elderly one, with the money gone, the health going, and the looks in disrepair, is something different—something intensely sad, futile and desperate, moving in a void. Rupert knew it himself. He had the remnants of a good mind, and he was afraid.

"Isn't Rupert wonderful?" said Gillian. "There he is, lurking in Peter's crumbly old castle (I suppose because he was mixed up in that Tangier smuggling racket) and almost immediately great droves of famous, fascinating people like us, darling, come and stay there too. It's black magic, and I'm sure he made it happen—he prob-ably said Mass backwards, or ate a Virgin, or something, bless him."

"Very likely," I said.

"How about Peter's child?"

"How about her?"

"She's *so* lovely."

"Well?"

"Too crazy for Rupert and Benny to make passes at?"

"One can only hope so," I said.

Gillian became very chummy with Mrs. Jake Hogan, a vaguely mid-European beauty called Sachi Gosztonyi, a great star of the gossip columns ("These names make news") and a lesser star of the cinema. She was reported to have driven two directors crazy and caused a third to shoot himself, owing to her great penchant for getting herself popped into good parts by interested producers, and her total inability to be anything but her simple self once in them. She had superb dark blue eyes with dusty

36

blonde lashes that hung absolutely straight down over them like a silky fringe—a trick of bountiful Nature which made her look withdrawn and thoughtful, and lent her a sad, appealing dignity, as baffling as the face of an El Greco Saint would be on a trained chimpanzee. Gillian reported to me that she was busy buying delicious pants in dark grey corded satin and silk tartans, for the *cinq à sept.* I tried to visualize the *cinq à sept* when we were all gathered together in the sixth Earl of Dungarvan's draughty, crumbling pile in October, and failed utterly.

"I adore Sachi, but won't she drive Benny crazy, like the others, trilling about in his film?"

"Is she going to trill about in it?"

"So she says."

"In what capacity?"

"I can't think—unless there could be a brief shot of Ascot. She could be in that, tremendously unsuitable in white lace?'

"There isn't *going* to be a brief shot of Ascot, damn it."

"Not yet, there isn't, darling."

But I didn't really believe that of Benny, who was a serious student of, and craftsman in, his profession, and belonged also to the neo-realistic school. He was, it seemed to me, far more likely to rely on Father Sweeney and Paddy Casey and Dr. Herlihy than on Sachi Gosztonyi—however excitingly clad. I put this hopefully to him, and he nodded seriously, for once appearing attentive, and even worried.

"I know, kid, I know, but I've got to use what I get given, haven't I? God knows I can't tread any harder on Louie's toes, or we don't get any dollars at all to do this thing."

"But why do we get given Jake and Sachi, for God's sake?"

"They were kind of tied up already, you see, on account of that Argentine picture."

"Oh!" I said, not seeing.

"And Sachi is Louie's girl-friend, too."

"Oh!"

"Yeah."

"Well," I said, "I'm mad to see how you fit Louie's girl-friend into the Tipperary scene."

I had only spoken quite idly, half-joking, half-ironical, but now, to my amazement, Benny abruptly crashed his fist down on to the table where leaves of the script were scattered between us, and stood up. He looked down at me, scowling, resting his finger-tips on the table, and his hands were trembling.

"You think it's all flipping funny, I know, but it's all bloody heartbreaking, let me tell you. I want to make a picture the way I want to make it, and everybody's always right in there buggering it up. I want it to be true, and it never is. I see what I want to do, and what sort of punishment do you think I take not being allowed to do it, while wise guys like you stand around thinking up their wisecracks about the result?"

"For heaven's sake, Benny," I said, startled, "calm down. I was only joking."

"Yeah? Well, stop joking, willya? I'm not just in the joking mood today."

He sat down again heavily and ran a hand wearily across his eyes, up his forehead, and through his greying hair, leaving it standing wildly on end. He looked tired and ill and rather dazed. Phillippa had told Gillian that he never slept without drugs.

All my adult life I had known Benny to say Hullo to, but up till this moment I had always looked upon him as more or less a figure of fun—with his Hemingway weaknesses, his sipping at the fashionable philosophies of pessimism, his schoolboy preoccupation with physical courage, his wine, his wives, his women, his gambling, and his art. An attractive figure enough, even a fascinating one, but clearly labelled "not to be taken seriously".

But perhaps I was, after all, quite wrong? Perhaps, after all, he was real enough to be forlorn; real enough, even, to be tragic; perhaps some of the tears which Gillian kept so lightly prophesying would be, this time, shed by him and not by his victims.

There was now a farewell party at the Savoy, where Louie himself appeared, unexpectedly. (I never made out if he had come straight from California or not)—a sad, bald, bright man, full of jokes and desperation, who was frightened of Benny, and alternatively flattered and bullied him without any success at either. Benny remained adamantinely morose throughout dinner, drew horses on the tablecloth, and only spoke to people in other parties. Afterwards we went and played chemin-de-fer in somebody's rich flat, always a fatal move, and won and lost far too much money. Benny had a tableau on his cigarette case, needless to say. He had a gold swizzle-stick for the champagne, and he also produced an infallible cure for headaches when somebody's girl developed a headache— he went with her to the bathroom to show her exactly how it should be taken, and Phillippa went on nobly trying to soothe Jake Hogan, whose wife was being rather too openly appreciated by Louie. Jake Hogan grunted inattentively and drank whiskey. Benny had said he was kind of a hard-drinking guy at times, and I saw now what he meant. About half-past three Gillian observed furtively to me that she wished she was on a wet mountain with dull, cosy sheep, and I saw what she meant too— but presently, mercifully, the party ended, long, long after I had finally decided that it never would.

39

Then we really were all assembled at London Airport, and the familiar Dakota of Aer Lingus,[1] with its painted shamrock, its little green flag fluttering, its saint's name, awaited us. Once more the indefatigable photographers crouched and bounced around Benny, who was managing to look incredibly exotic in a perfectly normal tweed overcoat and cap; around Sachi, triumphantly normal in sables; and around Jake, contentedly sub-normal in a tremendously woolly belted overcoat and a soft hat pulled down over his eyes and tilted sideways.

It was a cold, grey heartless day, and the airport smelt of old leaves and petrol fumes and frost and something burning on autumn evenings, sad as death. All the black depression and vague, formless, but dreadful fears that had assailed me during the last week, hovering and flitting jeeringly and horribly just beyond the horizon of my conscious thought, full of grief and betrayal, now over-whelmed me suddenly—as breath-taking as a blow in the solar plexus, and almost as unpleasant in its physical effect. I drew Gillian aside, as a surprised air hostess tried in vain to take my boarding card.

"Listen, my love. I'm not coming."

"Not *coming*?" Her voice held the elements of a scream in it.

"Not this moment, I mean. I'll probably take the boat tonight. I'll be with you tomorrow."

"For God's sake! What's wrong? Have you insured me and planted a bomb in the aircraft?"

"Partly that, of course, and partly—I don't know," I said heavily, feeling a fool. "I just don't know."

Gillian eyed me very narrowly, looking more like a wife than I had ever seen her look before.

"I could be angry, darling, easily," she said.

"No doubt about it, and no blame to you," I said.

[1] Before the day of the Viscount

40

"Are you absolutely certain that all you need isn't a big drink?"

"Absolutely certain. I've had two."

She continued to eye me.

In a successful marriage the whole becomes greater than its parts, in a less successful one the parts merely remain parts; and the tragedy of a totally unsuccessful one is that the parts are lessened by the whole. Gillian and I had always been parts, but we interlocked better as time went on, we worked more smoothly with less oiling; we moved, in fact, towards the whole rather than away from it, and so she might now, with no formula to guide her, feel a reason for my behaving in an apparently uncouth and intransigent manner, the reason for which I could barely formulate myself. She might—or she might, as she had just observed, be angry. We balanced uneasily, gazing at each other, while the photographers again fell earnestly to one knee, feeling that we had taken up a pose for them. Then the subtle, invisible gears between mind and mind engaged smoothly, without a tremor, without the jarring, distracting screech of an explanation. Gillian relaxed and sighed and shrugged her shoulders, in mocking resignation.

"And what, my little one, am I to tell all your chums?"

"Tell them I forgot it was Tuesday," I said, with an enormous sense of gratitude and relief.

"That certainly sounds splendidly ambiguous."

"I'll be with you to-morrow, I promise."

"You won't forget that tomorrow will be Wednesday?"

"No."

"Good-bye, then. It seems a pity about the bomb."

But we were both aware that something rare and moving had taken place between us.

Chapter Four

A steel-coloured sky; dark blue hills; no-coloured yet perhaps faintly green fields gleaming palely between brown-grey plough and grey-brown tattered lines of blackthorn topping the sodden banks; rooks blowing like ragged leaves in the air; real leaves trampled into the rain puddles, which reflect the steel sky in their muddy depths; and a sudden, small, dramatic splash of scarlet at the corner of the straggling covert. Smells of leather and mud and rain-water and sweating horses; a wind with a rumour of snow and dried bracken in it; wet chocolate turf freshly cut into by eager, plunging hooves; sounds; inexplicably stirring, shivering the spine, tingling the scalp; the crackling of undergrowth; the first hound speaking, in a voice shaking with eager uncertainty; the swelling, thrilling chorus, confirming, asserting—and then the high, heart-halting holler splitting the cold air, and all the blood leaping, with a fierce, joyous, frightening atavism, to the exultant, triumphant horn blowing them away.

And cub-hunting mornings, as bright and isolated as jewels, early star and lantern lit, and later cobwebby, midge-haunted, still breathing summer; the mists knee-high across the long grass; long blue shadows from stooked corn as the sun comes up; the gambolling, wagging, tender-limbed, grinning puppies suddenly ruthless, tasting death, and acquiring the taste for life; the young horses, shaggy, sweating and shapeless, staring with popping eyes and thumping hearts into the fearfully haunted wood, while their elders (who have been brought out to set a good example) behave quite appallingly, pouncing in all directions at once, spattering foam over their chests, seizing every opportunity to buck, and pulling like demons when requested to trot gently for a few yards down the side of the covert.

And perfectly terrifying mornings, with an east wind blowing flurries of stinging sleet cruelly into your face, and just not enough frost for anyone to go home with dignity; your heart in your too-tight boots, your stomach in your mouth, your nerves in shreds, and your head-shaking horse, made crazily irritable by the weather, preparing to take at least the first three obstacles by the roots. The unplaited reins on the wrong bridle (God help the lad when you get back) slipping wetly already through your frozen, clumsy fingers, which are too numb to tighten the girths, although the saddle is slipping farther back every minute—and why, in God's name, has that nit-wit boy put rings on this shocking green animal instead of a decent martingale, which you could at least clutch at in the emergency which is obviously bound to arise?

A terrible taste in your mouth, which may be purely due to fear, or may be because you drank too many port-and-brandies at the meet (although you did feel sick at breakfast—perhaps, after all, you really are not well enough to be out?). An aching back (kidney disease?) cut in two by the icy, unrelenting wind, numb nose, watering eyes—and some crass idiot hollering like a madman on the far side of that extremely high and narrow stone-faced one—why, oh, why can't he leave well (such as it is) alone? Your whole being is one long, silent, earnest plea to be transported immediately to southern Italy, which you will never leave again under any circumstances—or certainly not under any circumstances remotely resembling these. . . .

And muggy, damp, gilt mornings moving towards Spring, with horses in a cloud of steam, and the bitch pack infinitely dégagé and grinning, with lolling tongues, and an indulgent attitude towards their huntsman. "He seems to think—" (you can hear them say) "—that we can find a fox—my dear, isn't he a scream?" They gossip and roll about in abandoned, snake-like attitudes on the wonderful-smelling new grass, and shriek in an exaggeratedly female fashion when rated for their appalling behaviour—but nobody minds, and the horses idle along, sweating in their growing coats, snatching very rudely at tasty budding twigs and incipient crab-apples, thinking, if they are thinking at all, of the white clover in May, and falling heavily, out of sheer carelessness, when requested to pull themselves together and jump some small but slippery obstacle between coverts.

Snipe, too, flickering like illusions across the gold and mauve and chocolate coloured bog; yearlings galloping joyfully with ridiculously arched tails; foals boxing provocatively at the patient, fond, but bored, faces of their dams, in a hopeless attempt to make them play; salmon leaping in tumbling, tawny water; point-to-point horses circling edgily at the start, gingery with nerves, snatching at their bits, sidling anxiously into line; and an endless series of guilty, foolish, fawning hound puppies—Plato and Panda, Cottager and Challenger, Willing and Witness, meeting their varying fates with goodwill and complete lack of comprehension. Willing and Witness had killed a sheep and had been sent back to the kennels in disgrace

44

in the Land Rover; Willing was sick twice, on the way, and sincerely believed that the end of the world had come. Plato had run head-on into a tractor in the yard, and was not quite as others were in after life. He hunted indefatigably, but never a fox, and always in the opposite direction from his more orthodox colleagues. When he was drafted I was sorry, because I had been fond of him, and it was clear that no huntsman ever would be. Panda became the stallion hound, Challenger picked up poison and died, Cottager won glory and the champion dog cup at the puppy show; an occurrence that apparently adversely affected his character, for he hunted very jealously always, running mute, and determined, it seemed, to pick up for himself alone any further glory that might be going.

And Jameson and Paddy whiskey, smoky-tasting, glasses of stout at any hour (even when I was five, because I was small for my age, and it was well known that there was nothing like the porther for putting growth into a man), turf fires glowing flakily—"You could watch the fleas lep from them when they'd be lighting," one of the housemaids once assured me—I spent hours watching, but never saw anything so satisfactory. Nanny coming firmly into my bedroom for the Syrup of Figs ceremony. "Now, then, Anthony, up you sit, dear, you know as well as I do you're not asleep, and I've something nice for you afterwards, I'm sure I don't know what all this fuss is about, Roger just drinks his straight down and not a murmur, now dear, don't put on that ugly face, you know what will happen if the wind changes, don't you?"—and, discovering my early literary efforts—"How ever did you pick up an idea like that? I'm not sure but what I shouldn't take you straight to your father."

And my magnificent, port-faced father, splendidly letting himself go after retiring from the diplomatic service,

45

rollicking, cursing happily, across the West Tipperary country on his handsome hard-pulling heavyweights, closely followed by his travelling bar, driven with desperation and extreme acumen by his French valet—up and down narrow, rutted bohireens, across boggy fields, almost over banks. Once it took on a wall, but that was after the poor man, in greater desperation than usual, during a three-hour slow hunt across uncharted bogs, had taken to the bar himself. He was a thin, grey-haired man with troubled, intelligent eyes and philosophic leanings, and only his love for my father had enabled him to stand for a moment the extreme barbarism of the country. "Quelle abérration, le fox-hunt!" I would hear him murmur, pouring drinks like mad between coverts, to restore the nerves (he was convinced) of those who had been lucky enough to survive the previous run. "Et ces chasseurs de renards, quels types! Que c'est triste, la vie sportive—que de sécheresse!" The types stood heartily around him, men and women and horses all inextricably mingled, all panting, mud-splashed, sweating, spattered with foam, bloodstained from blackthorn and wire and stake, and all entirely delighted with themselves and not in the least sad—nor, indeed, secs—as was always joyously and abundantly proved at any hunt ball.

Only the odd casualty or two, who had taken really crucifying falls, and sat, sick and shaken, in somebody's car, saying they felt fine, and only wished they had a second horse out, experienced a sudden longing for a more civilized scene, and a great, late affinity with Oscar Wilde, and even then it only lasted until they had stopped feeling sick, which was usually after the third glass of brandy.

That valet was a charming person, and we were all sorry when he had to be sacked. "Charles," my mother

46

said to my father. "Charles, he must go. He runs through the housemaids as if they were your shirts. I simply cannot keep myself in housemaids, and now it's the cook—just when I had got her to make a quite perfect timbale, the work of years, I assure you, it really is too bad, and not an eligible farmer left in the district, after all those house-maids."

He had even once made a pass at Nanny, then a buxom little creature with silky brown hair scraped carefully into a neat bun—a very tactful pass—two civilized people with extraordinary affinity of soul, in a strange, barbarous country. Nanny had gone straight to my mother, flattered, but indignant. "Not but what he's not perfectly polite, my lady, but that's a one you wouldn't know what he might be up to next, polite or not polite, and I really couldn't feel myself safe in the same house, not after what he said."

My mother had been fascinated. "What did he say, Nanny?"

But Nanny had only pursed her lips and said it wasn't so much the actual words, if her ladyship knew what she meant.

Now, driving back from the airport to my club, the thought of my mother closed comfortably around my heart. Small, crumpled, bosomy, light and warm as a puffed-out sparrow; always smelling faintly of the flowers she misplaced with so much enthusiasm around the house; managing the ill-assorted household with amused toler-ance and tact; continually amazed at the wickedness of the world, and absolutely delighted with the resultant gossip (She would have had Rupert to dine the moment he set foot in Ireland, and obviously knew already about Benny and Rose Hillchester); wonderfully kind to the wicked ("Poor Rupert was always so very good-looking, and needed guiding" and "Of course, Rose's husband *is* dreadfully dull, poor darling"); bored with the self-styled good; herself upright, unselfrighteous, gay; as sweet and sound as brown bread, as stimulating as salt; as uncomplicated as only the rare, the truly charitable, dare let themselves become—I could rest in the thought of her, while Benny and Jake and Louie and Sachi lost their glossy, menacing charm, their ability to make me disintegrate, and became merely sad, bad, lost children who had never had the benefit of a good upbringing. It seemed at once infinitely peculiar to have been so blackly depressed, so formlessly fearful—to have felt, suddenly, that to lay the country of my childhood open to these strange, cold, calculating eyes was to betray some remote, half-forgotten trust, and to make it finally the land of lost content, to forbid myself forever the happy highways where I went—the innocent ambience of horse and hound, snipe and salmon, fox and foal, Nanny and Syrup of Figs, the milky breath of cows, tatty sheep caught in brambles, morning sun high-lighting the dust left by the bad, willing servants in square, shabby Regency rooms, dirty, Guinness-smelling bars at meets, summer rain driving across race-courses, huge fires and high teas after hunting, ferreting expeditions with squat, self-assured terriers, and with it all the secret, young, enthralled dreaming of my other true and tantalizing love, the theatre, who later proved to be false and unkind, yet none, the-less extremely profitable, a woman who would always slip you a gold cigarette case, even if that wasn't really what you had wanted from her. All that youthful world I had been afraid of losing—it was a world I returned to when I was tired and tightly wound and sick of myself, a world that it had never occurred to me to try and write about. Nobody wrote about without turning out either a classic or a crying shame, and there was only one classic, as far as

I was concerned. I had kept it very strictly alone, apart, until now, in a sulky don't-care mood, a small boy kicking stones, hands in pockets, shoulders hunched, I had signed the contract to write about it for Benny. Guilt-ridden and conscience-stricken, ("You're just bloody childish, chum," said my alter ego), I now tried to salve myself with the thought that Benny would not get near enough to the heart of the matter to hurt, and that many people in London and New York would be vastly entertained, and think the Anglo-Irish very cute numbers indeed. . . .

I had a calming, dull gossip in my club and then went to catch the Liverpool train at Euston—a soothing and familiar gesture. I realized now why I had said I was going to take the boat—it was because the boat was a part of my childhood. Half-way to Liverpool I glanced at my watch and realized that this was the hour of the *cinq à sept* and wondered if Sachi had her silk tartan pants on at Castle Saffron, which was the name of Peter Dungarvan's draughty pile, and, if so, whether Peter was being sufficiently appreciative, or had merely disappeared into the *Field*. He had always been inclined to be a bit shy and jungly, until he married his adorable Maria, who, as his racing friends rightly remarked, had brought him on a ton. "And of course, it was such a *relief* to us all," my mother had said, "we always thought Peter would get himself trapped by Rose or somebody—he had this dreadfully dangerous habit of thinking he ought to ask people to marry him. He was so *distractingly* honourable (Well, he still is, bless him)—he had that very close shave with Bella, you know—asked *her* at four o'clock in the Four Hundred, and at eight o'clock she rang everybody up and told them she and Peter were engaged, including *The Times*, if you can believe it!"

49

"I can, easily, knowing her."

"Luckily she did just make the tiny slip of telling Freddy. Freddy was always a very good friend, bless him, even at his worst, and he got up immediately—can you imagine him getting up at eight o'clock? I think it was so loyal and touching—and he went and shook up Peter and doctored him and forced him to deny it—poor Peter, Freddy said, was completely bewildered, he couldn't remember a thing about it, and had the most shocking hangover Freddy had ever seen—"

"Must have been something, then," I had said.

"Freddy said he kept telling him to try and think forward from the last thing he remembered—but that turned out to be tying his tie, which didn't help. So then Freddy asked him what was the last thing *before* he started to dress, and Peter just said"—here my mother assumed a quite entrancing expression of delighted disapproval— " 'Don't be a bloody fool'."

"One sees the pattern of the evening clearly."

"O, it was a *very* close thing," my mother had said, shaking her head.

It was a long time, I thought now, rather sadly, since Peter had been that young buck escaping.

Liverpool; the boat; and what had always been known in my family as A Great Fry for dinner: bacon and eggs and sausages; to sleep in the tiny cabin with its hissing ventilator and the ominous object that you could, if too weak to rise, fasten to the side of your berth; a disgusting cup of tea in the early, shivery dawn; the draughty, gloomy customs shed; the cobbled street outside where waited the rickety, expensive taxis with their chatty, professional Irish drivers; breakfast at the Shelbourne; the familiar, malt-smelling drive past the Guinness breweries to

Kingsbridge. I bought an *Irish Independent* and read a cosily familiar tirade about something underhand and irreligious the wicked English had done. And then the train pulled out of Dublin, and the stud farms went by, the bog, the Curragh, the white-washed, grimy cabins, the muddy bohireens, the stone walls, the undug ditches, the old women on donkey-carts, the tinker children waving at the train, the young horses galloping away from it—and always mountains on the horizon, washed in against the sky in dark blue and brown and purple, half-hidden in the drifting, gentle rain.

It was a soft day. The country was very open. I began to wonder what the date of the opening meet might be.

Chapter Five

Peter was on the platform to meet me, looking superbly shabby, and totally, delightfully, unlike anybody I had been seeing during the past few months. His angular, elegant, tough red face, untidy hair, amused blue eye, and tatty black patch which never stayed quite in the right place, all seemed highly satisfactory, and almost as reassuring as the boat had been; it really did not seem very likely that anything spectacularly dreadful would happen as long as Peter was around to deal with the situation.

"*Well*, boy," he said, with delight, as I took the acrobatic leap from step to platform required by Irish trains, "You *are* going to make me a lot of dollars—how on earth did you collect them all up? How long can you persuade them to stay?"

"They collected me," I said. "And I imagine they'll stay either for months or until tomorrow. Louie might decide on the Argentine, after all."

"I bet he might, too," said Peter, with a grin.

He had the always endearing characteristic of not having to have things explained to him.

A Labrador bitch, much broader across the back than she was high off the ground, apparently propelled towards me by a violent circular tail-motion, offered me, grinning and dribbling with affected embarrassment, something shapeless and disgusting she had just discovered under a porter's truck. Peter booted her gently in the stomach and advised her to shut up and take it away, and she turned her attention to him, and fainted with love on to his feet. "You're a fright," he told her, twiddling an ecstatic ear, "You've lost all sense of decency since you gave up working. Isn't she an awful old bag?" he said, proudly, to me. "Shameless bitch," he said, lovingly, to her. "I really ought to put you down, I suppose—take that bloody thing away."

She levered herself slightly off the ground by placing one knotty paw on him, firmly and reverently, with a holier-than-thou look in her eye. I haven't forgotten how to behave, she said, even if you have. Peter took what she offered, weakly. "She's got you by the short hairs, all right," I said.

Peter looked at her gift with awe, holding it between thumb and finger, "What do you suppose this was?" he asked.

"Throw it away, for God's sake."

"Where can I throw it to?" he looked round nervously. "*Just throw it.*"

"It's not a grenade, goddammit, I can't just throw it."

"Chuck it back where she found it."

He dropped it, and shuffled it back under the truck with a guilty sideways kick.

"We could put *her* under the train, now, and just go quietly away."

Peter grinned. "I might miss her," he said. "You never know. Your woman and Rupert came with me. They're boozing in Dwyer's—I suppose I could wash there," he added, doubtfully, sniffing at his hand.

"Will I put them bags inside, my lord?" now inquired a hopeful small boy with a gay, pimply face and very oily hands.

"Do," said Peter. "And look out for the terrier in the van," he said to me, "he's a devil for eating you.

I've just got to collect some bloody spare part or other here—I can't remember when I ordered it, or even if I did."

He limped off and I went in some trepidation towards the van, accompanied by the small boy, who was successfully ruining my suitcases and keeping up a cheery flow of question, answer, opinion, and commentary.

"Is it the fillum you'll be working at above at the castle? You will, so, 'tis a grand place for it, mind you, and I seen a gentleman came yesterday for the fillum, and a lady too, and didn't I see their pictures on the paper a whiles ago. Haven't you the great weather for it, now? Wait, you, while I'd give the dog beyond in the van a slap—he'd be cross, likely, and you to get in and his lordship not here."

The terrier was very cross indeed, but he was slapped relentlessly and bundled into the back of the van, where there was already a deeply shocked calf peering helplessly out of a sack, a drum of lubricating oil, a bundle of plough socks, a roll of bullock wire, a breaking roller, two sacks of oats, a very patched saddle, and a rather smart piece of tweed *boutiquerie* which I recognized as belonging to Gillian. I rescued this, which was half on the oil drum and half under the calf, and the terrier managed to eat me shrewdly as I did so. "That's a great little hunting dog now, mind you," said the small boy, slapping it again, more in sorrow than in anger, like a parent with too high-spirited a child.

"Did he eat you?" asked Peter cheerfully, appearing.

"He did," I said, and rewarded the small boy for allowing him to do it.

Peter drove fast and slaphappily, flipping his left hand casually back and forth from wheel to gear-lever. "Fear nothing," he said, "this is a lot safer than it looks."

I hoped it was, because the narrow, twisting main

street of Ballinakil was full of nonchalant, wobbly little boys on their mothers' bicycles, wobblier old women crouched on weaving donkey-carts, totally unaware of the existence of other traffic, very tiny children playing shrill games of hurley, hysterical car-eating dogs darting out of ambush suddenly, a young horse being steered precariously through the chaos in long reins, bullocks being as stupid as only bullocks can be, and gay lads indulging in chariot races on carts returning from the creamery.

The Labrador bitch, whose name was Suky, sat squatly on my lap, full of triumph, leaning warmly and heavily against my shoulder, gazing at Peter and breathing love at him. Once, overcome by passion, she poked her nose suddenly and enthusiastically into his ear, which caused him to swerve violently, say, "Don't, Goddamit, Suky," and then to pat her in case he had hurt her feelings, removing his hand from all controls in order to do it. I was delighted to arrive at the scruffy bar in a shop full of pigs'-heads and gumboots where Gillian and Rupert were said to be boozing. There, sure enough, they were, very cosy indeed—Rupert with his nobly *déclassé* air, and quick, glinting eyes that never missed a trick, Gillian with a diamond bracelet showing beneath the enormously turned-up cuff of what I presumed was an old coat of Peter's, in which she was almost totally submerged. "I just liked the smell," she said to me in explanation. Rupert had managed to take six cigarettes and a drink off Gillian, and was telling her about the sad mistakes made in Tangier. He hardly paused to say, "Hullo! Here's the dollar king—now, listen, Anto, I'm in this with you up to the hilt," before continuing his saga—which had to do with Bobo St. George; a perfectly delightful Arab girl, very good family, mind, you, nothing wrong there; and that high-class pansy photographing feller. I ordered drinks for Peter and myself. The turtle-like old man behind the counter made Peter's whiskey a double one, I observed, without hesitation or inquiry, and so far as I could see nobody had added any water when Peter picked it up and drained the glass casually. I watched with awe and admiration, and the old man, catching my eye, said with reverence, and all the fond pride of someone showing off a local monument, "Sure, 'tis but a daisy in the mouth of a bull to him."

I leant contentedly against the bar, smelling dust and bacon and stout, looking at the sunlight from the straggly street flickering through the window, and at Suky noisily engaged in licking a luscious, squashed sweet biscuit from the filthy floor; and Time, no longer the enemy, but a perfectly cosy member of the same house party, filtered soothingly through me, so that Gillian, apparently hanging on Rupert's every word, whispered sideways to me, "Darling, the boat *did* do you good—you've stopped looking like a haunted greyhound that can't remember how many times it's been round."

"I still can't remember," I said. "But just now it doesn't seem to matter."

Peter and the old man were discussing a horse, and the familiar, ridiculous jargon had at that moment to my receptive ear the true, the divine, dying fall, as elevating as a dry Martini, as soothing as a poultice.

"Ah, a goodish horse enough now, and a horse would be travelling on when some 'ud be bet, mind you."

"Takes hold, doesn't he?"

"He do catch on, right enough, but sure, where's a good horse that wouldn't, and hounds running?"

"Now tell me, Pat, did you ever know him give a fence a look?"

"I'll tell you straight. He'd the heart crosswise in me before now, the way he'd be shy to lay a foot to his fences before he'd settle—when he'd be faced in, now, there's no one would stop him, but sure, who'd want to? He never gave me a fall yet, mind you."

"Only a heart attack."

"True enough for you—I'm not saying now that's a horse everyone would ride—but for a gentleman would like to go on a bit! And lep! I'm telling you now, if 'twas the Lord himself, and the horse clapped an eye to Him, he'd lep."

He gave Peter a look of triumph, as of one who says you cannot, surely, require more?

Peter was silent, apparently weighing the tremendous responsibility of owning such a brash animal; and while he meditated, swinging the remains of his second drink gently round his glass and gazing down into it, a woman sauntered gaily across to the bar from where she had been buying cheese at the other counter, folded her arms lovingly around him and said: "Don't buy him, darling, he'll kill you. Besides, I want him myself."

Peter unwrapped himself calmly and said to me, "You know each other, I expect," with all the determination of the well educated not to make introductions if it can possibly be avoided, or if it cannot be avoided to couch them in ambiguous terms, "Well, but of course I know him, who doesn't, but why would he know me?"

"I do know you," I said. "Sarah Collingwood. You married Dan Nugent, and I haven't seen you since—are you living over here now?"

Before she could answer, Rupert detached himself from Gillian and put his arm round the new arrival. He was slightly drunk. "Ah!" he said, "Little Sarah—one of my few failures. But I was very young then."

"I distinctly remember thinking how very old you were," she retorted, smiling at me. "I thought, dear old Rupert, poor old thing." She gave him an unkind glance of mockery, but Rupert was unmoved. He merely tightened his hold around her, so he could get in a bit of thumb-work, and asked if she was going to give him a drink, if nothing else, and she did, affectionately contemptuous, delving into the tight pockets of her narrow corduroy pants for the money, deliberately leaning back against him to do it, cat-like, smiling to herself. Rupert's mouth twitched, and I didn't blame him. Sarah had always been one of those extremely rare women who carry the mysterious property of glamour within themselves, to whom a background can add nothing, and take nothing away. Many, only too wearisomely many, are the women who contrive to be glamorous in the cars, the jewels, the furs, the places, which are contrived for them to be glamorous in—few indeed, can fail entirely to be glamorous if supplied with sables, a Rolls Bentley and the Sporting Club—but none that I knew of save Sarah could carry that aura with her in a dirty roll-neck sweater, horsy pants, and a scruffy shop. Gillian, I thought, had something of the same quality, but it did not shine with quite this contemptuous, unwavering brilliance, and Sachi Gosztonyi—I realized suddenly—given the same clothes, the same situation, would merely look odd.

What was it I had kept hearing in London about Sarah —that the drums of the bush telegraph had relayed relentlessly? That she was making Dan unhappy, that you wouldn't know him for the same man, that he had lost his nerve, that Sarah was cruel, that he adored her, that he was drinking, that it was all Sarah's fault, or Dan's fault, or that it was really perfectly all right, they were fond of each other still? Something, anyway, had been tapped out—the throbbing had been heard in the Four Hundred; the first faint sounds of certain doom approaching slowly through the jungle.

And not surprising, I thought now, watching Sarah tease Rupert. She looked like an arrogant, superb black whippet, with her slender length of leg; her snipey, ugly,

58

fascinating face with its golden, light-reflecting self-absorbed eyes. No wonder, I thought, that she needs more than a successful steeplechase jockey whose great days are over, to keep her in check. . . .

Dan had won the National twice in succession, the second time riding a horse belonging to Sarah's father, and that night, at the Adelphi, he and Sarah had abruptly announced their engagement—causing one of the most ringing family rows of all time—and then rather quickly eloped.

I remembered Dan as a gay, swarthy, tough Irishman —not tough as the Jake Hogans are tough, but tough enough to drink milk if he needed it; tough enough not to play poker unless he wanted to play it: to dance all night if he wasn't riding the next day, and to go to bed at ten o'clock if he was; at all times ready to boot the faintest-hearted horse over the worst obstacles; tough enough to collect Sarah Collingwood, and tough enough to hold his place in her world—by the vitality, the virility, the sheer physical prowess which were the bootlaces by which he had lifted himself into it.

If those bootlaces are failing him now, I thought, still watching Sarah, and his wife is a highly desirable woman who might, I think, find it not unamusing to be cruel . . . he's in for a hell of a time, poor chap. . . .

Peter asked, breaking into my thoughts:

"Did you know Dan?"

"I'd met him a few times at parties after racing."

"Nice chap."

"So I thought."

"He and Sarah have bought Drumshannon, you know. They've done it up in a big way, you won't recognize it— it's a kind of cross between Beckhampton and Buckingham Palace these days. He trains there—hullo, here he is."

Here was Dan—and I saw at once that the bush tele-

59

graph had not been without reason in its dark forebodings. His dark gamin face, that had been gay and mobile, full of swiftly-changing expression, seemed, even now, as he smiled and greeted me and indulged in a polite what-a-long-time-it's-been conversation, to be set in the strained and sullen lines of a spiritual exhaustion that was quite frightening to see. He looked like someone who, having entered upon a race which he has no hope of winning, yet continues to run in a fog of desperation; too proud, too stubborn, and too bewildered to pull up, or to remember that to pull up would be perfectly simple, and wise, and even possible. When, as he chatted to me, his tired eyes flickered and changed focus, looking over my shoulder at Sarah and Rupert, and then shifted uneasily back to my face, watching narrowly to see if I had noticed, I began to realize just exactly how punishing a race he was running. To keep Sarah faithful might be a difficult enough task, tackled in however robust and detached a spirit, but to try and do it while in such a vulnerable state that he was uneasy because Rupert Chichester —"the joke rake", as Gillian called him—had managed to get his arm round her and was massaging her ribs with his thumb; this seemed to be a task more certain to end in tears than anything that Benny or I might devise to torture ourselves with. I was quite relieved for Dan's sake when Sarah detached herself lovingly from Rupert, patting his cheek in mockery as she did so, and said did we realize it was two o'clock for heaven's sake, how about luncheon? The Spaniards were really much more sensible, bless them, but she had ordered it for one-thirty and her cook was distinctly uppity already, so come along, darling, do, and did you remember to order the grass-meal?—will you all come over for drinks this evening— and do bring that divine director, I couldn't fancy him more. They went.

"Lord! . . ." said Peter gently, half to himself, settling himself underneath Suky in the passenger seat of the van, presumably in kindly deference to my unstable nervous system. The terrier immediately leapt jealously, in an evil, scrabbling manner on to his shoulders, teetered there for a moment, and then, finding no space on Peter unfilled by Suky, fell deliberately on to the gear-lever, from which I snatched away my hand only just in time to avoid a shrewd, witty nip.

"Shut up, you," said Peter. He lifted him cunningly up on his foot, still snarling, shifted him into his hand, and settled him soothingly at the base of Suky's cart-horse back. "Drive away, now. Fear nothing, boy."

In the back Gillian, who had refused the front seat in order to protect the calf from Rupert, crouched precariously over it, while Rupert, who didn't care what he sat on as long as he was comfortable, complained bitterly.

"We'd have much more room," he pointed out. "I didn't know you were an animal-loving woman—such a bore they are, with all their cats, perfectly dreadful carry-on, I call it."

"I have only one calf at the moment, and I only love that enough to prevent you from sitting on it. I'm quite normal really—do take care as we go round this corner—its poor legs."

"What about *my* poor legs?"

"Well, darling, they've had their day, after all."

At the lodge gates they unanimously demanded to be let out, and I saw what they meant—the very long avenue was in a state of considerable disrepair. As we shuddered and rocked up it, in low gear, Peter said suddenly, "Poor old Dan."

"So I thought," I said.

"Sarah bitches him all the time—I don't know what might not happen this season."

"This season?"

"Hunting—he's lost his nerve."

"Why doesn't he stop then?"

"Can't. She won't let him."

"Poor chap—I must say, I thought he looked like hell."

We drove over the last rise of the rutted avenue, that wound now between fields of rutilant stubble, and saw below us the wonderfully proportioned, porticoed, nobly winged pile of limestone that was called Castle Saffron, and was in fact a huge, aloof, early Georgian house, superbly beautiful and recklessly uncomfortable.

Painted magnificently against pale, towering clouds, darkening sky above it, rooks blowing over it, winter trees lacily enclosing it—"I must look at it a moment," I said, and stopped the van.

"Better to look at than live in," said Peter, and lit a cigarette and then said, suddenly, "What sort of a chap is this film chap?"

"Which one?" I knew perfectly well.

"The one called Benny."

"I honestly have no idea."

"He says he's known you for ever."

"Yes, but I still have no idea what sort of a chap he is— I can quote you the surface stuff."

"Quote away."

"He tries to lead a sort of pagan, heedless, instinctive life, to be a god to himself, but he only succeeds in achieving a rather unhappy compromise between the fashionable and the bohemian."

"Sounds like hell to me," said Peter gloomily.

"I think it probably is."

Peter tilted his cap forward and scratched his head thoughtfully.

He said: "I just got the impression that he might be—" he hesitated—"—well—perhaps *capable de tout*."

62

"Such as?" I asked, knowing what he was thinking.

"Such as seducing a child," he said, quietly and reluctantly, twiddling Suky's responsive ear. I said nothing, so he went on. "Trouble is, she's so pretty now, she's bloody well lovely, and she's not a child any more, in years you know. She's seventeen. Lord, it makes me feel old."

He did look rather old, suddenly.

Hell, I thought.

I said: "Beauty and innocence is a well-known dangerous combination."

"Exactly. And I just got the impression that your pal might find it an amusing one to destroy—God knows I'm probably wrong."

"I hope you are."

"But you wouldn't be certain?"

"No."

"H-m," he said, and sighed. "Drive away, now, or we'll have Rupert catching up on the calf."

We drove on to the semi-gravelled, weed-ridden, uneven sweep before the wonderful, high spreading fan of wide, shallow, donkey-coloured steps. Peter opened his door and tipped Suky and the terrier gently out backwards, breaking their fall with his foot. They were immediately set upon by the foolish hound puppies that Phillippa had hungered for, who were hysterical with emotion at seeing their friends again after so fearfully long and cruel an absence. Suky was indulgent, and the terrier rather bored. He nipped one of them in an absent-minded way, and it set up a sad, shrill protesting, and then licked him lavishly, so that he did it again.

"Funny thing . . ." said Peter thoughtfully, half out of the van.

"What is?"

"The way people can't leave other people alone."

"If they did," I said, "I'd have nothing to write about."
Peter grinned.

"You won't lack something to write about with this bunch, boy."

"Gillian keeps telling me that it will end in tears," I said.

"I wouldn't be surprised," said Peter.

Chapter Six

I shall not easily forget the opening day of the West Tipperary fox-hounds that year. It had about it that quality of nightmare that haunts the imagination and refuses the mercy of oblivion to the memory. Even now, in moments of depression, I may recall suddenly, with a shudder, the peculiarly penetrating qualities of the east wind carrying the sleet before it; the expressions of patient, unnecessary martyrdom on the faces of lame and shivering horses; the wet roads stretching into cold, unkind distances; the sourness of mid-morning champagne in the mouth at two o'clock; the appearance of Rupert's waistcoat after he had spilt a bottle of port down it, and of my brother Roger's face after he had hit a road with it —they looked much the same; the manic-depressive behaviour of Benry; the green-white tinge of Dan's dark face at the meet; the agony and exhaustion of staggering through sucking, half-frozen mud in boots; the gloom, confusion, and futility of the whole sporting scene; the baffled efforts of the protagonists to do something constructive; the ground covered to no purpose; the tendency for any piece of the puzzle to refuse to fit into another; drama piled relentlessly upon exhaustion; lost hounds, lost wives, lost children, loose horses—of it all only Kafka could write, I think, with the mastery necessary to convey the full and bitter claustrophobic sense of nightmare.

We had started off badly, of course, by going to dine

quietly with Dan and Sarah the night before, and ending up playing poker until half-past three—at which hour Phillippa and Peter and Gillian and I had come determinedly away, nagged at by Benny, looking frighteningly ill, who said it was only just getting interesting, and we could sleep any time, for Chrissakes.

It had been getting only too interesting. Rupert had lost a lot more of his uncle's money, and drunk a good deal too much of everything he had been offered, and he was beginning to move his hands about restively and chat to himself. I knew that movement of Rupert's hands, and that confidential self-encouragement, and it meant one of two things—either he was going to accuse somebody of cheating or else he was going to cheat himself. In either case, there would be trouble. Already he had failed on several occasions to put into the pool during jackpots, and the merriment with which the other players had at first pointed this out was now becoming distinctly strained.

We had been playing rounds of dealer's choice for some time, and the choices were becoming more and more wild and complicated.

"Tens are kings", we heard someone grimly announcing, after the low cards had been removed and the glasses topped up, as we nimbly closed the door on them, "Tens are kings, one-eyed knaves are wild, threes or better to open"—and then Rupert's voice, slurred, thick, and aggressive, "Tha's not poker, tha's bloody *pelmanism*".

"We're well out of *that* circus," Peter had remarked happily, as he helped Phillippa into her coat in the hall.

"O, dear," said Phillippa, "Benny will be so tired tomorrow." She tied a silk scarf round her head and looked divinely resigned and tender. Peter gave her a shrewd, compassionate glance. "Do you want me to go and winkle him out of it?"

66

"He wouldn't come, he gets absolutely hypnotized, he might easily go on playing for days."

"They're all hunting tomorrow, so he can't really go on playing much after ten o'clock," said Peter, comfortingly.

"I know, but if they weren't, he would," she said tiredly, and then broke into sad, loving, unwilling laughter. "And tomorrow he'll be hotfoot for going to join Albert Schweitzer—he always wants to do that when he's tired, particularly if he has a hangover."

"Well, that sounds like a very beautiful reaction," said Peter, with a grin. "I always want to clock somebody personally." He was struggling into his coat, and Phillippa reached up gently, and draped it round his maimed shoulder—upon which the match-making fire kindled at once in Gillian's eye, and glowed brighter still when Peter gave Phillippa his hand down the frost-rimed steps outside.

"O, they are such poppets together . . . admit?"

"You have the mind of a woman's magazine," I said severely.

"But don't you think, darling . . ."

"What about Benny?"

"O, *Benny*—he doesn't notice who he happens to be married to, anyway."

"But Phillippa does, like anything."

"I suppose so, poor sweetie."

Phillippa had once said to me sadly, "I have a dreadful feeling I shall love Benny always, no matter what he does, you can't imagine how frightening that is."

"I can," I had said.

"Yes . . . perhaps you can, darling, you *are* very good at that sort of thing. . . O, dear, I never know why people seem to think that love is such a *relief*. . . ."

I had waited, because she was wanting to talk.

"Once, when Benny was going to New York—only for a week—O, dear, will you laugh, I wonder, Anto?"

"No."

"Perhaps you won't . . . anyway, the night before, after we had made love, Benny went to sleep lying on my arm; it was *excruciating*, and my arm was so stiff in the morning I could hardly move it, and I wanted it to stay stiff until he came back—I kept moving it about and feeling very glad when it still hurt—for *days*—I couldn't bear the stiffness to go off, because it was as if he was still with me. . . ." She had looked at me nervously, but I felt very disinclined to laugh. I said, instead, "Ma chère et douce peine. . . ."

"*Yes*," she had said, gratefully, "*Exactly* that—who said it?"

"Ronsard."

"Well, he knew."

"O, yes," I said, now, to Gillian, "Phillippa notices, all right."

Much later, or earlier, cosily semi-conscious for a moment, we heard, vaguely, the rest of the party arrive back—and later still, less cosy, and more irritated, with unwelcome light threatening round the curtains, we were again disturbed: this time by gruesome sounds of distress from some far bathroom that was nevertheless still too near.

"O dear," Gillian murmured. "Rupert or Benny?"

"Both," I said into the pillow.

"Ought we to help?"

"Certainly not."

"O, the poor sweets, they *are* ill," said Gillian, listening, betrayed, as always, by her curious combination of tough mind and tender heart.

"Go to sleep."

After a few minutes she spoke again, thoughtfully.

"I wonder if Albert Schweitzer would *like* Benny to join him?"

"I suppose it would be all right if he stayed tired," I said. "Go to sleep."

"But it's morning."

Horribly enough, it was.

A bright, cruel morning, with the mountains looking as if they had been cut out of wet cardboard, and a threat of sleet in the icy wind. A bad scenting morning, and a bad morning after—a bad morning altogether, in fact. A morning for tugs breaking in boots agonizingly half-on and half-off, for stock ties wilfully slewing into curious, crumpled knots, for studs lost out of hunting shirts, for spur straps inextricably tangled, for strategic buttons to be missing from too-tight breeches, for total lack of small change, and a tendency to feel sick when bending down —a morning, in short, on which to give up hunting; a morning which everybody has experienced, and a morning on which nobody has yet had the moral courage to speak up and say that, after all, they have decided not to hunt today. I didn't have it now.

Tremendously complicated arrangements had been made. Dan was providing me with a horse. Gillian was being mounted from my home. Sarah was trying Pat Dwyer's horse, who would lep the Lord himself. Peter was giving Benny his old hunter and riding a four-year-old himself.

("O, darling, I think that's too dangerous," Gillian had said to this.

"So does the four-year-old," said Peter.)

Dangerous or not, it was only allowed to do half a day, and Gillian and I, our endurance weakened by our effete non-sporting existence, were also quite unfit to do more, in spite of our more mature age. The secretary had been rung up and forced to give us the order of the draw. He had warned us very seriously as he did so that old George would cut our throats with his own hands, every bleeding one of them, if we went on to them before hounds, see? Horse boxes were to be left here and there in strategic positions. Dan's man was to follow in the Land Rover which pulled Dan's trailer, and Pat Dwyer's lad would, it was said hopefully, be around. Peter's child, who hated hunting, was going to drive with Jake and Sachi in the van, and was already glowing with delight at this enthralling plan, and fascinated—as, indeed, we all were—by Sachi's simple outfit for following hounds; a small leopardskin tent, with cloche and boots to match. Phillippa and her young and Nurse Simmons were going with my mamma in the car from Knockmoree. Phillippa's young, whom I had at last discovered was called Patrick (he had been called Peewee and Paddy in London, and at the moment answered to Possum) stout and self-reliant in a blue duffle coat and rubber boots, had fallen delightedly down the front steps before breakfast, and been completely submerged beneath an eager wave of thrilled and loving hound puppies, who thought he had been specially invented for them to play with. He had been snatched from their jaws by Nurse Simmons—"Get away with your great dirty paws, I never did!"—and put into a different duffle coat, in which he teetered provocatively at the top of the steps while we ate breakfast—trying hard to make the whole wonderful episode happen again, and ruining what little peace of mind had been left to Phillippa by Benny.

Benny's hangover seemed, this morning, to produce a particularly strong destructive urge, which I could not feel would have been welcomed at Lambaréné. He chewed his way fiercely and doggedly through eggs and bacon, hating every mouthful, but determined not to appear faint-hearted, and announced that he was certainly going to stay out all day, why wouldn't he, for Chrissakes?

Phillippa said reasonably that I was only meaning to do half a day, and I was a lot fitter than he was, and Benny gave me an insolent, unfocused look through half-closed eyes and said he guessed I was wise, and asked immediately for some more bacon.

"O, dear . . ," murmured Gillian, who was twitchy anyway at opening meets, and at that moment in wandered Rupert, clad in shirt and breeches, a half-tied stock tie, and flapping slippers. One of his eyes was closed and much blackened, and he was, plainly, still living in a world of his own. He wandered slowly twice round the table, with his hands in his breeches pockets and his head sunk on his breast, glanced out of the windows each time he came by, and said "No smell", to himself in a dispirited voice. Then he sat down heavily by Peter, leaned back in his chair, ran a hand over his face and through his scanty, unkempt hair—rather questioningly, as if he wasn't certain they would be there—yawned very loudly, and slowly closed his other eye. Benny said with delight to Sachi, showing off Irish Life to her, "Isn't he just a wonderful guy?" and Sachi, as determinedly appreciative of everything as her husband was stolidly unappreciative, agreed with great animation that he sure was just that, a real old Irish comic.

"Rupert, who clocked you?" called Gillian, unreticently, down the table. Rupert opened his eye swimmily and shut it again. He said repressively:

"I fell down something."

Peter got up and put a comforting hand on his shoulder.

"Hair of the dog, old boy?" he asked. "Or coffee? Or would some tea stay down better?"

Rupert opened his eye again and said, "You're a lovely

71

man. . . . Isn't that the expression they use around here?"

Peter said patiently, "Which do you want?"

"Could your excellent boy provide me with a gin and peppermint? A large one?"

"This is something, now this is really something," said Benny delightedly, able at last to give up his bacon with honour.

"O, Rupert, love, your *guts* . . ." said Gillian in dismay.

Rupert looked up the table at her, with difficulty, stiffly turning his whole head in order not to move his one workable eye.

"My guts," he said, with dignity, "like my legs, as you recently unkindly remarked, have had their day."

He then slumped back and withdrew into his confused private world—once or twice he felt suddenly and anxiously through some non-existent pockets in his shirt, several times he hiccupped threateningly, once he hummed a few bars of *Swan Lake*.

Peter's very young, bad, willing houseboy, who had recently replaced his very old, good, unwilling, and now dead butler, appeared with the large gin and peppermint and a face of holy revelation.

"Mr. Chichester," said Peter, nodding towards the wreck.

Rupert reached out an unsteady hand, seized the glass, tilted back his head, and drained it without swallowing. Then he replaced it inaccurately, and the boy caught it in mid-air.

"Will I give ye the fill of it again, sir?" he breathed reverently.

"You're a good boy," said Rupert judiciously. "Do."

He slumped again, but not quite so irrevocably, and toying now with a piece of dry toast. "That's right, darling, eat up," said Gillian. Rupert looked consideringly at her and began to hum again, in case she was real.

72

After the second gin and peppermint, which he downed in the same way, thus making the entranced boy his slave for life, he began to come round slightly.

"I'm drunk," he told Peter, sadly.

"Stale drunk," said Peter comfortingly. "Better eat some more toast. No, don't butter it."

He put a piece firmly into Rupert's hand, and Rupert champed his way vaguely through it, hardly noticing that he was eating at all, still less that he hadn't put his teeth in. "I wonder who I insulted last night?" he asked himself, blowing crumbs about.

"Did you insult somebody?"

Rupert fingered his eye tenderly.

"You said you fell down something."

"I hope I was right."

"You hadn't insulted anybody up to the time we left, so it must have been Dan, or his trainer pal."

"Was the trainer pal about seven foot high?"

"About that."

"I hope it was Dan," said Rupert, with deep gloom. "Why can't I stay out of trouble?"

He rose, with a long, whuffling groan, stood very still for a moment, and shuffled off unsteadily to find his boots —a perversely gallant and curiously touching figure.

"He *can't* hunt," said Gillian, nervously, in her best maternal form. "He'll die at our feet."

"Not at all," said Peter bracingly. "It'll do him good. He'll be able to eat by two o'clock, you'll see."

But Peter was wrong, as it turned out.

He had not reckoned on champagne at the meet; and champagne at the meet there was—provided by the considerably surprised Rupert, who was informed by Dan that this was the *amende honorable*, and had been decided upon at the break up of the poker school. Dan's trainer pal, who seemed even now to be seven foot high, and was ruddy, cheerful, quite impervious to insults, and disinclined to bear malice, said to Rupert, "You need a steak for that eye," and Rupert said he couldn't stand the sight of food, and they became close friends and toasted each other, and Rupert was given a good thing for Leopardstown, which he wrote down illegibly at the bottom of the bill, and told the indulgent old woman behind the counter that if it won he would be able to pay.

"Sure, any friend of his lordship's now, would be welcome, indeed."

"*I'm* not going to pay," said Peter.

But I had a feeling that in the end, after Rupert's good thing had gone down, he would.

Now in came my mamma and Phillippa and Possum and my brother Roger, and my mamma fell upon me and wanted to know if my collar-bone had really mended completely ᴛʜis time, were they absolutely certain it had knitted itself properly, was that the word? Roger fell upon the champagne; and Gillian's eye fell upon Roger; and I knew, then, at once, that what she saw was still not the same Roger Kavanagh that the other, detached eyes saw —but, instead, that sad, wild, tender mirage of the heart, unbearably sweet and forlorn, and forever just out of reach, with which the heart so tends to nourish, delude and betray, and finally break itself. I watched her with warm affection, and thought, rather sadly, that perhaps the best recipe for a lasting marriage is that there should be a little aversion to start with.

I also watched, without affection, Benny busily charming Peter's lovely child with glowing tales of gallant Kentucky colts racing their hearts out for the equally gallant lads on their backs, and bearing away the glittering prize to save the old Kentucky home. It could not possibly have sounded, or looked, more entirely innocent and delightful. Benny was radiating kindly warmth and charm, making the day for the child, who was enchanted, looking and listening with the grave and holy stare, the withdrawn, dreaming smile with which a very young child will silently regard the lighted candles of Christmas. Perhaps, I thought, rather wearily, the evil is in the eye of the beholder—perhaps my eye today is altogether too cold, too disenchanted and suspicious, after all these years of observation and deduction. Benny, perhaps, is just being disinterestedly kind, for God's sake, he *is* kind, maybe, why not? Too bloody ready to see the worst, I thought, rather confusedly, on my third glass. But then I saw Peter's stilled and watchful glance as he leaned across them to put his own glass down, and I knew that if Peter, who was the least evil of men, saw something wrong, then the wrong was there. I remembered how, curiously, he had seen it at once, and I remembered how often before this I had seen Benny charm in order to destroy; be movingly kind in order to make the betrayal the more cruel. Poor bastard, I thought, pitying in my god-like mood, how he hates things to be whole! I must remember, I thought, listening to Sarah flirting with Rupert, to have a word with Peter. . . . "Ah, a great-hearted horse, mind you," said Dan's trainer pal, finishing some story he had been telling me and I agreed with him warmly. "Good man yourself, now," said somebody else—it turned out to be Dr. Paddy Herlihy—and placed a glass of port and brandy in my unwilling hand. I gave it to Dan, who swallowed it down gratefully. He gave me a cigarette and took one for himself, and when he lit them his hand shook. "This fellow I'm giving you, now," he said, "he might make you think he'd be going in to them too fast, if you didn't know him, but don't touch him, he'll watch himself, he knows it all."

He was watching Sarah as he talked, with strained and

anxious eyes. Sarah's eyes were mocking delightedly, and Rupert's only visible one, although still dulled, was nevertheless glinting with happy and unashamed lust.

Possum sat rollickingly on one of the bar stools, showing off rather. He had drunk tonic water, and also a pretty good swig of Phillippa's champagne, which he had downed very neatly while supposedly smelling it only. Now he had excitingly violent hiccups. After each convulsion he threw his head back, roared with laughter, and tried hard to fall off the stool backwards—a design that was thwarted by Nurse Simmons, who had the back of his duffle coat bunched tightly in her capable fist. Every time she played him skilfully, as if he was a fish, hauled him sternly upright, and set him relentlessly in place again.

"Well, I never, what will the ladies and gentlemen think of you?"

"Fine little fellow," said Rupert, with total lack of interest, vaguely patting the air in the region of Possum's head. "I hate children," he added confidentially to me. "They do joggle you so when you're shaving, and they're too small."

I could see that my mamma was longing to know whose children had recently been in a position to joggle Rupert while he was shaving, and that she was about to ask him, so I moved over to talk to Phillippa, who was happily hypnotized by the shameless behaviour of her son.

"Why aren't you attacking today?" I asked her.

"O, darling, I would so much rather some day when Benny isn't—he does hunt so *virulently*, and I'm always certain he'll break his neck. He doesn't know the horse, or the country—well, he doesn't know anything about it anyway, really—just the odd rather bogus Long Island day, you know, and occasionally at home, and once with the Quorn, when we were staying with the Beaumonts.

76

That was sheer hell, he and Simon Beaumont very nearly came to blows. You would have loved it, darling, it was so wonderfully funny really, Benny was convinced that Simon was despising him for being a film director, and Simon was convinced Benny was despising *him* for being a hard man to hounds—O, *very* stiff-legged, it was—they were really rather touching, if they hadn't been so maddening."

She looked tenderly at Benny, and sighed.

"Do you think he looks ill, Anto?"

"Not as ill as Rupert."

"Do look after him today."

"He might not like that."

"But do try?"

Chapter Seven

As it turned out, I had no chance to look after anyone. A fox broke at once from Kilteely in a flurry of discouraging sleet, and ran downhill. Dan had stolen a start, the drink nicely alive in him, and was some way ahead as we all bucketed on our snatching, humped-backed, over-eager, sworn-at horses towards the rather serious wall at the bottom.

"*Hold* up, you. . . . Ah, *stop* that, willyer . . . easy, easy, ye joker. . . ." Somebody got bucked off and the loose horse had the obstacle first, bouncing madly over it with reins and irons flying, an impertinent kick-back expressing its joy in behaving so wrongly and recklessly. My own horse was raking like a demon. Having seen his stable companion ahead, he had at once been seized by that hysterical desire not to be parted from it at any cost which is so much a part of what Gillian called "the divine silliness" of horses, and causes them to gallop with their despairing, popping eyes glued to the loved one's vanishing quarters, half a field or so ahead, and to forget completely what they are supposed to be doing with their own feet.

So it was with us.

It was a satisfying fall. A full-blooded, whole-hearted, unequivocal somersault—none of your little slipping, scrambly, timid, on-your-knees-and-up-again falls.

"Bigod," announced a lad of no consequence on a wild young animal, who landed over it after, and nearly on top

78

of me, "he never laid an eye to it, whatever came to him."

I knew exactly what had come to him; it had happened purely because his eye had been laid only to those distant, beckoning hocks; it was still laid to them as he thrashed to his feet, and as he stood beside me, quivering, and whinnied after them in a tragically hopeless falsetto. But he had lost his chum, and I my hunt. Blood was already oozing thickly from long ragged cuts just above his knees, clearly showing how light-heartedly he had failed to rise at an obstacle far too stout to be treated in such an off-hand fashion—it had, unfortunately, been one of those walls, only rarely met with, whose top stones, large and ragged, are cemented together to form a coping.

The hunt had now gone from us; disappearing entirely in that blackly magical fashion so bitterly well known to those left behind. One moment the whole world is filled with noise and rush and energy—hound voices clamouring like bells, huntsman throatily cheering them forrard-forrard-forrard, the pelting thunder of hooves smacking into wet turf, the eager bit-snatching heads and swinging shoulders all around you, the rush of cold air and wild spattering of mud—the next, as you rise shaken and surprised to your feet, spitting that same mud out of your mouth, the whole theatrically stirring scene has completely dissolved. You can vaguely recall that one or two people who landed close to you (one, indeed, was frighteningly close—the mud now in your mouth was flung there from his horse's hoof) had called, kindly, "Are you all right?"—gallantly making a gesture as if to pull up, defying you to be not all right, turning their frantically disapproving horses' heads for a second back towards you, and you had shouted "Go on" and they had gone on with enormous relief and celerity.

And now, nothing.

Nothing but a small boy belabouring a smaller, sour,

self-righteous pony who is determinedly not jumping the wall, and two men with a greyhound standing on a bank to your right, gazing into the distance. No sound but the soughing of the cold wind, nothing stirring but the bullocks, who have already settled to their grazing again. The hunt has passed like a furious dream; only the tremendous torn track of hoofmarks down the field is there to prove that it ever passed at all, and you and your limping horse must find a way back to dull normality and a road as best you can.

So, again, it was with us.

I plodded drearily down the field, the almost-freezing mud sucking at my boots, stumbling crossly in and out of hoofmarks, while my horse pulled furiously and eagerly at me, treading heavily on me from time to time, and smearing green froth over my already mud-plastered shoulder.

The gate into the bohireen, when I finally got to it, turned out to consist of an elaborate iron bed-head threaded with stakes, with two strands of rusty barbed wire added for good measure, and the gateway was liquid, bullock-poached bog—I stood drearily surveying it, an unrelenting sleet shower stinging my ears, while my horse circled restlessly around me, grinding its teeth in acute anxiety, and being as unhelpful as only a horse knows how to be. Finally I decided to lead him over the bank, which was a low stone-faced one, simple and solid, so I crawled painfully to the top of it, and urged him to follow me. He looked wilfully in the opposite direction, pulling the bit through his mouth, and me very nearly off the bank, and whinnied again in the same helpless, worried manner. I swore horribly at him, and a small boy appeared, as small boys invariably do in such circumstances, and inquired with ill-concealed contempt, "Will I let a belt at him for ye, misther?"

I made the mistake of swearing at him, too, so he went away, and after a further fruitless few minutes, during which my horse took up the tranced stance of one who hears voices, I had shamefacedly to yell at him to come back again. He advanced, looking, under cover of a large branch of blackthorn, like Burnham Woods. The horse rolled an eye back at this unfair apparition, switched his tail, and lifted a hind leg threateningly, but Birnam Woods plodded determinedly forward, making odd hissing noises, and finally the horse lost his nerve abruptly and plunged wildly to the top of the bank, catching me neatly with the point of his shoulder, and knocking me off into the bohireen, whose ruts were even muddier than the gateway had been. As I rose, speechless, and with a numbed nose already beginning to trickle blood, the small boy peered over the bank at me, and announced without hope or despair, but with the mild, fatalistic interest in disaster of his race, "Bigod, he'd have ye quinched, mind, if he'd jump on ye".

I contorted my face into what I hoped the horse would consider a reassuring expression, and took hold of the dangling reins again. He was hunched unhappily on the top of the bank like a circus elephant on a tub, all four feet together, enormously elongating his neck as he peered down into the fearful dangers awaiting him, with all the horror and despair of Dante looking into a particularly displeasing circle of the Inferno. These dangers consisted of myself, two depressed hens, several scraps of paper and sodden rags, and a broken wheel under the opposite bank —the remnants of some tinker's camp.

"Are ye right, now, misther?" inquired the small boy, and without waiting for an answer dealt the horse a shrewd swipe across the hocks with the thorny branch— upon which, true to the divine silliness of his kind, he launched himself wildly out across the bohireen, in a desperate attempt to clear all the dangerous pieces of paper lying in ambush for him, and landed right on the wheel—which gave way further with a splintering crack, leaving one piece arrayed round his fetlock, like a prisoner's spiked ankle chain. He backed away in a sort of mad, prancing shuffle, squinting down at this new adversary, and uttering a series of shocked snorts, while I, clutching the reins by the buckle, slithered after him through the ruts, making, with enormous self-control, soothing noises, wiping the blood from my face with a hand stiff and aching with cold, and, calm and calculating in despair, considering the question of how little I could decently offer Dan for him after he had become a complete cripple. The small boy once more saved the situation.

He had climbed over the bank, and now appeared behind the horse in the bohireen, hissing in a masterly manner and further uttering the magic formula of "Ah, there, ye thief, ye!" The horse—again like all his kind, when they have realized that there is no possibility of losing their heads any further with any success—immediately stood stock-still, and became kindly and wise. He gave me a friendly nudge with his head, like one who says, "Not quite so much fuss, next time, *please*," and offered me his foot, so I could remove his fetter, like a dear old doggie shaking hands. I felt a great longing for a thin, stinging whip, and a sudden acute sympathy with cruel Italian peasants, particularly as the small boy remarked, reprovingly, to me, "By dam, misther, ye have that one reared very pettish".

When I straightened up I put a numb hand strugglingly into my breeches pocket to find a reward for him, and found a pound note. Just that. I remembered, then, how I had failed to get any change that morning. I had counted on buying drinks at the meet, and poor, surprised Rupert had forestalled me. It was the pound or nothing for this kindly, energetic and deserving child. I gave it to him. He called excitedly upon the saints to witness my generosity, and bolted like a hare, in case I should come to my senses before he got clear. I was left alone with my now quiet and depressed horse, my sweating body, enclosed in the muddy and clammy clothes that would soon effectively chill it, my numb feet and hands, my steadily bleeding nose, and my empty pockets.

The sleet had stopped momentarily. A great stillness fell upon us, while my horse nibbled in a half-hearted manner at a twig, and relied on me to do something.

Alas, the profound and inexplicable difference between those who are well away in a bustling hunt and those who have early come to grief and are out of it!

To those in the first category life is—for half an hour or so, anyway—merry, frightening, fascinating, gallant, full of urgency and purpose, high, strange and moving in the extreme—but to the sorrowing fallen all seems drier than dust, more futile than the fall of dice, older than Egypt; they are surrounded heavily by tomorrow and tomorrow and tomorrow and even Macbeth after the murder felt more cheerful. Why, oh why, does anyone wish to ride, trumpeting, after these yelling dogs, across these hideously dangerous obstacles which bar the benighted country? Oscar Wilde, dear, civilized fellow, was so dead right, so full of sensibility in his opinion of the whole monstrous business. The small, unstable soul yearns in the void for something both elevating and soothing, such as Beethoven's Fifth or a large glass of whisky, but nobody offers either, nothing in the least comforting occurs, the soul receives only its familiar dusty answer—which was, on this occasion, that the horse was still bleeding and would soon be chilled, and something constructive would have to be done. But what? We moved dispiritedly up the bohireen. I realized suddenly that I had no idea where

83

Dan had finally intended to leave his trailer. I had meant to ask at the meet what the latest plan was, and in the general alcoholic whirl and daze I had done nothing. The champagne was now sour and cold within me, and the intense, self-despising gloom of a midday hangover settled heavily upon my defenceless heart and stomach. I cursed God and man and Benny and the film industry and anyone mad and childish enough to have anything to do with a pack of foxhounds, and, cursing, I emerged on to a pot-holed side road, deserted save for an old, tatty figure who was engaged in the interminable Irish game of filling in the holes with small stones ladled on an even smaller shovel out of a donkey cart. He raised a gay, toothless face at my approach and inquired kindly, "What happened ye at all?" I explained, and he said sadly, Bigod, didn't he seen them hunting, now, all days and weathers, but times, now, it would be a very bad-paying game for the health, mind you. I agreed heartily with this acute summing-up, and asked him if he had seen any cars following on the road. He had not, and I plodded on vaguely, hoping that perhaps the trailer had been left where we met, when an eerie screech echoing after me told me that he had suddenly remembered something. He came hurrying up to tell me, leaving the road-mending apparatus to look after itself, and the donkey walked meditatively into the ditch with its load of stones tilting precariously behind it, and began to eat the hedge gratefully.

"Bigod, I seen a gentleman only a minute gone, go back the road and he leading his horse the very same that it could be yourself, now—only for the grand red coat he'd on him," he added, reproachfully glancing at my very old black one.

So I started "back the road"—mainly because it had begun sleeting again, and if I went the other way the sleet would be in our faces, and the horse would begin to walk like a crab and tread all over me—and presently now he cocked his ears and began to jiggle about and snatch at his bit, and finally whinnied—a hopeful, cheery burbling this time—and an answering, excited scream came back, and round a bend we came upon the best friend who had caused all the trouble, looking over a gate beside Dan Nugent, in his grand red coat.

The desolate droop of the shoulders in that coat told me what had happened; warned me to be careful about asking questions; the drumming in the Four Hundred came back to me abruptly, and Peter's compassionate voice beside me in the van—"lost his nerve"—"lost his nerve"—"lost his nerve"—echoing in my brain like the disembodied, booming memory which haunts the hero in a film flash-back. The face Dan now turned towards me; the smile, the inquiry, utterly failing to break up its frozen misery; told me the same. The supremely ridiculous, the tragic, the disgraceful thing, unimportant and world-shaking.

"I'm afraid I've ruined your horse," I said.

"Are you hurt?" he asked, looking in amazement at my face.

"Not at all. My nose bled."

"What happened?"

"He somersaulted over that first wall out of Kilteely—he never looked at it—he was looking after your horse."

"Ah, the silly bastard! And he's a great wall horse, too. I'm sorry, Anthony, 'tis a shame for you, they looked like having a hunt." He pointed over the gate. "They swung right-handed and ran into Greystown, but you can't see them now, they've gone right up over the hill."

In the pause that followed I hesitated, and then asked the question that it would be even more awkward to leave unasked—"What happened to you?"

His face froze again, became wary, and pathetic in its wariness.

"I got into wire." He pointed at the horse's off hind leg. A long, shallow scratch ran from stifle to hock on the inside. The blood had already dried on it. It was a scratch and nothing more. Dan was watching me. He said "It's nothing, but he was feeling it at the time, the clown."

"It looks nasty," I said, thinking ridiculously of Walter Mitty—("Only a scratch. I set it myself.") I could so clearly imagine the sort of thing that had happened; I could almost see the tall, innocent-looking bank, and feel the horse's confident pounce up on to it—Dan quite happy then, a good start stolen and kept, the drink not dead in him, the first few obstacles tackled with courage and flung behind, the horse going well—and then the trap springing; the wire rising up at them, glinting and coldly wicked, set a couple of feet out in the farther field; the guts dissolving, icy-cold in that horrifying split second; the upflung hand and automatic shout of warning to those behind; too late to stop himself, now, the horse already coming off it; now, for Christ's sake, give him his head, sit still, leave him alone, all so difficult to do; Dan's overstrained nerves, clamouring their frantic warning to his too-often-hurt body, had probably betrayed him, made him clutch hopelessly at the horse's head, his own hands pulling them down to what might have been disaster. But the horse had jumped right out, only dropped a hind leg, kicked back out of it cleverly instead of pulling away, he had been to his nose (I could see the mud on it, now) and up again with a lurch, ready to gallop on; but Dan, suddenly sick, cold, trembling, had pulled up, and, looking back and down, seen with a surge of terrible relief the thin, bright, welcome trickle of blood; a red badge of courage which would allow him to pull out of the hunt with honour.

86

Something like that, anyway, had happened, and Dan was now shaken and miserable and furious with himself.

"Shall we hack on?" he asked wearily, turning away from the gate. "They've run right away from us."

As we moved on drearily up the road, my horse, stiffened up by the brief halt, began to hobble painfully—but Dan's horse, I saw with embarrassment, with compassion, without surprise, strode out gaily. He was not in the least lame, he wasn't in fact feeling it at all, he could have gone on all day.

We slogged along.

Dan said, "I told my man to take the trailer to Knockmore and unhitch there and then follow us round. When he picks up the hunt and finds we're out of it he'll be looking for us. We'll just keep going for Knockmore, God help us, he's quite bright, unlike most of them, God knows, and he'll likely realize what road we'd be on."

"I'm very sorry about the horse," I said. He was becoming rapidly lamer and more martyred, trailing sadly behind me with a patient, ill-used air, bobbing his head wearily up and down at each painful step. Dan's horse, meanwhile, slightly bewildered by the strange turn of events, but convinced we should see hounds again at any moment, and excited by his brief gallop, jiggled tiringly about with cocked ears and shining eyes, shamelessly displaying his soundness in a most embarrassing manner.

"Ah, what the hell," said Dan wearily, in reply, "These things happen—it'll teach him not to bloody brush through a wall next time." He looked down at my horse's knees and smiled unhappily and said defensively, "My fellow seems fair enough now—I reckon I should have gone on."

"I hate a chap who goes on with a hurt horse," I said. "People seem to think that it shows how tough they are

87

—well, maybe it does, but it shows a hell of a lot more about them as well."

He glanced at me sharply, and seemed about to say something, but changed his mind.

We slogged along.

Dan's man did, indeed, seem to be quicker-witted than the majority of his kind, for we were still three miles out of Knockmore when the Land Rover roared triumphantly towards us from round a bend, its blunt and unlovely countenance a thing of remarkable beauty to the grateful eye of its beholders. A little paragon of a man skipped out of it and said he was sorry he'd missed, like, and what happened us? Dan said curtly that he'd done well enough, and he was to hack the horses quietly on towards Knockmore—we would go and hitch up the trailer and bring it back to meet them. There was a briefly sticky moment when the man inquired, as he took the horses from our willing hands, "Will I sit up on this feller?" I saw what he meant. There is no prospect more purgatorial than that of walking between two horses one of which pulls madly to the front, while the other trails sulkily behind—particularly if there is no need to be walking at all.

Dan said shortly, "You can. Don't hurry them", and his man led them off, hurling himself up into the saddle as he went, with the curious squirrel-like and gravity-defying action of his kind. Dan looked heavily after them, standing in the sleet with his coat collar turned up, his hat tipped over his eyes, his shoulders hunched, depression and defeat in every drooping line of his figure. I longed to do or say something of comfort, but for him at this moment there was no comfort in the world.

After a pause, appearing almost to shake himself, he turned back towards the Land Rover; from whose mysterious back depths, thick with the odorous ghosts of hounds and mackintoshs, terriers and oil, and many little, horsy men, he pulled a very comforting hamper which looked as if it had come straight out of Beatrix Potter, but actually contained whisky, port, brandy, bacon sandwiches, and black plum cake.

I felt myself drooling like Suky.

"Ball of malt?" Dan asked, pouring it recklessly. "Warm you up."

"Doctors will tell you," I said, pompously, snatching it "that alcohol in fact makes you colder; the warmth is an illusion, see?"

"Ah, well, 'tis a great illusion to have—and what class of a doctor would tell you a damn fool tale like that when he'd be sacked for it? God, wouldn't some people say anything, now?"

He had given me a very generous glassful of Paddy, and I drank to all illusions of warmth and gaiety, and tranquillity. The whisky hurried warmly and gaily down and through me, and whispered as it went that tranquillity was not far off.

Maybe Dan was very unhappy, and Sarah a bitch, Rupert a ruin, Benny an egocentric madman, and myself (as I had so often been told), a dangerous combination of weakness and recklessness—but if so, what the hell? Why, tomorrow I may be myself with yesterday's seven thousand years, I thought vaguely, with a sweeping mental gesture, and meanwhile what about another glass of whisky and a bacon sandwich to go with it?

Some space or time later Dan up-ended his third glass, and said in a self-testing voice, as if he didn't really believe he was going to move at all, "Better hack on, hadn't we?"

Alcohol always has on me the comforting effect of total detachment from myself. I stand some distance away, watching with tolerance, sympathy, and wisdom the capers of the curious chap pretending to be me. So, now, I watched him, this sporting figure with his bloody face

89

and muddy coat, climb stiffly into the Land Rover, and sprawl there as comfortably as the high seat permitted, light a cigarette, and laugh when Dan reversed it too far and too violently on to the muddy verge, and only got off after a desperate struggle in the lowest low-ratio gear. We had gone churning noisily past the horses, whose attendant looked at us with self-conscious rectitude, before he remembered to change the ratio.

"Tell you what," he said confidentially to me, "those damfool doctors were wrong—they were just a bunch of spoil-sports."

"Of course they were," I said happily, eating plum cake sodden with richness, and getting it slightly muddled with my cigarette.

We went on, less noisy, but rather too fast.

Dan said suddenly, "That bastard knows."

"What?" I asked, startled out of a dream of brilliant dialogue in a Pirandello-like plot which was approaching philosophy in the purity of its mathematical precision. Hell, I thought, I had something there.

"My man. He knows."

"Knows what?" I asked, coming round, and stalling.

"Knows I had no bloody reason not to go on."

"You wanted to stop," I said. "Reason enough for him or anyone else, isn't it?"

"I stopped because I was scared," said Dan, savagely. "I was plain bloody scared stiff because I had nearly been on the floor. And he knows. You know. Tomorrow everyone will know."

Tomorrow! Why, tomorrow you may be yourself with yesterday's seven thousand years. . . . But how to apply the philosophy of a Persian mystic to heal the raw wounds of an Irish ex-steeplechase jockey?

"What the hell?" I said. "They say. What do they say? Let them say."

"O, Jesus," he said. "They say, all right. I'll bet you heard it in London."

I said nothing.

He asked, furiously, "*Did* you?"

"You know what the bush telegraph is like. I heard that Peter was never sober, and Jane Harrington was making a strong pass at a priest, and that Euphemia Coke had really finally turned into a man, and was going to make his fortune writing about it for the Sunday papers. For God's sake, Dan, you know what it's like."

He hadn't listened.

"What the hell am I going to do?" he inquired, not particularly of me, staring ahead, wrapped in the illusionary, glowing safety of alcoholic confidences.

"Give up," I said.

"Sarah would leave me," he said, with a tragic simplicity.

"I don't believe that. But, if she would, you'd only be well rid of her."

"That's a bloody silly thing to say."

"But true."

"True, maybe. No comfort."

"Comfort, hell!" I said, trying to brace him up a bit. "Since when have you been looking for comfort? When you were faced into Becher's, I suppose, you looked around for it? Or on some green, star-gazing brute in a novice chase, you asked the chap next to you to hold your hand as you came into the regulation?"

"I didn't give a damn, mind you. I'd never had a horse on top of me. I didn't know it hurt, God help me. I didn't know anything hurt. I was feeling my bloody oats and nothing else."

I said: "Nobody ever accused you of lack of guts—but I'll do it now, if you don't give up. This is just a different class of an obstacle you're faced into—but it still won't be any good looking around for comfort."

"I love the bitch," he said, drearily, as if I would neither believe nor understand him, and as if it hardly mattered anyway. He had to say all this some time, and this was the time. The shaking he had received, the whisky, the presence of someone reassuringly outside his world; all these had betrayed him. He might or might not remember he had confided in me, but it ought, anyway, I hoped, to lessen the strain a bit for him.

"Look," I said. "I do know a bit about the way people's minds work—that's how I earn my living, anyway. If you tell Sarah you'll see her damned before you'll hunt longer, and mean it, and beat her if necessary, the odds are she won't leave you. And what's the alternative? Endless dreary, frightening seasons, and she'll give you progressive hell, and leave you anyway in the end. And you've got to give it up. You know that. God knows I'm scared and you're scared and everyone's scared before they get going—but when you go on being scared while they *are* going, that's the time to stop. You know that, too. You go on, and you'll have all the crucifying falls you're dreading, every one of 'em. You'll give yourself falls. You know that, too. You'll pull your horse down."

Outside the muddied, bloodied, authoritative and sporting figure another Anthony Kavanagh watched, detached and tolerant, somewhat amused and rather touched by this excellent if self-assured advice.

Dan looked across at me, for the first time.

"True enough for you. I know it all."

"Well, then. . . ."

"People are so narky. They're bloody ruthless. Maybe you don't know the hunting crowd as well as I do."

"I know the theatre," I said. "And let me tell you, Melton before the war was down the course to it."

We had swung suddenly, in carefree fashion, off down another pot-holed little road, and now a yellow sign-post

92

flickered suddenly past my eyes, written (as an Irishman had once explained it to me) "In Irish to annoy the English, and in English so the Irish can understand it."

"Hold hard," I said, "You're not right for Knockmore."

Dan braked screechingly.

"That signpost says carry straight on."

"Don't you know this country? They twist 'em round for gas—it's the national game." But he backed up, nevertheless, and we stared at the signpost which pointed, as I had said, straight ahead. A sign on the other side of the road advised us to call in to McCarthy's Hotel.

"You're in the right of it," Dan said, and backed out on to the other road.

It was as we were halted, just as Dan's hand reached for the lever, to engage a forward gear again, that the incredible and beautiful thing happened.

The fox jumped out into the middle of the road from the drop and ditch on our right—a long, sure, curving leap like a swimmer swallow-diving. He was big, dark, handsome, and undistressed, and his bushy brush was flauntingly tagged with white. He took off again from the road as if he had landed on springs, and sailed superbly to the top of the farther, stone-faced bank, where he halted a moment, calmly arrogant, and stared at us without fear, consideringly. Then he whisked his brush, dismissing us with the gesture, and dropped delicate as a cat down the far side and was gone like a ghost, leaving behind him a strong, disturbing rumour of the wild. The whole thing took perhaps five seconds, and I was not even very sure that I had really seen him at all.

"Christ!" Dan said, open-mouthed, his hand poised above the gear-lever like a child playing statues, "Charlie!"

"Himself," I said.

Then we were out of the Land Rover and scrambling to

93

the top of the bank. The fox was holding his point straight across the middle of the far field, despising all hedge-running, gliding on with that easy, loping foxy gait that looks so slow and is so fast. We watched him float like a dark lump of thistledown to the top of the next bank. There, again, he paused and looked back at us for a second before he disappeared, almost as if he was amused, as if he said, "I wish these hounds of yours would give me a run for my money."

"Bigod," said Dan lovingly to him, "You're a bold fellow enough."

"I wonder if he's the hunted fox?"

"If he is, they're not pressing him."

We shuffled ourselves round on the razor-backed bank and looked back the way the fox had come. The place from which he had jumped out into our startled vision was a plain, stone-faced drop into the road, with a dirty ditch. Beyond it the ground sloped, field after field, down to what appeared to be a stream, and straggling woodland, and beyond that rose again gently, colourless in the cold light. Nothing stirred but the rooks and bullocks and the wind.

"Listen," said Dan.

We listened.

Nothing. The cold sighing of that wind, the faint movement of leaves, the grind of a lorry labouring somewhere up a hill out of sight. Nothing. A bullock bawling, a dog barking, a child shouting shrilly from a cabin. Nothing of what we wanted to hear. A bird chittering suddenly, our own breathing, the shuffle of our boots as we shifted position. No other sound.

"They're likely not on that fellow at all," said Dan.

"Wait—listen . . ." I thought I had heard it then, and a moment later we both heard it for certain—unmistakable, unforgettable, unfailingly shivering the scalp; the true, throaty clamour and crying, faint, far off, but rapidly swelling. "Aha!" said Dan, with the peculiar exultation that that rather frightening sound arouses in its devotees, "Running hard, too—who'd have thought there'd be this much smell on a day like this?"

"Must be going to snow," I said, in the manner of the cognoscenti.

A moment later I saw the hunt coming down the slope of the far ground, little, moving, multi-coloured, dots that might have been cattle, but were not; and then, taking a line down from them, with straining eyes, I could just see hounds running, like a handful of pearls being rolled down a giant backcloth.

"That's the hell of a water-jump they're going into," said Dan. "It'll stop some of them. There's no way round within miles, God help them."

We waited, while the hunt went down into the valley out of our sight, the little toy figures, men and horses and dogs, crossing the country with that deceptive ease which distance lends to the view of a hunt, a point-to-point, or even a National.

The cry grew stronger all the time.

"The water-jump doesn't seem to be stopping the dogs, anyway," said Dan. "Wouldn't it amaze you, now, that the smell's so good?"

"Snow," I murmured, stubbornly, with that tendency to know more about scent than anyone else that is so curiously apt to afflict even the most ignorant and retiring.

Behind us a creamery lorry had pulled up, and the driver had got out and was now standing on the bonnet, alternately straining on tiptoe to see, and bending down to cuff two little boys, who had appeared from nowhere, and wanted to stand on the bonnet also. "God help us!" I heard him say, "And can't you rise yourselves on the

bank beyant? Is it no use of yourselves you have at all?"
So, with shifty glances at Dan and myself they clambered
up on to the Land Rover instead, and bounced about on
it, very much above themselves, and shrieking imagina-
tively that they could see the fox's self, and a felly in the
ditch below, and he clear mad at it. We couldn't—but in
another moment we could see the leading hounds coming
up from the stream, driving forward grimly, lean, intent,
destructive and superb, even as the fox had been superb.
The body of the pack came crying together just behind
them, and on their flank two horses laboured, rolling
towards each other and away again as they attacked the
hill, and after them again came a loose horse, bucketing
along wildly with his saddle slipping, and intimidating a
couple of tail hounds who were already depressed and
guilt-ridden by their inability to get to head.

"Old George and Roger," said Dan. "And Peter's
young one going spare, bigod. We'll try and catch him
before he goes and gets himself into wire or something.
I hope he hasn't crucified Peter."

Striving, tense, muddy wet coats plastered close to
their ribby hard-muscled bodies, scratched and bloody
ears pinned back by the wind, delicate noses drinking a
scent that flowed like wine to their fox-haunted brains,
hounds came down into the road off the drop, shouting
like bells. A first season dog was leading, delirious with
the glory of it, but as soon as he hit the road and the
gorgeous smell vanished somewhat his confident cry
changed to shrill, agonized inquiry: "Where? Help!" he
shrieked woefully, "Gone!"—but the old hound behind
him drove straight to the top of the far bank, and owned
to it there gruffly: "Here, fool, here!" and the rest shouted
"Right, right, right!" in triumphant chorus, and the
whole bank for a second swirled and shuddered and
shimmered with black and white and tan bodies, and then

they were clamouring on across the far field, their cry shaking the cold air, and our hearts.

And now here came old George, launched into the air above us, off the drop, a second's vision of a set, mulberry face, watering eyes narrowed against the wind, a battered cap blue with age tilted somewhat over them, mud-spattered breeches, and a spur gone. The old, clever horse, sweating, breathing like a steam-engine, indomitably in command of the situation, slithered as he landed, and collected himself and faced himself straight into the bank with no help at all from his entirely uninterested rider—old George never knew, or cared, what he happened to be jumping; his mind was always far ahead, catching his fox. His horse took in, now, the stone face of the bank, and its razor back, and the fact that he must get right to the top of it and kick straight off again, and his wise head, as he lowered it to measure the exact amount of effort required, was a lovely heart-stirring sight—ears cocked, wide, delicate, nostrils pulsing, a study in noble determination and courage. He leaped with a grunt of self-congratulation, kicking a stone crashingly back down into the road as he launched himself out into the field, and Roger's horse, landing on to it from the drop, crashed with all the sickening, slipping, skidding flurry which makes a fall on tarmac so horrifying to behold, and the loose young horse, jumping wildly out after them, and then trying to avoid them, also slipped, skidded, flurried, but managed not to fall, ending up with its chest against the Land Rover's mudguard, and its horrified nose resting gaspingly on the bonnet, at the little boys' feet.

"Holy Mother of God!" said Dan, reverently.

"Ah, now, whoa there, the good fellow!" said the lorry driver, unnecessarily.

"The gintlemen is quinched for sure!" shrieked one of

the boys, ecstatically. Roger was not quite quinched, but he was fairly groggy when I disentangled him from his horse. He sat on the front bumper of the lorry, saying in a sick voice that he would be all right in a minute—a prophecy correctly traditional in the circumstances, but only too often, alas, untrue. I was trying to find out how bad he really was, preventing Dan from giving him brandy, and holding on to Peter's horse, while the lorry driver encouraged the other one to rise—"Sure, you couldn't lie there all day, at all, so you couldn't. Have you the leg hurt on you? You have not, then, 'tis codding you are, taking your ease that way"—when we were all electrified suddenly by the passage of Sarah on the horse who would lep the Lord Himself; and who now, by lepping into the road, over Roger's horse; and out again, proved himself worthy of the honour. He came like a lion, an acrobat, a kangaroo, all rolled into one, turning and twisting like a minnow and was gone with the surge of a south-westerly gale.

Sarah sat absolutely still on him, in a trance of danger and delight, unseeing, smiling, her hands resting quiet and confident on his snaky, muscular neck.

"Jesus Christ," said Dan, heavily, with the same reverence with which he had called upon His Mother. His dark face wore an almost tearful expression of fury, love, and despair. Roger, who had opened his eyes briefly, shut them again and leaned his head weakly back against the lorry, and the lorry driver, who had had to skip out of the way very quick indeed, said admiringly wasn't that a horse, now, who had a great heart to go on, and with a lady, too, mind you!

Now here came Benny, down into the road a little higher up, and battering towards us with a quite extraordinarily dramatic air of blood-on-the-sand about him. He looked bemused and intense, the look of one determined to practise a mystique in the proper manner. I saw what Phillippa meant about his hunting virulently, but whether this particular piece of hunting was that of Sarah or the fox I was not sure.

"Are you O.K.?" he shouted.

"No," I said.

"Great, that's great," he said absently, and pressed wildly on.

"Who the hell was that?" asked Roger, with his eyes shut.

"How are you feeling?" I asked him back.

"Sick," he said, faintly. "All-right-in-a-minute."

"You'll be all right in a minute," Dan told him, helpfully.

I was much relieved when the little wreck of a car in which my mother always drove to hounds chuggered round the corner and drew up in surprise. Four faces came out of it at us—my mother's, used to hunting casualties, alarmed but resigned—Rupert's, with an air of bemused beatitude—Phillippa's, fearing the worst—and Possum's, dreamily detached. My mother said, "Don't give him anything to drink," Rupert said disinterestedly, "Feller here's got a fall," Phillippa said, "Oh, it's not Benny," with surprise, and added belatedly "*Poor* Roger" —and Possum asked me very seriously, "Did you ever see a saxophone?"

The sleet had changed to a thin, bitter, driving snow (even at this moment I congratulated myself) and out of the comparatively cosy little car my mamma and Phillippa came gallantly, while Rupert and Possum—those children of nature—seized the opportunity respectively to take a long pull at a bottle of port and to blow the horn shatteringly. Roger put his head in his hands. My mamma, even having now seen the state of his face, managed to look back and say sternly, "I told you to eat

99

a sandwich, Rupert dear," to which he replied with dignity, "I'm not an eating man," before re-applying the bottle to his face. Phillippa said to her son, more feebly, "Stop making that noise, and I'll play a game of snakes and ladders with you before you go to bed"—upon which he left the horn, and experimented with how far he could lean out of the window without falling. It turned out to be not very far, and the lorry driver, profiting by his recent practice in swift movement, caught him as he fell, and set him on his feet with an admonition not to be worrying his mammy that way. Possum looked up into my face with holy ecstasy and said, "You've got a bleed."

"I know," I told him.

"Are you hunting?" he asked, rather sternly, pinning me down.

"I was," I said.

"Is this the hunt?"

"No," I said.

"Why isn't it?"

I found I was quite unable to work out why it wasn't, or, if, indeed, it was, and Roger was now being sick, tenderly and expertly ministered to by my mamma and Phillippa. Possum looked consideringly at them, unmoved, and said, "Once, I had sick on my sock."

"Oh," I said.

The lorry driver, whose tact and resource seemed to be bottomless, said comfortingly that he had no call to be thinking of them ugly things—look at the grand horses, now. Possum continued to look fixedly and enjoyably at Roger. Rupert stretched himself luxuriously out along the back seat of the car with the bottle of port, like somebody attending an unexpected but nevertheless delightful orgy, and shut the window firmly, dissociating himself from disaster. My mamma told Roger gently that he would be all right in a minute, and turned briskly back towards the car.

"Come out of there at once, Rupert."

Rupert let the window down an inch, and said he wasn't a man for all this ridiculous battling with the elements—they were too big, he added, to make his point.

"If only he would eat at least a sandwich," said my mamma sadly. "Come out at once, Rupert, dear."

Rupert emerged with difficulty from the little car, still clutching the bottle of port. " 'Straordinary thing," he said loftily to the lorry driver, "All women want you to eat all the time. 'Straordinary idea. Even you——" he said, sorrowfully, to my mamma, swaying over her, and patting the air magnanimously just above her shoulder, "even you, lovely Sophia, indiscretion of my youth."

"Not *really*," said my mamma, with regret. "And you were so attractive, Rupert dear."

"All my teeth in those days," said Rupert succinctly. "Well—where do we go from here? Why do we stand around in these elements so much? Has no one any initiative?" He began to climb, with an unnecessary amount of groaning and laborious acrobatics, into the back of the Land Rover, caught his foot in the spare wheel, and disappeared from view. My mamma looked after him with tenderness, softened by memories of the discreet indiscretion, and then re-applied herself to Roger; who was still saying in a fixed voice how absolutely all right he would be in a minute.

"Anto, dear," she said, "I must take him into Knockmore hospital, I think—will you and Dan look after Rupert? He's being dreadfully irresponsible, and quite apart from being drunk, I really think he isn't at all well."

"I daresay not," I said rather coldly.

"Where's his horse?"

"I really don't know—I don't even really know if he ever had one."

"Sour brute," said Rupert hollowly, from the back, "Threw itself down in the first ditch, the sod. Wouldn't dream of paying for it. May be dead, for all I know. Hope it is. Anyway, I've given up hunting."

At this moment Peter appeared at the top of the drop, very wet and muddy, and leading what I could only feel, with a sinking of the heart, must be Rupert's horse—a common animal with large feet and a surly air of confirmed disillusionment.

"Your woman's in the water-jump," he said cheerfully to me.

"Oh," I said. My nose had begun to bleed again and Possum, planted solemnly exactly in front of me, stared up at it as if he was seeing the Beatific Vision.

"What *is* all this, anyway?" asked Peter. "The Teddy Bear's picnic?"

He slithered awkwardly down off the drop and fell in a resigned manner into the ditch. Rupert's horse refused doggedly to follow him, and Peter cursed him fluently and dispassionately, his language causing Possum at last to take an interest in someone who wasn't actually being sick or bleeding.

"Peter, *dear*," said my mamma.

"Sorry, Sophia."

Rupert looked briefly out of the Land Rover and said, "Take that frightful animal away, can't you?" and sank back again out of sight. My mother and Phillippa now coerced and supported Roger off the front bumper of the lorry and into the awful little car, where he sat stiffly upright, pale green and rather unfocused—looking, obviously unlikely to be all right in a minute, and my mother, who always knew exactly on what to concentrate in an unpromising general situation called, "Come along, dears" to Phillippa and Possum, and prepared to abandon the rest of us.

"Oh, dear . . ." said Phillippa uncertainly, "I do hope Benny. . . ."

"Is Gillian all right?" I asked Peter.

"Yes, fine, but the horse is still swimming, she's trying to fish him out, she's got about fifty locals hindering her—I see you caught mine—good."

"Animal lovers," said a slurred, contemptuous voice from the back of the Land Rover.

My mother had turned the awful little car around. "Come along, dears," she called again.

"Oh. . . ."

Peter looked at Phillippa and grinned. "We'll bring him back alive," he said, comfortingly. Phillippa gave him a look of glowing gratitude and said, "Peter, you're *soaking*; don't get pneumonia, promise?" and I longed for Gillian to be there, so that I could observe the matchmaking fire kindle in her eye. Phillippa led the reluctant Possum away, and bundled him in beside my mother, putting herself gallantly behind with Roger, who might well be sick on her. Possum hung back as he was led off, not looking where his feet were going, still held in thrall to the fascinating behaviour of my magically unusual nose. His round blue eye, its beam piercing between Phillippa and Roger from the front seat was the last thing I saw as they chuggered away from us.

"Jesus, such a circus," said Dan gloomily. "This would be a day that you wouldn't mind was it over." He poured out a drink for Peter, who accepted it gratefully and gulped it down eagerly. His face, I noticed suddenly, was rather drawn beneath the mud splashes, and I wondered if he had fallen on his bad shoulder, and if so, how much it was now hurting him. Then we gave a drink to the lorry driver, who had by now persuaded Roger's horse to get to its feet. He was a kindly man, but I felt that his reluctance to leave us was due less to kindliness than to the tendency of his race to involve themselves eagerly in any confused situation which has in it the elements of drama, and may, with a little luck, become disastrous. I wondered who, or what train, was waiting for the milk. My nose ceased to bleed for a moment and I endeavoured to pull myself together and take stock. "We now have three horses, one lame, and a Land Rover," I said to Dan.

"And Rupert," he said gloomily. "We've got *him*, God help us."

There was now a curious, piggy noise from the back of the Land Rover, and I peered in. Rupert was sleeping the sleep of the just and innocent; his head lolling forward and down on his port-stained waistcoat; his long legs in their filthy boots crossed comfortably upon the hamper; the bottle of port still clutched in a protective hand. He looked like an exhausted naughty child with a rag doll. "What a wonderful thing it must be to have a clear conscience," said Peter, looking in beside me.

Rupert's horse was still standing on the top of the drop, ravenously tearing at some very unattractive-looking tufts of old grass. He seemed determined to move as little as possible, and kept one eye rolled towards us, watching for any further attempt to make him jump down, which he intended to thwart. Suddenly he swung his head up from the grass and cocked his ears, and a moment later we heard it, too—the hollow slapping of trotting hooves, coming towards us from beyond the bend of the road. "And who the hell's *this*, now?" asked Dan, "God, wouldn't you think there might be one of us up with hounds and not playing games in the road this way?"

It was Gillian, the animal lover—wettish but triumphant, with her rescued animal. Rupert's horse seemed unduly moved. He plunged heavily and unexpectedly down off the drop, and greeted them skittishly. Gillian's mare gave him a haughty but not entirely unpromising eye, and allowed him to touch noses for a minute. She then gave a shrill, affected scream, and struck at him violently with a forefoot.

"*Don't!*" squeaked Gillian, taken by surprise.

"Mare's in use very late," said Dan, trapping Rupert's horse skilfully.

"Darling, what can you mean? No, don't explain, just take that horse right away, please. . . . What *are* you all doing, hiding in the road like this and letting the dogs escape you? I thought you were all hard men to hounds?"

"We are," I said. "We've all taken crucifying falls on account of it."

"Darling—your face!"

"I know. I had a bleed."

She gave me a strict look.

"If I was a wife I'd say you'd been drinking."

"You are, and I have."

"Well, no need for complete lack of chivalry—how about one for the little woman?"

The whiskey was finished. Peter skilfully disengaged the port from Rupert's nerveless hand, which was left clutched pathetically around air, and mixed it deliciously with some brandy. Gillian golloped it down happily. "Now I feel a lovely glow, just like in an advertisement."

"You don't really—it's just an illusion."

"Don't keep on saying that," said Dan. "We might get to believe it, and then we couldn't stand the cold, mind you."

Again, I tried to take stock.

"Is your mare sound?" I asked Gillian, rather pompously.

"She seems a tiny bit vulgar to me."

"Never mind," said Peter. "She can still walk. That makes four horses: two sound, one lame, one vulgar, to be got somewhere, somehow, God help us."

"Ours must have been in Knockmore some time, by now," I said to Dan. "Your man has probably given up hope."

"He has fair sense," said Dan. "He'll have boxed them up. We shall have to unbox them while we hitch up, and then box them again," he added, musingly.

"That will be fun," I said.

The lorry driver, observing that the situation was deteriorating into one that looked like being dealt with fairly sensibly, and in which no further fruitful disasters would be involved said now that Bigod, there was them beyant at the station would be lepping afther the milk, and withdrew, after being tactfully rewarded by Peter. Gillian, who had gone around to the back of the Land Rover to peer in fascinatedly at Rupert, gave a sudden squeak.

"There's *blood* on the road!"

"That was Roger, poor chap," said Dan.

"Roger?" Gillian went immediately and frighteningly white. Her treacherous guts, it was obvious, had gone into one great, hard, cold knot again.

"Pretty shook, he was," went on Dan, not noticing. "He took a shocker."

Peter had noticed, gently, on the instant. He said comfortingly, "He got a bit of a crack on the head, that's all. Sophia and Phillippa took him off in the car—he'll be flying in a few hours."

"I can't think why anybody ever hunts, can you?" said Gillian, mastering her guts.

I suppose, I thought, still confused with whiskey, that I ought to be angry—or at least upset. My wife in love with my brother—is it something wrong or right with me that makes me feel merely sorry? Am I full of compassion, or just passionless? Perhaps my passion is only for people and situations I create myself, and not for

106

those already created—perhaps a line of dialogue; an effect; a silence superbly eloquent; the subtle impressions of entry and exit: the boundless reality of the imagination, may always mean more to me emotionally than any one self-energizing figure of flesh and blood and beating, uncertain heart. What's Hecuba to me, or I to Hecuba? Infinitely more, perhaps, than these breathing, unpredictable, half-realized types around me? A wife—as Gillian had pointed out—a peer—a retired steeplechase jockey—asleep in the Land Rover a determinedly unretired rake—off stage, a mother, a brother—all making their entries and exits with such untidiness, and so appallingly little sense of occasion. All of us the bloody same, I thought, resentfully—some god's handful of salts and calcium and iron; swayed by stars and tides and passions, changed by ideas and electrical storms; touched by grace; marred by gravity; curious if we feel ourselves to be animals, yet more curious if we believe ourselves to be angels; carrying within ourselves our familiar hell and our rare heaven; still standing only precariously upright, belly deep in earth and crying for the moon. . . . And what the hell are we doing here in this road at this moment? Am I, I thought, by no means for the first time, really raving mad?

"Darling, you're looking mad," said Gillian.

"Brace up, boy," said Peter. "We have to apply our minds."

"I was," I said.

"The thing is," said Gillian, "we all need a drink."

We all had some port and brandy. The wind rose, developing a slight, eerie howl as it did so, and driving a further flurry of snow before it. Peter turned up the collar of his coat and tried to disappear into it. He was very wet, and so was Gillian. Rupert snored on happily in the back of the Land Rover, and Gillian peered in at him again, and announced ecstatically that he had taken his teeth out. "He probably thinks that he's shacked up cosily with that Arab girl of very good family."

"In Tangier . . . so beautifully warm . . .", I heard myself, to my surprise, say wistfully.

Dan said, "Ah, listen now—we ain't tucked up anywhere, and it's bloody cold, and we've got to press on."

"But where the hell to?"

Where, indeed? Four horses, one lame, all miserable, five people, two probably with incipient pneumonia, one drunk, one (myself, I had just realized) slightly concussed.

"We'll go in to Poodle," said Dan suddenly, brilliantly. "It's only a mile up the road from here."

"*Darling*," said Gillian, "of course we will—straight into her delicious, cosy lair, with those great, welcoming puffs of heat coming out of it, and all those bathrooms, endless hot water—oh, the heaven—*quick*, come on."

Poodle was the Lucy Glitters of the West Tipperary country, and had, lucky girl, a tremendous talent for living in sin and luxury. Gillian sometimes complained that she was too blonde and too pneumatic and too fashionable to be allowed to go on getting away with it, but nobody seemed to be able to stop her. Nor, indeed, would anybody of any sense have wished to do so—she was a person who deserved to be heavily subsidized by her neighbours in return for the vast amount of entertainment and gossip she provided them with freely and generously throughout each hunting season, and for the even more fascinating—because tantalizingly non-proven—messages that the bush telegraph would relay tirelessly in the summer about appreciation of Primitives in Italy, the moment of truth in Spain, and even, sometimes, less glamorously, sailing close to the wind in Kerry.

"But wait a minute," I said. "What about the current boy friend? Will *he* give out any great welcoming puffs of anything if we all suddenly arrive on him like this, while Poodle's hunting?"

"Of course he will, darling. I know him. You do, too. He's that lovely blond Canadian dolly that Rose had last year, lucky her. He can move his eyes, and all his clothes take on and off. Filthy rich. He'll love us. He'll think we're Irish Life."

"Irish Life, where are you?" said Dan gloomily. " 'Tis a bloody circus we are. But we can put the horses in there and get 'em dry, and rugs across 'em, anyway."

"But what about the other horses?" said Peter.

"The *other* horses?"

"Yes—*your* horse, and Dan's—where are they?"

"Dear Lord," I said. "They just happened to have slipped my mind. We seem to have so many horses anyway."

"Here's the way we'll work it," said Dan, masterfully. "You three take these horses and yourselves to Poodle's, and get cleaned up and warm—them and you. I'll take the Land Rover to Knockmore and get hitched up and take our horses home."

"But Rupert—what about him? He's *in* the Land Rover."

"Drop him at the hospital in Knockmore," said Peter, catching some of Dan's brilliance. "Phillippa and Sophia will be there still with Roger—those two could look after anybody, even without a hospital to do it in."

"Was Roger so bad?" asked Gillian, in an off-hand way, practically humming a tune, which made me feel a strong desire both to laugh at and to comfort her.

"He was all right," said Peter. "A bit groggy. Come on, now."

Dan roared off, still masterful, bumping Rupert about rather unkindly, and the rest of us plodded urgently on our depressed, shivering and bewildered horses, towards

Poodle's gorgeous, hot, scented jungle of a house, which seemed at that moment more than likely to be a myth. The snow had become thin, wet, and savage, and our horses walked unenthusiastically sideways into it, very slowly, with heads down below their knees and cold ears laid flat back. Occasionally one or other of them would summon up enough hope and courage to try and whip round from it, or else to stand stock-still and suffer. Our progress was purgatorial, and it seemed unlikely that any of us would ever be warm or dry again, or, indeed, ever had been within memory. But suddenly, at last, there was Poodle's yard—rather splendidly two-toned in Poodle's racing colours—there were boxes strawed down hock deep, there were many hideous little lads scampering about with wisps and rubbers and rugs, with gruel and stout and hot water and antiseptics and linseed mashes and soft, comforting exclamations and professional hissing noises—so that Gillian and I were able to persuade even Peter that the horses could really be quite safely left in these capable hands while we attended to our own very badly needed comfort. So we struggled wearily out of the yard, and down the path by the side of the house, past Poodle's drawing-room windows on our way to the front door. Head down against the snow, numb with misery, desiring only a hot bath or death, I ran suddenly into Peter, who was in front of me, cursed him savagely for stopping, heard him draw in his breath sharply, and looking up, saw that he had gone a very curious colour indeed. I wondered again if he had hurt himself much in his fall, and, if so, whether he was now about to pass out on us, and thought selfishly, that it really would be the very final straw if he did—couldn't he at least wait now, for God's sake, until we were inside the house?

Then, following his gaze, I found myself staring, equally horrified, into Poodle's lovely great forcing house of a drawing-room; at the superbly roaring gilt and scarlet fire in her glittering Adam grate; at her enormous golden invitation of a sofa—what Gillian always rather crudely referred to as Poodle's casting couch.

Upon this now, slightly entangled with two fawn-coloured Italian greyhounds, but none the less rather seriously entwined themselves, lay Benny and Peter's lovely child—entranced and oblivious.

Chapter Eight

Luckily, mercifully, Benny went down with flu. Not, of course, at that very moment—a moment which I often think—and hope—must have represented the very nadir of discomfort and embarrassment in my life—but twenty-four hours later. It was Gillian who had saved the situation at the actual moment of its acute development—Gillian, staggering a little in front of us through the snow in her sodden, squeaking boots and sopping breeches, her hair dripping in depressed rats' tails from beneath the cap she had tilted irritably over her eyes. How sad it is, she had observed to me later, that we so seldom face up to our zeniths and nadirs superbly coiffed, full of incomparable *tenue*, spiritually armoured by great principles; she had been merely annoyed at the time, she said, by the interruption of her journey towards Poodle's baths and fires and drinks—and I remember that I thought how sore my upper lip was going to be, as I kept licking the mingled dried blood and melting snow away from it.

"Gillian," I had called, faintly. Gillian had looked very irritably over her shoulder at me, and I had pointed, speechlessly, and she had looked and said, "Oh, *no!*" more faintly still, and seized Peter by his arm without hesitation and said "*Poor Phillippa!*" fiercely.

Peter said something obscene.

He had become an even more curious colour, and he now took an unsteady step forward, with a frightening face. Gillian bent down, scooped up some gravel, and flung it at the window, and a frosty star crackled out sharply across one pane of the thin, old glass. The Italian greyhounds unplaited themselves in one sinuous movement of shock and amazement, and curvetted shrilly in the air, and so, more or less, did Benny and Peter's child; demon face and angel face arising from the depths, with the entrancement sliding visibly off them, like water. Gillian seized Peter again. "Don't, don't, *don't*," she hissed rapidly. "*Poor* Phillippa, *think*, darling, wait, *don't. Do* something," she added, to me, stamping her squelching foot. I suppose I must have been looking particularly foolish, standing there, licking my lip, shivering, with the glazed air of mild concussion over all.

"Better go in," I heard myself say, thickly.

Inside, Poodle's lovely blond Canadian dolly received us with amazement, and the small boy in a white coat who was following him across the hall dropped the tray of drinks he was carrying and caught it again in mid-air; a decanter of whiskey slid to one side, one glass turned over and shattered. "Jesus God!" he muttered, righting the whiskey and breathing hard.

"Say! Has there been an accident?"

"About eight accidents," said Gillian wildly. She always swore, afterwards, that she did *not* add, "One in your drawing-room," but I still think she did. She now pulled herself together neatly and said rather pompously, "Don't you remember me? Staying with Rose and Guy?"

"Why . . . why, of course . . . well, of course. . . . Mrs. Lodwick, isn't it?"

"Mrs. Kavanagh now, darling. You know Anthony? I married him—here he is."

"Well . . . why, of course I do. . . ." A lovely, blond hand seized mine. "Why, this is great, just great . . . well, why ever didn't I know you were over here? We must certainly celebrate this—why, I remember—" he went on, with exquisite courtesy, to remember the first night of a play of mine he had seen in New York. Smiling numbly, I saw out of the corner of my eye Peter stalk grimly and purposefully past us towards the drawing-room door. His tough, battered face, usually so gentle and amused, was stony and rigid with anger. This, I thought, must be either a film or a nightmare—perhaps Benny has made the film already, and this is it? Or has he just made the nightmare? Gillian went after Peter like a terrier, and the lovely Canadian dolly half-turned in amazement.

"Why . . ."

"You know Lord Dungarvan," I said, automatically.

"Why . . ."

"He isn't feeling well," I said.

"Why . . ."

"He's just had a very bad fall."

"Why . . ."

"He needs a drink," I said, wildly, and seized the decanter from the hard-breathing small boy and hurried after Gillian.

"Why, yes, why, of course, . . ." said the blond Canadian dolly helplessly, following me. "If there's anything at all I can do. . . . Delighted to be of service . . . Poodle. . . ."

I had forgotten quite how unutterably bland Benny could manage to be under these sorts of circumstances. He stood at ease in front of the gorgeous fire with his legs apart and his hands behind his back, and beamed indulgently at us, as we entered, like one who endeavours to cover up and excuse the hopelessly uncouth behaviour and manners of well-loved but irritating friends. He wore some tight pink pants and an Italian shirt that undoubtedly belonged to his temporary host. Dry and warm, blast his soul, and how did he get here, anyway?

He drawled sympathetically, "Gee, you po-o-or things, you're so-o-o wet and cold."

Gillian, she told me later, had been about to say, "You skunk"—but had stopped because it seemed so much the right thing to say, and she suddenly felt sure that Benny had written the script for her.

Peter said, "I should like a word with you. Outside."

He looked intensely dangerous.

"He's ill," I said to Poodle's astonished dolly. "He hit his head."

"OUTSIDE," said Peter very loudly.

"Peter, *love*, . . ." said Gillian, very softly, still holding him, terrier-like. The Italian greyhounds and Peter's lovely child stood and quivered together; all divinely beautiful, innocent, and alarmed. Snuffing the air, they smelt anger, and didn't at all care for it. Their wonderful dark eyes flickered this way and that, piteously, as they hoped against hope that everything would be lovely again quite soon, and they could all go back to the sofa.

Peter said nothing, very eloquently, waiting for Benny.

Gillian said more loudly, with a tinge of exasperation, "My head . . ." and staggered, not ungracefully, against Peter—and I took my cue smartly, sat down in what I hoped was a groggy fashion, and put my luckily blood-smeared face in my hands. After all, Peter had only one arm, and he could hardly hold up Gillian and take Benny outside at the same time, and, being a chivalrous chap, he would, I hoped, feel forced to put Gillian first.

"Why . . . gosh, this is just terrible . . . hold on a minute . . . why, you poor things, . . ." said Poodle's dolly, and hastened to the brandy. Peter knelt down, angrily, so that he could support Gillian comfortably against his shoulder. He was not certain whether he was being fooled or not but he was far too kind to risk letting Gillian fall with a heavy bump to the floor, in case he wasn't—luckily she looked very peaky indeed, cold, wet, and exhausted as she was. I considered her from between my fingers, and found her acting deplorably good, as she lolled her head back, and let her mouth hang slightly open. "*Here*," said the Canadian frantically. (He was called Archie, I remembered, suddenly. Archie West—something to do with biscuits—or copper?) He knelt beside Gillian and Peter and thrust a glass at her teeth. Gillian chattered them in a mad, pathetic manner, and the brandy went down her chin. "Here, . . ." said someone to me. I squinnied up at Benny, bland as ever, very kindly offering me a drink. I snatched it, and said, ungratefully, "Beat it, quick, you bastard."

"You mean he's really upset?"

Benny had the look of a hurt schoolboy, who has been taken up too sharply and very unfairly over a harmless practical joke. Innocent pain in the face of an uncomprehending world. How well I know it, I thought, and choked on the brandy, rather seriously, in my anger, and took some time to recover. When I looked up again the room was absolutely full of people—Poodle, my mother, Phillippa, Possum, Jake, Sachi—a mad whirl around the furious, defeated Peter and the triumphant Gillian, who felt it now safe to open an eye, but still clung piteously to him, thwarting any move he might make to get after Benny.

"*Darling*," shrieked Poodle. "Are you all right?"

"I shall be in a moment," said Gillian, bravely and truthfully. Peter looked across at me, an indescribable glance, and I quickly felt very groggy again. Poodle swept sparklingly here and there, talking, touching things, kissing people, telling everyone about the hunt, ordering tea, ordering baths, asking everyone to dinner on Friday, selling a spectacular four-year-old to Benny as he went, arranging how we could all lunch on Sunday; finally picking up Gillian, who had felt it safe to recover fairly fully, and taking her away to a bath, ordering Peter and myself to tell Archie, darling, to bring you along, will you, darlings?

My whole soul longed for a hot bath as the soul of the mystic longs for union with its maker. I trapped my mamma into a corner. "Listen, darling, take Peter's child home with you? We'll collect her this evening."

She gave me rather a strict look.

"I shall have to go back to the hospital, Anto. Roger isn't too good."

I had forgotten about Roger, preoccupied as I was with my own hideous physical misery.

"Darling, I'm sorry. I'll take you there. But I think we'd better take the child along with us, because there's nearly been a very ugly little scene indeed."

"Such a terrible pity, in a way, that she's *so* lovely," said my mother thoughtfully. "Wouldn't it do just as well if Phillippa took Benny home?" She gave me a beady-eyed glance.

"In the olden days," I said, "you would have been fried up as a witch."

"Well," said my mother, pleased, "one still isn't entirely without perception, I hope, even at my age. Now darling, don't worry. Go and have your bath, and take Peter with you—if necessary into the same bath—yes, that would be wisest—and I shall deal with the others. You both look terrible, really dreadful, and you must get those wet clothes off at once, don't just stand about drinking, Peter doesn't look after himself at all, and you're rather stupid about it, too, and you could easily both get rheumatic fever, so just do what you're both told. Straight into a bath. When you feel better—not before, mind you, take your time, you can both come along to the hospital and collect Rupert."

"Rupert?"

"I think it would really be advisable for him to stay the night there and have his stomach washed out, but he won't, of course."

"I suppose not."

Peter and I lay enclosed in a heavy and glorious golden haze of steam, essence of everything, oil of something else, Archie's very good Bourbon whiskey, and mental and physical exhaustion. I must remember, I kept telling myself, that this is what heaven is like. *All you need is this.* Just analyse it, can't yer? The golden dolphin tap endlessly burbled miraculous boiling hot water, and Peter's stomach slowly assumed the normal fiery hue of his face. He closed his eye, sank slowly and luxuriously down until his mouth and nose were under the surface, and began to drown happily, bubbling rather as he did so.

"Oy!" I said, and kicked him in his roasting ribs. He came up, equally slowly, opened his eye, focused it on me with some difficulty, and said, in a very dignified manner that really lost very little by the fact that he was inclined to run his words together, "Must apologize. Lost my temper."

"Not at all," I said, equally dignified. "Every-reason-to-do-so."

"Wonderful-woman-your-mother. Like to marry her, y'know."

"So would I," I said.

"Getting a bit-close-to-the-bone, old boy," said Peter, reprovingly. "Some-things-too-sacred to jest about."

"Must apologise."

"No, no, say-nothing-more. That chap's a shit, anyway. See-that-shirt?"

"That's Archie's shirt."

"Whose?"

"Your host's."

"Hosts, yes. . . . Doesn't signify. They're all alike. Shits. Shirts. Shit's-shirts. See?"

"Does your shoulder hurt?" I asked, muzzily, belatedly discovering a lack of logic in our conversation, and trying to account for it.

"Bloodily. I fell on it. Where's this shit with the drinks?"

"Why, I'm right here beside you, Lord Dungarvan." There was a hint of panic in the voice. "Poodle says won't you both come down now and have some tea?" it pleaded.

Peter closed his eye and sank again.

Gillian told me afterwards that Archie, who was really an extremely nice person, even if a dolly, had come endlessly in and out of *all* the bathrooms, bearing drinks. Poodle had said once, "You don't mind Archie, do you darling?" and Gillian had said that as long as someone was willing to bring her a drink in a hot bath at that moment she didn't care if it was the Pope. She didn't feel so absolutely certain later on, she told me.

Presently an extremely smooth number who perhaps was Archie's valet came into the bathroom and began to collect up our sopping, muddy clothing from the highly carpeted floor in a manner which was totally lost on us.

"Her ladyship asked me to inquire if you gentlemen would like your tea served here?"

His voice was chilly.

"We'll have four eggs," said Peter, quelling him effortlessly.

After that we explained life pretty wisely to each other for a bit, and ran out some absolutely filthy water and ran a lot more, very hot, in.

"Let's try the bath-salts," said Peter, who was relaxing very nicely. "Mauve. Wouldn't you know?"

Presently Poodle and Gillian came round the door with

119

a plate of hot buttered toast, and Archie followed with four eggs, and the smooth number, very sulkily, with a quite charming silver tea-pot and cups.

"You can put them on that thing that goes across us," Peter said, loftily.

"For Godssakes, darlings, *do you know how long you've been here?*"

"No."

"You're so *decent*, which is dull," said Gillian. "Lying there in that disgusting mauve *bog*—absolutely impenetrable, it's sickening."

We had tea, and the eggs, and cigarettes, and presently some more Bourbon and lots more hot water. Archie then hopefully brought us some shirts and pants, and the girls withdrew. Peter eyed the clothes provided for him. He looked prepared to be pretty nappy, so I kicked him shrewdly and frowned at him, and he struggled into them muttering slightly. I thought I caught the word dagoes, and kicked him again.

"Very-much-obliged. Wonderful-hospitality.Extremely kind," he said, still dignified.

When we came down Gillian said, "Oh, Peter darling, you are quite, quite, ravishing—why don't you wear things like that more often? *Now* don't you see how one worships Italians?"

"No," said Peter.

Roger lay very flat in the Spartan hospital bed, and tried not to move his eyes. He looked beige and remote.

"How do you feel?" I asked.

"Bloody," he said.

"Sure, you'll be flying in the morning," said Dr. Paddy Herlihy cheerfully, rising up from the floor, where he had been sitting astride his bag in order to demonstrate to me exactly how J. J. Connors had remained aboard Royal

120

Spain when the horse was already down, right down, mind you, at the last in the National, sure, there's no other jock would have stayed with him.

Peter had told me that Dr. Paddy had once informed a hunting casualty that it would be flying in the morning and this had proved to be only too hideously true—the body had been flown back to its loved ones in England. But, in fact, as we all knew well, Dr. Paddy, in spite of his alarmingly unreliable appearance and behaviour, was an extremely clever doctor, and always knew to an inch exactly when to prescribe complete rest, and when a tremendous party and champagne. He now herded us firmly out of Roger's room, and told my mother that he would be getting a special nurse for the night—"The way we could be quite sure, now, that he wouldn't be taking it into his head to move around. There could be a skull fracture there, mind you."

"Is there anything else we can do, Paddy?"

"There's nothing. He needs quietness, darkness, rest. Later on we'll X-ray, but just now I don't want him moved."

"Can we just go and kiss him good night?" asked Gillian.

"God, Mrs. Anthony, 'twould be best leave him lie, the way he'd rest easy."

"You see?" I said, rather unkindly, restored by my bath.

"Come on," said Peter. "We have to collect Rupert, wherever he is."

"You'll find him having tea with the nurses," said my mother.

"Tea?"

"Gallons and gallons of it. If only he would eat something. . . . Peter, dear, I hear there's been a little trouble. If only she wasn't *so* lovely, bless her."

"Yes," said Peter.

"Would you like her to come to me for a few days, just until you can get things sorted out a little?"

"Yes, please, Sophia darling—she'd love that, and so would I."

"That's all right, then, I'll take her straight on when I've dropped Phillippa and Possum and Gillian. You'll look after Rupert, then, won't you, darlings?" She kissed us fondly.

"Where are the film stars, by the way?"

"I think they got bored, having tea with the nurses, and Sachi was worried about her clothes."

"Her clothes?"

"Yes—you know—she thought them unsuitable for the occasion, and I think Dr. Paddy took them off in his car."

"*Her clothes?*"

"You know perfectly well what I meant, Anto."

"Well, if they've gone off with Paddy she'll find herself playing forty-five in the pub—much more unsuitable, in leopardskin."

"And where's that shit in the pink pants?——" Peter broke off and said, "Sorry, Sophia."

"My dear, you must remember he never had the benefit of a good upbringing. Nobody seems to know where he got to. Phillippa, poor love, is quite worried, but she says she simply must get Possum and his nurse back. You'll have to look after Mr. Benoit."

"I'll look after him," said Peter. He looked suddenly intensely autocratic and arrogant, and as if he was quite capable of ruling Empires, regiments, or Benny. He was, too.

"Yes, dear, I know how you feel, but you will remember poor darling Phillippa's feelings, too, won't you?"

His face softened. "Of course."

My mamma bustled away, and Peter and I went in search of the nurses' dining-room; from which noises of a curious, wild merriment floated to our ears. When we entered, we found a great group of normal, healthy Colleens, each one plainer and gayer than the last, crowding eagerly around Rupert—the most eager amongst them having attained his knee. They all held great ghastly doorsteps of bread and butter and large china mugs of tea in their great, capable fists. Rupert also held a large china mug of tea, but it was tea with a difference. The fierce fumes reached our amazed nostrils as we came through the door. Rupert looked round at us and smiled beatifically.

"Finished with the elements at last, eh? Good boys, good boys, just in time for a cup of tea with all these lovely creatures."

Rupert's boots were lying in a corner. Below his muddy breeches his thin legs were clad in much-laddered nylon stockings—a present from Gillian's hunting store—and rather dirty woollen socks. His feet looked quite enormous, and somehow obscene. His coat and port-stained waistcoat were open, and also the top three buttons of his breeches, which was allowing him to relax his illtreated stomach nicely. He seemed to have mislaid his teeth again, and his face was a threatening purple colour, but indestructible wickedness and delight gleamed in his one workable eye, while the nurse who sat upon his knee applied a very unattractive piece of unidentifiable meat to the other one.

"It's no good," said Peter to me, resignedly, "One simply can't help being fond of the old bastard."

"That's what's always been his downfall. You're fond of him. I'm fond of him. Rich women are fond of him. Arab girls of good family, and high-class pansy photographing fellers and Rose Hillchester are fond of him. So what hope has he?"

"None, of course."

"Dear boys, don't just stand there, in your gauche way," said Rupert. He seemed much refreshed. "Come in, come in, and meet the little women." He waved a hand towards us in an expansive gesture. "Lord Dungarvan, girls—*Earl* of Dungarvan, mind you—and my very old friend the great dollar-earner Mr. Anthony Kavanagh. Now don't say I don't bring a little joy into your drab lives—worthy they may be—self-sacrificing, yes, I grant you—but drab, drab!"

"God help us, but he's fierce funny," squeaked one of the little women. "Wait now, 'til Matron 'ud hear him at it."

Peter gave the little women a general, melting, nervous smile, and put his hand on Rupert's shoulder.

"Come along home, boy," he said.

"Have some tea," said Rupert. He pushed towards us a very large and sinister bottle, half-full of a colourless liquid.

Peter smelt it cautiously.

"For God's sake, what is it?"

" 'Tis the stuff we'd be rubbing the backs of the old yins beyant with, what else?" piped a little woman, merrily.

"*The backs of the old ones . . . ?*"

"Dear boy," said Rupert, "Try not to be so naïf. This is a hospital, or so they tell me, and where there's a hospital there's alcohol, right?"

"Rubbing alcohol! Well, of course, you'll just die, old boy, no doubt about it at all."

"Never felt fresher in me life."

"Please, wouldn't your Lordship take a cup of tea?" asked an eager colleen who would have been very pretty if permanent waving had never been discovered.

Peter accepted, since there was clearly nothing else to

be done, in a manner which curiously combined the hunted and the gracious air.

("I felt like the Queen Mum," he said to me afterwards.

"You didn't look at all the same.")

He was still rather upset about his clothes, and kept backing and filing. Rupert took him in, suddenly, and put down his mug and leant forward, peering.

Then he sat very upright and peered again, as one who uses a quizzing glass.

"Look," said Peter, defensively. "One word, just one, and we don't take you home."

"I'm perfectly happy here. I was just wondering when you joined the Commedia delle'Arte. It seems out of character, that's all; but don't let my kindly interest embarrass you."

Peter went crossly behind his mug of tea.

"I seen your play, all right," said a Colleen to me, "And 'tis a fright the way you'd think up thim things. 'Twill be great dee-varsion for you to be reading them through in your latter end, indeed."

This was a new aspect of playwriting, which, up till now, had not occurred to me, and I pondered, not unpleasurably, upon it. Rupert stretched out his legs to a non-existent fire, and poured some more alcohol into his tea. He seemed to fancy himself at his own hearthside, for presently he began to tell a story of quite petrifying unsuitability, concerning certain aberrations of sex encountered in Tangier. Luckily, it was all rather above the heads of the little women, who, I think, imagined they were hearing a rather touching tale of the love of a dear little Arab boy for his dear little white goat, in the style of Gallico. Nevertheless, Peter and I were sufficiently alarmed to make a grand effort and sweep Rupert, his boots, and his teeth, out as far as the hall; where we lowered him not very gently on to an out-patients' bench and stood above him, breathing heavily, to consider our next move.

We had no means of transport. Poodle had brought us to the hospital and, after asking everyone indiscriminately to dinner, had driven off again, saying that she must get back to Archie, who seemed just the smallest touch edgy, she couldn't think why, and, goodness, she had forgotten they were dining with George, could we all come on Thursday? I decided to ring up Dan. His voice, when I got him, sounded rough, almost as if with tears. He said God help us wasn't it nearly seven o'clock, and had we seen Sarah? Oh, yes, he'd come along and collect us, he'd a lost hound, anyway, he could take back to old George on the way, and maybe Sarah had gone into the kennels for a drink, they must have had a whale of a hunt, wait, now, he'd be right over.

"Sarah's missing," I said to Peter.

"Aha."

"Poor old Dan."

"I think you could be right about this ending in tears, boy."

Dan arrived, and we shovelled Rupert, happily bemused, into the back of the Land Rover once more, with the lost hound. "Animal-lovers," he mumbled, huffily. I felt, indeed, slightly sorry for Rupert—because nothing in this world can smell so horrifyingly carnivorous as a fully-grown foxhound in a small, confined space, particularly if it happens also to be very wet. Sunk in the self-pitying gloom and horror of all its kind when separated from their fellows, it lolled its heavy, panting face helplessly upon Rupert's chest and awaited its certain end, looking noble and misused, like Sydney Carton. But Rupert was too far gone really to care, even when, very soon, it was rather sick.

126

We jolted on through the cold, dark evening. The mad whirring of the Land Rover's heater, and the roaring of its engine, made speech almost impossible, which was lucky, because I was exhausted and Peter was worried and in pain and Dan was quite clearly in hell. I tried to keep my mind on great, universal, soothing matters like the Unified Field or the Four Last Things, and failed utterly.

Sarah was not at the kennels. Later on, when we were gathered together for dinner at Castle Saffron, Benny was also missing.

Chapter Nine

To be here, in this November morning, was like standing in the middle of a luminous, milky pearl. It was windless, and the gilt winter sun was sucking up the mists very slowly. Black hedges were delicately decorated with star-like gossamer webs, the grass was crisped with rimy white hoar frost, but beneath it the ground was soft, dark, earth-smelling, full of goodness and a magic foreseeing of the Spring. The smoke from our cigarettes hung across the air in thin blue layers, smelling like dawn in Paradise, looking like the form of content. All my body felt light and warm and relaxed, as I smoked and enjoyed being alive, watching the horses move around the big field in twos and threes. They drifted like flames through the misty air, champing, chopping, flirting, jogging, side-stepping, switching tails —heads flung snortingly up and down, shining, shifting eyes, bit-ringing, a wicked grunt or two, a hunched back there, an ear moving ominously there, a smell of salty sweat, the hollow clap of a hand against a shoulder, the soapy squeak of old, tatty saddles, the lads calling to each other, one of them singing, one laughing.

Every few minutes some little group would break up into a mad whirl, like leaves raised by a sudden gust of wind, as an uppity youngster decided to play up, and saw a ghost in a thistle or a white bullock four fields away— both excellent excuses for whipping round and cunningly dropping a shoulder with a squeal, or making a sudden, mad plunge sideways and upsetting all its comrades, who were just longing to be upset, anyway. The head lad, on an old hurdler, would come hurrying up to the disorganized group, and, with advice and admonition— "God help us, Francie, is it a rocking horse you think you're sitting up on?"—herd them on their way around the field; walking, jogging, walking, jogging; the slow, thorough warming-up and loosening process before the serious work began.

"Very settled, this morning," said Dan, happily. "They like the sun, the brutes. Soft as hell, all of 'em." Even Dan looked settled. His dark face was tranquil, he was contentedly absorbed in the horses he knew exactly how to deal with. Peter was happy, too, or, anyway, what he referred to as bloody carefree, briefly insulated by the morning from his wearing household. He breathed the milky air in heavily like someone tasting wine, and said, "Makes you want to skip about like a lamb."

"And have the yearlings in fits," said Dan. "Wait till they go in." He trained under both rules, and so now the yearlings were staggering around at a walk in their long coats, their ears, eyes, legs and tails going all ways at once, and the tiniest lads—the youngest and the most withered—tucked up very still behind their immature shoulders, talking soothingly and hopefully to those mad, flickering ears. "Ah, there now, there, have sinse, now, will ye, be easy now, ye thief, ye. . . ." All punctuated with soothing whistling. Soon, two by two, they went off into the next field to do their cantering and we followed Dan to watch them rolling about, amazed at their own ability, weaving, bumping each other on purpose, and bouncing off with laid back ears and an attempt at kicking, trying on sudden mad bursts of acceleration, and, when thwarted in this by their sweating lads, sulking, and thinking it would be fun to stop altogether, then suddenly deciding to be good, settling earnestly into their baby stride, and feeling, it was clear, exactly like race-horses. Afterwards, with loosened girths, blowing and sweating in great disproportion to the work they had done, trying to nip each other's behinds, and showing off terribly, they were walked in a shifting circle around Dan and his head lad, while Dan brooded silently over them, absorbing and diagnosing their abilities, necessities, anxieties, with the strange seventh sense of the good trainer. The head lad's mount, who had won good hurdle races, regarded them with an indulgent, ironic eye, and sighed shatteringly at human stupidity when he was not allowed to put his head down and pick at the rimy grass.

"Backward bastards, the lot," said Dan finally, contentedly. At this royal word of dismissal, and a nod from the head lad, they were led away to cool off somewhere where they would not be unduly elevated by the thrilling sight of their elders doing their gallops.

The old horse now suddenly threw his handsome head up and gazed fixedly, with cocked ears and pulsing, inquisitive nostrils at a bright, moving chestnut splash against the hill—a horse, actually another horse!—jogging easily down towards us. On its back would be my dear Aunt Emmy, who was hacking her latest young one (O, Cheltenham; O, Aintree; but, O, alas, how often not) from Knockmoree to do a school over hurdles with the old horse, and had immediately had the kindly thought of how very nice it would be for me to have the fun of riding it—it would take the look of the city from me, she had said, totally unmoved by my protestations of unfitness and general lack of suitability—"Sure, you'll have been hunting all the while—" (she had applied her heaviest idiom) "—you'll be grand and fit, and the filly's a dote, just a dote. All you've to do is sit on her." O, famous last Irish words, so soothing, so tempting, so often inapplicable! "All you've to do is sit there." Yes, indeed. "Jesus!" says a soft, injured voice, as you pick yourself up. "I never seen him (or her) *offer* before— whatever took her (or him) I couldn't tell at all." And neither can you, owing to the unbelievable speed and wickedness with which she (or he) has done whatever it did, and is now careering triumphantly about with its reins round a foreleg, thinking of jumping something unjumpable, and deliberately breaking its foolish flighty neck.

So now I was not in the least taken in by the gentle manner in which the chestnut filly came jogging up to us, flirting her superbly beautiful head, and putting her feet down like a ballet dancer, with my Aunt Emmy slumped beamingly in the saddle, the reins hooked in a lacka-daisical manner over one finger while she patted vaguely around the bulging pockets of her frightful coat to see if she had remembered to bring her cigar. I knew very well that my dear Aunt Emmy had a soporific effect on young horses, and also that this wore off as soon as she removed herself from their sensitive backs. She did this now, bumping down heavily, and adjuring the filly to stand still while she disentangled her large gumboot from the small iron. Anybody else would have been dragged and killed at once, but the filly stood like a dog for Aunt Emmy, only turning her head to give her a loving, help-ful shove in the ribs.

"I'd give you gold, mind, to come and ride out my yearlings," said Dan admiringly.

"Ah, well now, I'm a bit heavy for that, you know. Old, too," said my aunt happily, finding her cigar. "Good morning, Peter. How are all your invalids?"

Everyone at Castle Saffron except Peter and I and Gil-lian was down with 'flu—at least, Benny and Phillippa and Possum had 'flu. Rupert we suspected of having alcoholic poisoning, and Sachi of having a strong urge not to follow hounds again ever—Irish Life was wearing a touch thin, we thought—and Jake very wisely just wanted to stay in a warm room with some whiskey, well away from outdoor sport of any kind; a delicious alcoholic womb, observed Gillian.

Gillian, this morning, was going to fetch Roger from the hospital and take him back to Knockmoree, and we were all going to meet there for luncheon and bring Nanny back to Castle Saffron with us to help with the invalids. But before this thoroughly cosy plan could materialize I was faced with the schooling of Aunt Emmy's lovely filly, who, walked around us now by a lad, was already beginning to look unreliable, as she absorbed the thrilling sights, scents, and sounds around her. "Hurdles!" her ears twittered excitedly. "Galloping! Coo!"

"Perhaps you'd like to sit up on her and jog round, Anto dear, just to get the feel of her?"

I took off my coat, and the lad brought her in and threw me up. She swerved about in jittery circles, tossed her head, declared her nerves to be in shreds, squealed slightly, and rushed backwards at what seemed to be a gallop, dragging the lad along with her.

"Let her *go*, damn you," I snapped irritably, endeavouring to nose my feet gently into irons that refused to materialize—Aunt Emmy seemed to ride at cowboy length. Peter and Dan were roaring with laughter, slapping each other delightedly on the back, and the head lad was snickering politely down his nose.

"There's a grand girl, now," said Aunt Emmy happily, puffing out great clouds of rich smoke. "Isn't she grand and strong under you, Anto?"

I rode off sulkily, stroking the filly's shoulder and longing to hit her instead. But she was indeed a lovely ride, she drifted like a cloud around the field, gently shaking her head, chewing her bit thoughtfully, wondering about me, summing me up, and all my early morning happiness rushed back, light and warm. I hummed contentedly to her, and pulled up Aunt Emmy's leathers to a more suitable length for galloping and rode back to where Aunt Emmy and Dan were discussing what work the filly was to do with the old hurdler, who was to be her schoolmaster this morning.

Peter stood by them, and he looked suddenly a little bleak and weary, I thought. In his dashing days before the war, he had owned and trained a wonderful character with an evil sense of humour, called Mr. Tod, on whom he had won the Liverpool Foxhunters, and even got round in the National, being, in fact, sixth, or, as he described it, an easy last. Life was far from being the fun it had been then, and it must have seemed to him, and indeed was, a very long time ago indeed since he had ridden work on mornings like this one, and had been young and whole and bloody carefree, and had a future. He looked at me now and smiled, and said encouragingly, "J.J. is down the course to you, boy," and Dan said to him suddenly, with a perceptive sympathy that was moving. "Why don't you sit up on the old fellow, Peter? Good for your liver."

"Couldn't hold him. Couldn't keep him straight. My liver's past repair," said Peter. But he looked hopeful.

I saw the words "You've only got to sit there" tremble on Dan's lips, but the head lad was before him, with a rather more elaborate version of the spiel.

"Sure, this one's a terrible lazy horse in his work, my lord. He'd never take hold of you at all, you'd need to be punching him around and you couldn't pull him out from lepping if you'd want to, once he'd see where he'd be going, he'd like the fun of it, the thief," with which siren song he slipped down off the big, old horse and waited alertly to put Peter up, delighted with the un-orthodox turn the morning was taking.

"Ah, well," said Peter, equally delighted, "tie a knot in the reins, and don't blame me if we don't stay in the groove," and allowed himself to be thrown up on the big horse, who sidled pleasantly about, grinding his teeth, anticipating fun, while Dan gave us our instructions.

"Start over the far side, by those bushes, just hack along, no jumping off. You'll come right round and down the hill, jump the three hurdles on the straight, then round and the same again. Half speed all the way. Anthony, Emmy wants you to stay behind the old boy and give the filly plenty of time and room. If she settles down nicely you can move upsides with him on the second round. Right? Off you pop."

"Bloody brisk," I said to Peter, as we moved off.

"He's a great chap, Dan," said Peter. "Pity Sarah's bitching him so—does she really think your chum will put her on the fillums?"

"On a morning like this, who cares?"

"You're dead right."

Extremely happy now, he began very inappropriately to sing the boating song. The big horse had a superb, long, slouching walk, and Peter slouched also, contentedly perched up behind those swinging shoulders, and looked very much younger now, and not bleak at all. He broke off from his singing to say, "I'm no judge of pace these days—shout if you don't fancy my half speed."

"I don't suppose I shall be in any state to shout."

"Bit of a handful?"

"I don't know yet, but I'd say, by the look in her ears, yes."

We jogged gently on towards the bushes; all around us the gilded mists; the singing; the blue mountains; the pale, vaulting sky; the bright horses flickering in the far field; the gentle, moving air; every scent and sound and sensation a delight to be infinitely praised, the very blood beating in the body a celebration of the beauty of the morning. But what makes the picture up, I thought? Dan in a hell of a state, and the lad with the voice is the biggest twister in Tipperary, and not one of the ruddy horses, I suppose, but hasn't been run crooked at some time and done some poor silly bugger out of his week's wages . . . but the sum of it, good Lord, is perfect, and how about that? Curiouser and curiouser. But Peter began to trot up towards the bushes ahead of me, and I was immediately entirely engaged with the filly, who wished to take off into the gentle sky. Peter glanced round and asked "Right?" and let the big horse stride away quietly in front of me, and the filly, snorting, bounced unquietly after him, with her beautiful, wilful face in the air.

In the air it stayed, too, over the first hurdle, across which we skittered in a strange, last second sort of step dance which I found very unsettling, and which I hoped Dan and Aunt Emmy hadn't been able to view very closely. The second one she consented to glance at, with a swift, shy curtsey just before she took off, but at the third she lowered her head and reached for it properly, nearly jumping up to her imperturbable leader over it. Peter looked briefly round again and grinned, and we sailed on up to the bushes, up the hill, round, down, and into them again. The filly's shoulders slid forward and back, forward and back, superbly lovely pieces of intricate machinery, functioning flawlessly beneath the glowing chestnut coat now beginning to darken a little with sweat; her floating gilt mane blew up and tickled my nose; her velvet mouth, now that she had lowered her head and was behaving herself, played a subtle, silken game with my hands; her delicately curving little ears, carved on the air ahead of me, nearly met at their keen tips with excitement, as she measured the next hurdle and reached for it like an old hand, and I told her "now" and she believed me, and we were gloriously right. She swept across it like a flame, a poem, taking my heart and my breath away with her, and so I let her stride delightedly and impertinently up alongside her indulgent teacher, who rolled an eye back and could have been said to smile.

Peter and I, breathing much too hard, grinned sideways at each other, numb-nosed and red-wristed in the rushing chill of our passage, sweating everywhere else, the beginnings of cramp in our unfit backs and thighs, care traditionally left behind, happiness singing in our ears with the wind of our going.

"I have her in the four-year-old hurdle at Peppardstown," said Aunt Emmy, eating with a hearty appetite the confusing stew that always resulted when my nevertheless unvanquished mamma endeavoured to produce *pot-au-feu* from an Irish kitchen. It was quite delicious always, never quite the same twice running, and never stood close investigation—there was a theory that whenever Bridget found that "the stock had weakened on her" —a euphemism for not having prepared any—she tossed in great handfuls of the hound puppies' bone meal. My brother Roger always held that he had in fact once found a hound puppy in it; but this was considered to be going too far—it had only been a kitten, my mother had said firmly, and there had been a perfectly reasonable explanation. When pressed for this explanation she would bustle off to do the flowers.

There was no doubt, however, that the Knockmoree Stew, ladled from a huge, ancient, odorous marmite, and washed down with Guinness, was a tremendously revivifying experience, always provided you had taken sufficiently severe physical exercise beforehand to enable you to cope with it, and Peter and I now coped with it easily, golloping it down deliriously, rather in the hound puppy style, while Roger, sitting pallidly opposite, begged us to take our paws out of the trough, and Nanny, guest of honour at her farewell luncheon party, decently clad for travel in her good nigger (any student of Nannydom will understand the phrase) said she did like to see the gentlemen eat up nicely, it was really quite a treat, and she'd say Anthony had put on a little weight, but not his Lordship, who was too thin for his height.

"Nanny means you're getting podgy, darling," Gillian explained helpfully to us. "And Peter is skinny."

Nanny said pleasedly that Mrs. Anthony had taken her up wrong, but she was always a one for her joke, and Peter, rather disgustingly engaged now in polishing round his plate with an enormous chunk of wholemeal bread, said indistinctly and indignantly that he rode at fourteen stone, what more did Nanny want? Nanny said placidly that his Lordship looked very well really, but—she added darkly—not but what he couldn't be a little fatter in places. Peter looked alarmed and Gillian choked into her stout with a burbling sound. Peter said afterwards that he had really thought that Nanny might come round the table and start pinching him as if he had been something hanging in a poulterer's—she had such a considering look in her eye, he said.

After these splendid nursery exchanges, Aunt Emmy, who throughout had been murmuring happily away, unnoticed, about her filly, and had got as far as Cheltenham two years later, announced triumphantly that I was mad keen to ride her in her races, didn't she go for me a perfect dream?

"You're a wicked woman," I said, after I had swallowed sufficiently to be able to say anything.

"I'm sure Miss Emmy knows what's best," said Nanny, reprovingly.

"Aunt Emmy, you do remember what happened the last time I rode a horse for you?"

"You fell off it," said Roger, in a brotherly way.

"I had a crucifying fall," I said coldly.

"Your own fault," said Roger, cheerfully. "If you will take on the top toughs at their own game. . . . You shouldn't be so dashing."

"I've never been the same since," I said.

"I told you at the time, dear, and it's true what I said. You shouldn't never have gone flying about in aeroplanes directly—there's nobody has concussion but needs rest after it, and a nice long rest, too; but you were never a one to heed your elders, you'll only learn by experience, dear," Nanny concluded, triumphantly.

"You're dead right, Nanny," said Gillian. "And I really do think," she added to Peter, "that he *has* been a touch odd since—otherwise how did we find ourselves in this *galère*? I don't mean your house, of course, darling," she added, hastily, to my mamma.

"Mine then, I suppose?" said Peter.

"Well, darling, admit."

"I do admit. First a film studio—except there isn't a film, only Anto and his chum squabbling over the script —I always thought you had to have cameras—and now a bloody hospital. Sorry, Sophia. What next?"

"The location manager next," said Gillian, with the smug air of a conjuror who has just pulled off something pretty fancy.

"What?"

"The location manager."

"Who?"

"Darling, *stop* it. That's the man who comes and decides where is the best place to film a point-to-point."

"Wouldn't a point-to-point course be the best place?"

"My dear, the *least* likely place in the world."

"Oh!" said Peter. "Well, of course, I'm just an ignorant, dishonest lodging-house keeper. Does the location manager have dollars?"

"Bound to stink of them."

"That's all I need to know," he said, and attacked a delicious toasted apple muddle that had tried to be a Flan de Pommes Grillées, with a vigour that obviously afforded Nanny tremendous satisfaction.

Across the table from him, astoundingly painted against the panelling behind her by Botticelli, his child sat, giving him each time he glanced at her a slow, blazing smile and the full heart-halting impact of her Mediterranean stone angel eyes—a shining look of unguarded love, as disconcerting to witness as only innocence and truth can be. She adored him. That was that. Adoration, I thought, in the oldest and fullest and purest sense of the word. She watched him as Suky would have watched, to see what he might say or do next, and how best she could please him. To be the subject of such adoration, I thought, must be almost too frightening and exhausting a responsibility to be borne—it's a good thing Peter isn't much given to thinking about himself. Before luncheon, over drinks, Gillian had said to her, "You're so lovely, darling," and she had replied gravely and sweetly, "You are too, in quite a different way." She had the fatal, direct touch.

"She's fey, you see?" Gillian had said to me after the first meeting. "And I *don't* want to know what Freud or Jung or Adler would tell me about feyness. I know perfectly well what *I* mean, and you don't need the smallest touch of intellect to recognize it at once. What's so difficult is to *protect* it—what a pity she can't marry Peter."

A pity, indeed, I thought now, since they don't come that way very often. A very remarkable man indeed, and apparently one of the most ordinary. I looked at him now, contentedly dealing with some more of the apple muddle —a long, lean, brick-coloured, untidy chap with greying blond hair, a filthy, elegant tweed coat, and a frightful stringy tie. Sometimes, nowadays, he had about him a fine-drawn look, an air of settled endurance, of accepted loss and pain, that was moving, as all resignation is moving; but today he was relaxed, he had had nothing to cope with but horses and old chums and the stew—what have we here but a jungly peer without a thought in his head but steeplechasers and bed? Anyone might have been forgiven for thinking so—but what, in fact, I wonder, have we here? Something rare, something difficult to pin down . . . a gentleman that was brought up proper Nanny considered, anyway—not, she had added, darkly, like That Lord Arranmore; a neighbour—as neighbours go in Ireland—who had lamentably failed to emerge from the chrysalis of adolescence, and lived in a sad whirl of publicity and bogus princesses. Still, I thought, there can't be many gentlemen, however well brought up, who would be prepared to look after their crazy child like this. Peter had been brutally knocked about in every way; no one would have blamed him if he had shoved the child into a home and got as far away from the ruins of his life as he could get; he had a perfectly good cousin for an heir, he could have got the hell out of it, or tried to, at least. A responsible man, a compassionate man. . . . Something more. My mother had said to me when I had just come home after Maria had been killed, "It's very difficult to talk about, Anto, because there just are not the right words. What words there are mean so little, and she and Peter . . . if I said he was heart-broken, if I said a part of him died then, it sounds as if I was writing a novel—but his heart *was* broken, some part of him *did* die; it doesn't happen much, but you can't mistake it when you see it. There just aren't any other words, you see."

"It does happen," I had said. "The reason why the words mean so little is because they are so often used when nothing like that has happened at all."

"And they are applied to the wrong people. Really extraordinarily few people, you know, are capable of love. The older I get, the more I see that it just is not an atmosphere in which most people move at all—it simply is not a thing which happens very much, it's just talked about a great deal. I don't know how Peter picked himself up, or how he goes on now. Fortitude . . . it's so unspectacular. Such a tremendous virtue, I think, and perhaps the most rare."

I had said, "Poor old Peter."

"O no, not at all, darling, that's the very last thing he is, I assure you—I should have hoped you would know better."

"I do really know better. I just said it."

"Well, don't, darling. I do so dislike slipshod thinking."

"Was she very pretty?" Peter had married just before the war, and I had been in New York then, and after that, like most people, in a lot of different places, and had never even met her.

"I suppose not at all, really. One would call her *pire que jolie*, only I always think myself that that implies a certain amount of nastiness, don't you, and she was the most heavenly person, as nice as Peter and even kinder, if that was possible. She had that wonderful, warm intense femininity that women from the Midi sometimes do have —oh, dear, it's so awful how one can't explain again. I'm making her sound dreadful."

"It's all right, Mamma. I understand exactly what you mean."

Fool, I said to myself now, it's the stout after all that exercise, making you sleepy and sentimental, and what's more, your imagination is over-active. But I knew I was wrong—and right. If Peter hadn't had to look after his child he'd be doing much the same thing, anyway. The same thing? my *alter ego* echoed—Why? Where? O, I don't know—he'd be living in the desert, or with lepers, or looking after someone on Skid Row. F—— that, said my *alter ego*. He'd be in the Four Hundred with Rose. Well, maybe. He'd be very welcome either place, which is really the astonishing thing. . . .

"Darling, do wake up," said Gillian. "I always knew exercise was bad for you. You've gone into one of your trances."

"And I'll give you the odds to a monkey your brilliant mind was a total blank just then," added Peter, still eating away, but now on the cheese.

"I don't bet on certainties," I said.

"*Goodness*," said Gillian, watching Peter with fascination. "You *are* going to be a little fatter in parts, any minute now."

"Don't make me self-conscious. Nanny's on my side, anyway."

"That's all good, home stuff, now, Mrs. Anthony," said Nanny reprovingly. "Not like those nasty restaurants. His lordship could eat twice as much and it wouldn't do him nothing but good."

"See?" He took a lot more cheese, and my mother gave up. "Go on eating as long as you like, darling. I'll take Gillian away."

As we sat down again the child doubled back and stood by him, sweet, anxious, relentless. He held out his hand to her and said easily, "What's the worry, my love?"

"Don't go without saying good-bye to me."

"No."

She went then, reassured and perfectly happy, agog to watch Nanny packing her Useful Little Case, and Peter settled cosily on the port and began to talk to Roger about hound breeding; a subject which should be barred as rigidly from the table as any other form of religion. Pretty soon they were shouting at each other with great enjoyment, and I left them to it and went to pay the filly a visit in her box.

Very much later my mother said, "Are Roger and Peter *still* in the dining-room?"

They were, it seemed. I went and winkled them out of it. They were splendidly expansive. Peter was reasonably steady, and Roger, speaking very much for himself, said that he was, too. They had, apparently, reached an agreement; mapped out the general lines on which old George was to proceed in future; and felt that there was now some hope for the West Tipperary foxhounds. They rather thought of going to call on him at once, to give him the good news, but we dissuaded them, not without difficulty. As we were finally about to leave, Peter said, "Where's my child?"

"She's gone out to the Windy Hill with Emmy to help her get in the mares."

"Oh, Lord!"

"Why, Peter?"

He looked shy and muddled. "Thing is, I said I'd see her again before I went."

My mamma said gently: "Come back in, then, darling. They'll be some time."

"Tell you what. I can walk across there, and if Anto and Gillian bring the car in about ten minutes I can meet them on the road."

"It's rather a long way."

"Good for me after the port. Sorry to be such a bore." He weaved off.

He was very lame after his galloping. "Goodness," said Gillian. "What a great sweetie he is. He'll never make it. I bet we'll have to go and quarter the plough for him."

"He can't be beat," I said, feeling triumphant, as if I had won a bet; allowed to see, for once, shining clearly even to my cold and questioning eye, a love and trust that were not misplaced. Oh, be your bloody age, can't you? said my *alter ego*, crossly. Just because a chap who has drink taken doesn't forget a promise, do you have to get starry-eyed? Yes, I said, wholehearted for once. I do. So shut up.

My mamma said, looking after Peter tenderly, "You and Gillian give him a little fun while you're there, won't you?"

Fun, I thought, or flaming awful bother. Peter had dealt brilliantly with Benny, who had arrived back at 3 a.m. after the hunt, and after whatever he had been up to with Sarah. Peter waited grimly in the library, and forced me to wait as well. "You can witness this—I'm not going to have him saying I didn't make myself clear."

Benny arrived looking unbelievably ill and awful, still in his pink pants, sickening for flu, and spoiling for a fight. I really felt rather sorry for him. The people he generally had to deal with had not emerged so far from the jungle as his host—who, after the first atavistic desire to take Benny outside and chew him up, was perfectly prepared to think of Phillippa's feelings. He had given Benny a whisky and soda and settled him comfortably before the fire before proceeding to tell him, with all the tremendous authority he could so frighteningly command, exactly what he thought of him, and on what terms he would be allowed to remain in his, Peter's, house. Benny sat still, staring at him, uncertain what line to take, and he hadn't actually taken any line, or spoken a word, when Peter wished him a courteous good night, asked him to turn out the lights in the library and scatter the fire when he had finished his drink, and took Suky out for her final, rather affected, stroll.

Benny appeared slighty dazed and quiet at breakfast, and it wasn't only his 'flu coming on, because when, a little later, we were battling wearily over the script together, he said to me suddenly, "That's a great guy."

I didn't have to ask who he meant. Maddening, Benny was. Just when you had decided that he really was very far beyond the pale indeed he would always show himself to have some nice feeling. He asked now, wistfully, "Was he *really* upset?"

"Well, hell, of course he was, for Chrissakes." (I must remember not to talk like that, I thought.) "He'd have thrown you out of here, but for Phillippa."

"Gee, I dunno, I dunno . . ." murmured Benny, running his hands worriedly through his hair, astonished at such eccentricity. "But he's a great guy, any way he comes—you think I ought to apologize to him, kid?"

"*Haven't* you?"

"Well, gee, he didn't give me a chance."

"Well, then, don't."

But he did, before luncheon, publicly, formally, and rather muzzily, just before finally collapsing with his 'flu. I have never seen a more embarrassed man than Peter. "My God," he said to me later, "your chum's mad. What was I supposed to say? I felt like m' Tutor."

"I think you are, from now on, as far as Benny's concerned."

Peter stared at me, alarmed, told me it was catching, and wandered off, sighing, to comfort himself by going round the horses and having a soothing discussion about the state of their feet and digestions with his head man.

145

Chapter Ten

Peter and Gillian and I now had a perfectly splendid few days in hiding, while Nanny and Peter's housekeeper (a sterling Nanny figure who had received the courtesy title of a married woman on becoming housekeeper, and reigned with placid tyranny as Mrs. Thomas, or Nanny Tom), and Nurse Simmons got to grips with each other over the invalids.

During this welcome time out we were always either hunting or recovering from and boasting about hunting in what Peter said loftily was his office—a messy and delightful lair haunted by the hound puppies, who had decided on their own authority that it hardly counted as being in the house. They were regularly spoken rudely to by Suky, and nipped by the terrier, and pushed out by whichever one of us wasn't too tired or too happy or too whiskified to bother; but back they sidled every time, innocent and ill treated, looking at us with holy depths of hope and sorrow and love, bullying without mercy. "Oh, your beautiful insincere eyes!" said Gillian to them. "I know *such* a lot of people just like you." To which they replied, very sincerely, that they only wanted, honestly, one thing in their sad lives, and that was to lie much too close to the fire and be no trouble to anyone. So they did just that, getting their own way by a timid but relentless wearing-down process, and we rested our feet on them, and told each other exactly how we had ridden each hunt —none of us listening to any other one for a second—and then had a splendid, unkind gossip about exactly how everybody else had ridden it, to which we all listened like anything, eating shameless quantities of tea. Then we would go and lie for a long time in our baths; come down and start drinking about eight o'clock; and finally, about ten o'clock, when the invalids had been settled down, and the servants had stopped willingly and dramatically whizzing about with trays, delighted with the disruption of routine, Peter's boy, breathing hard, would place a rickety card table over the recumbent puppies and give us whatever it had been decided would be good for us to eat, and we would eat it in front of the fire and then go to sleep. Later still, Nanny would come and bring us some Ovaltine and tell us to go to bed as soon as we had drunk it up, as we should need our strength. When she had gone we gave the Ovaltine to the puppies, who we thought needed their strength more—and could not, poor things, keep it up with whiskey, like us—and did not go to bed, but played chess and nostalgic gramophone records and the splendid, unfailingly exciting game of when did you last see old so-and-so and how dreadful did he look? It was all wonderfully relaxing, and we went to pieces cheerfully and thankfully, refusing to dine out at all because, we said firmly, we were so infectious, except in the open air.

Peter had a long telephone chat with his child every evening, and Gillian had one with Roger, fretfully convalescent at Knockmoree, and furious with us for having got away with Nanny. He made Gillian report every detail that we could scrape up of the truly epic battle of wits, principles, protocol, and general nursery-worlddom that was taking place between Nanny, Nanny Tom and Nurse Simmons, and we had a competition as to who could report the best episode from the field of honour each evening. The protagonists were fairly well matched, and the fortunes of war swung backwards and forwards in an enthralling manner. Nanny Tom had been Peter's nanny, and so was in the very strong tactical position of owning both him and the whole of Castle Saffron; but Nanny owned me, and, through me, Gillian—glamorous London figures both—and also a perfectly good establishment of her own at Knockmoree, to give her the solid background required. While it might thus appear to the indifferent student of Nannydom that poor Nurse Simmons, who had merely been to what Nanny called "one of those nasty colleges, dear, you couldn't credit the things they'd get taught there," might as well surrender at once, she was, in fact, in the absolutely unassailable position of owning the only available genuine child. Peace with honour seemed possible, and Nanny and Nanny Tom made cautious overtures to each other, in the hope of forming a grand alliance. Nanny was allowed to be present while Nanny Thomas engaged in the frightening pursuit of "going right through her linen". Then Nanny was allowed even to go through the pillow-slips herself, when they came back from the laundry. Peter seemed unduly nervous while this was going on. "They never let you alone," he complained, obscurely. Later, when Nanny had been given the freedom of the linen cupboard, and was having lovely, melancholy chats about how gentlemen didn't rightly appreciate good linen, she was told a tale of gothic horror (reported to Gillian), concerning the time when Nanny Tom, returning from her hols.—she had never gone on them again—had found the kitchenmaid luxuriously lapped in glossy, coroneted, hand-woven linen; while Peter had made himself very cosy in some curious twill numbers, which he had bitterly resented being parted from.

Nanny then honourably allowed Nanny Tom to take away Gillian's nightdress, as she had some lace which would just match up nice to that little piece the nuns tore. (This was not a reference to some Freudian frenzy in the convent, but to the Good Shepherd Laundry in Knock-long.) Nanny held a watching brief over the matching up, and then allowed her one of my shirts, and was in return given some socks of Peter's, and was even allowed to say without fear or favour that she had never known a gentleman harder on them.

At this point the Nannies felt themselves sufficiently dug in to allow the Nurse into the housekeeper's room for her supper—during which they could tell her how much naughtier, cleverer, more amusing, fuller of little ways, and generally more satisfactory and difficult Peter and I had been at Possum's age—and see what a credit we had turned out. Gillian would inveigle herself into these parties by means of a cunning passion for looking at happy snaps, and then would return to upset Peter and myself, who were trying to play rather serious chess.

"I say, Peter!" She would come sidling up to us with glittering eyes. "Did you know that you were never really dry, not to be relied on, that is, until you were six?"

"Check," said Peter, ignoring this with enormous self-control.

"And Anto, darling, how I do wish you would wear a white fur bonnet sometimes now—very low over your eyes—I can't tell you how beastly sweet it made you look."

"*You can't do that*, Anto—you're in check to my knight."

"Hell, I'm upset."

"Concentrate."

"How can I? Do you realize that those three monstrous women sit up there every evening going right through us as if we were the sheets?"

"And what's more, Peter—wait for it—" Gillian was

149

hugging herself with delight, "let me tell you *this*——"
She broke into helpless giggles, and Peter eyed her nervously, and achieved the seemingly impossible feat of going a good three shades redder. "You had the dearest little——" she became convulsed, "the sweetest——"

Peter lunged suddenly, and trapped her, and pulled her down, slowly and relentlessly, across his knees. The serious game of chess slid into chaos.

"Now, Anto," he said grimly, "swipe her."

"The sweetest little *ways!*" shrieked Gillian, head downwards, suffocating under Suky's excited and thorough face-licking. "It's *all* I was going to say, Peter, *honestly* it was. Ow! The dearest little *ways*—heavens! how you've changed—ow! You brutes! *Don't,* Suky! Help!"

"Mr. Eyeworks," Peter's boy announced from the door, his own eyes popping.

We had forgotten about the expected arrival of the threatened location manager, and it now seemed likely that he would go away again at once. To understand the full, fearful impact of the scene upon him, it should be remembered that we had been hunting, and were at that strange stage of semi-undress that can occur before getting as far as a bath. Peter was looking particularly odd. He had got out of his boots, and replaced them with some very peculiar slippers with curly toes, which he had looted in Tunisia—he had also removed his coat and stock tie, and had replaced *them* with, respectively, an old battle-dress jacket and a very tatty Leander scarf, which he had wound vaguely around his neck like a muffler. It clashed terribly with his face. The jacket had no buttons, the yellow check waistcoat beneath it looked curiously formal and incompatible—or would have done if it had not been spattered with dried blood, as was Peter's face, which had been rather thoroughly ploughed up by blackthorn that afternoon. Even so, I think it was Gillian who really created the worst impression on poor Mr. Eye-works. (We never, ever, knew if that was really his name.) For some reason known only to herself, bless her, she had not taken off her boots, but had merely removed her coat, and then wrapped herself cosily in my dressing-gown before stumping off to the Nannies' symposium. This, to some extent, might have made matters appear, if not exactly normal, at least not too acutely, horrifyingly abnormal—it must have seemed, at first, to Mr. Eye-works, so bright and dapper in his Brooks Brothers suit and his best Young Executive smile, that Peter and I were merely attacking another man—but when Gillian kicked herself desperately upright and turned to face him the young executive smile changed, as his eye slid un-believingly from her ruffled, silky hair to her booted and spurred feet—I must say, the effect was quite extra-ordinarily *louche*—to a look of the wildest surmise I have ever seen on a human countenance.

He glanced swiftly over his shoulder seeking help, but the boy had gone—full speed, no doubt, to the servants's hall with the glad tidings. Scenting panic, the hound puppies gave tongue clamorously, and Suky and the ter-rier advanced stiffly towards him, hackles up, while Peter cursed the lot of them, and Gillian, advancing with them graciously, smiling sweetly, wordlessly, shook Mr. Eye-work's unresponsive hand, and slithered out through the door behind him, turning to give us an indescribable glance of leering, gleeful triumph, before she disappeared.

"I was to ask for Lord Dungarvan," said Mr. Eye-works, in a thin, helpless voice, flapping his hands at the puppies, who were getting braver and noisier every second, much impressed by the sound of their own voices.

"Anything I can do," said Peter, with courteous am-biguity, rising, seizing the terrier by the scruff of his neck, and pushing Suky behind him with his foot. "Turn those damn puppies out," he shouted at me, above their clamour.

He had a good voice, and he was rather looming over Mr. Eyeworks, who shrank back, taking him in fully for the first time—blood, black patch, slippers and all. I saw all hope die in him, and all the cloud-capped visions of gracious living in which he had been nurtured piteously dissolve, leaving not a rack behind.

"You are Lord Dungarvan?" he inquired, in the voice of a child who has been given the wrong sort of birthday present.

"I'm sorry I can't shake hands," said Peter, "but if I let this chap go he'll eat you. They'll all calm down in a minute. Come in and have a drink."

A man invited to drink with the Borgias might have worn Mr. Eyeworks' expression of terrified dismay, of determination not to have a drink, and, at the same time, not to offend by not having one.

"Can you tell me if Mr. Benoit is here?" he inquired, piteously, still flapping at the puppies, who were utterly refusing to be called off, turned out, or in any way to have this splendid game spoilt.

"Oh, yes, he's here," said Peter cheerily, "but he's ill."

"Ill?"

"Yes."

"Very ill?"

"Well, he looked fairly groggy the last time I saw him."

Mr. Eyeworks did not seem to find this surprising. "I—I guess I'd better go see him," he said, beginning to back out.

"Ah, no," said Peter, kind and soothing, and genuinely sorry for the little man. "Have a drink first. You'd never be allowed to see him, anyway; he's got such a lot of nurses."

"O, my gracious, is he that ill?"

152

"No, no, not at all—it's just that we've got a lot of nurses in the house."

The eyes of Mr. Eyeworks went to and fro like clockwork mice, seeking something reassuring, and not finding it.

"I expect you know Mr. Kavanagh?" Peter suggested helpfully.

But Mr. Eyeworks was neither helped nor reassured. He had seen me beating Gillian.

"Here," said Peter to me, "hold Pigg while I get the drinks going." He threw the terrier to me, and I promptly let him fall, knowing perfectly well that if I did not he would nip me. He made a silent, evil rush at Mr. Eyeworks' feet, but Peter swung round and fielded him just before he achieved them.

"I'm awfully sorry," he said. "He doesn't generally behave like this." But Mr. Eyeworks had gone.

"Damn it, Anto," said Peter, quite upset, feeling himself to be lacking in hospitality. "Why didn't you hold him?"

"He would have bitten me."

"*Nonsense.*"

"It's not nonsense. And he always behaves *exactly* like that—I never heard a more bare-faced lie."

"He does *not*," said Peter, quite huffily, and then lapsed into helpless laughter. "Oh, Lord, poor little man. . . ."

"If you could only *see* yourself," I quavered. "Enough to frighten the blackymoors, as Nanny would say."

"Gillian's spurs . . ."

"Those slippers . . ."

"I wonder what in hell he thinks we were up to?"

"I bet he's pretty worried now about sex life in Europe, anyway."

We began to re-arrange the serious game of chess, exchanging schoolboy ribaldry as we did so.

All this sort of nonsense did Peter a world of good, in nice contrast as it was to the long, intimidating talks he was always having with his steward, who came in every morning to give him the bad news. There is never any good news on an Irish estate, everything falls to pieces in an incredibly ill-wished manner. If a day can be got through without anything actually going disastrously wrong, and nothing dying, that is good enough, but generally it can't. There are the bullocks (red-water, ring-worm and timber tongue), the bull (bad fertility percen-age), the Cacador mare (slipped her foal), the milking herd (half of them not in calf, the rest with mastitis), the ten acre (too wet to get the winter wheat in), the stony meadow (too wet to get the beet out), the bogged tractor, the punctured trailer wheel, the diseased trees and the ragwort and the broken gaps and the yearling that has got into wire—as well as all the agricultural machinery that breaks down instantly, as its kind does, when called upon to do the job for which it is intended. Peter was always having long-drawn-out battles with Spares De-partments who hadn't got a sprocket for driving the finger bar on the manure distributor—"not right this minyit"—which meant that they had probably never had one, and certainly wouldn't have one for weeks, even if they remembered to order it, or were capable of recognizing it when it arrived.

This was his life—this frustrating struggle, and the lodgers ("God bless the bastards, I couldn't afford to hunt without 'em"), and the endless financial worries, and the determination to keep his child happy in the only place in the world where she could be so. Because he was so un-self-pitying I found myself too apt to forget—as everyone always did—that he had had a tough and tragic war and a lot of pain and loneliness since, as well as all the worry; and that he was hacking on for fifty: but I remembered

all this one night when I came down again to the messy
lair to collect some cigarettes, after having gone to bed,
and found Peter still there, long after midnight, slumped
over his desk, laboriously scrawling his signature on
cheques and transfer deeds and income-tax returns, and
trying to deal with farm accounts and wages and fodder
bills. He had pushed his black patch somewhere up into
his hair—which needed cutting—and was wearing horn-
rimmed spectacles. He looked very odd, too thin (as
Nanny had noted) and (as I noted now) quite exhausted,
and I thought with a pang of the *on dit* in London, the
glossy members of the Establishment telling each other in
White's how Peter Dungarvan had gone native, and was
now damn near as crazy as the child. He certainly badly
needed an agent and a secretary, and his right arm and his
wife—even one of them, I thought, would be a help.

He said, scrawling away, "Half a minute, boy. The
whiskey's over there, feed yourself. If I don't get this lot
finished now I never will."

I fed myself, and sat and watched him struggling on,
cursing under his breath. "I never could add things," he
said, crossly, finally, "I sat at the bottom of every damn
division trying to do it." He pushed the papers into a mad
heap, threw his spectacles on top of it, rubbed his hand
across his forehead, re-arranged his patch, and came over
to the whiskey. "Trouble is," he said, pouring it, "my
eye's beginning to feel the going a bit."

Oh, my God, *no*, I thought. Aloud I said, "Badly?"

"Ah, no, it battles on well enough."

Gillian came in suddenly, looking a touch wan, her
eyes bruised with sleep, wearing, for once, her own
dressing-gown.

"I woke up and you weren't there," she said to me,
accusingly.

"He wasn't here, either," said Peter. "He'd gone to see

if he could make Phillippa's temperature go any higher."

"Beast," said Gillian. She looked at him, and saw what I had seen. She said, "You look as if you needed Nanny to put you to bed."

"Not Nanny, I don't. How about you taking me on?"

"I shall, darling, without any doubt, don't worry. You look distinctly peaky, and I have very motherly instincts, whatever Anto may say."

"She's a very keen match-maker, too," I said. "She's got a lot of wives lined up for you—eight, at the last count, I think."

"Well," said Peter, "I'm certainly a tremendous catch. Absolutely the top star on the Christmas tree. I bet they're falling over themselves to get at me."

He turned, and came over to her with the drink he had made for her—lame, smiling, shabby, and indomitable. I distinctly felt—practically saw—the quiver of Gillian's tender heart. She ignored the proffered drink, ducked under it, and folded him—or as much of him as she could —lovingly in her arms. She said, "I just would like to tell you, anyway, that you're the sweetest person in the world, and the bravest, and we love you dearly, see?" She kissed him.

"She can say that again," I said.

Peter looked down at her. "And she can kiss me again," he said—adding, to me, "Take the drink, spoilsport."

I took it, and Gillian kissed him again with a refreshing lack of inhibition, to which he responded with enthusiasm.

"Shall I leave you two alone together?" I asked.

"Do just that," said Peter cordially.

The true, the moving, moment had passed, the emotion the more powerful because it was unacknowledged and beautifully controlled, although known to us all. Peter had come close to tears when Gillian had so suddenly and sweetly spoken her thoughts to him. I had watched his face as he had looked down at her. He had been badly in need of a little appreciation just then, and it had put fresh heart into him. When Gillian emerged from his embrace he looked years younger. He said to me, grinning, "Still here? You've got no tact, boy."

"I know," I said. "That's why I married this tactful woman. But still, I'm so what they call innately decent, I'll help you do your sums tomorrow."

"The whole thing is almost too beautiful," said Gillian. "We must sup up these drinks and put this Peter to bed —O, no, *don't* settle there," she said to him in dismay, as he stretched himself at full length on the old, baggy sofa. "We'll never get you going out of that."

Suky, who had been apparently deeply unconscious in front of the fire, rose as if electrified, floppered over to him, and looked at him with piercing love and egotism. "No," said Peter feebly. She vibrated slightly, and laid a tentative but commanding paw on him, keeping him in bondage to her beaming gaze at the same time. "No," said Peter helplessly. She continued to beam and vibrate, and wished only to share his simple pleasures, holding him firmly in place with eye and paw. I have few days left to me, she suggested. "Don't give in," I said. She gave me a mild glance of amused contempt and got both her elbows as far as his stomach and breathed expectantly. "Shameless bitch," he said, and smiled. She immediately jumped very heavily on top of him, turned round several times in what was obviously an agonizing manner and flumped herself ponderously down, tilting herself backwards so she could wash his left ear rather thoroughly.

"O, my God, stop it," said Peter, clutching his slopping drink.

"If I ever saw a chap who got himself imposed on . . ." I said.

157

"I know, I know, but what can I do when the woman's mad about me? Silly, shameless bitch, old bag, gorgeous girl, Suky," he said to her, encouragingly, and she went into further ecstasies.

"Revolting," I said.

"I know." He lifted his glass, with some difficulty, over her gyrating, seal-like head, and drank the whiskey in one long gulp, and held the glass silently and demandingly out to me.

I very unkindly took it away and said to Gillian, "Now roust him out."

Mr. Eyeworks, whom we never again heard called anything but Joe, turned out to be a very nice little man indeed, who was absolutely terrified of dogs, horses, and Peter. This upset Peter, who already felt guilty about Mr. Eyeworks's reception, and his attempts to woo the little man threw Gillian and me into a state of barely suppressed hysteria, during which we did not dare to catch each other's eye.

"You two ought to be at St. Trinian's," said Peter crossly to us. "Do stop this awful sniggering in corners. You're upsetting him."

"*We* are? O, no, Peter, he feels perfectly safe with *us*," said Gillian wickedly.

"Can't understand it. I at least stopped the dogs from eating him. You two just sniggered, as usual."

"It was the way you looked, darling. It's given him a trauma."

"A what?"

"It was the way you looked, that's all."

"I can't help what the devil I look like."

"Tell you what, Peter," I said. "He's mad about orchids—try talking to him about them."

"I suppose you'd like me to try giving him one? That

158

ought to finish him off, but I haven't got one handy."

"He likes petit-point, too," said Gillian.

"I'm not that sort of a chap."

"Well, my goodness, you *are* difficult—you'll just have to tell him about the smashing finishes you used to ride on Mr. Tod, that's all."

"I'll beat you again in a moment, my girl."

Gillian twined herself lovingly round him and said, "*Do*, you brute."

Mr. Eyeworks took to hiding in Benny's room and shooting craps endlessly and drearily—a game which he had never really appreciated (I gathered, from what he didn't say) even when there were a lot of people playing, and none of them were Benny.

Rupert was now slightly recovering, and so was Possum. They were both rather irritable, and both apt, also, to wander about the house in their dressing-gowns, until caught by some Nanny and put back to bed with a good talking-to. Rupert was inclined to leave his teeth about, and Possum his toothbrush. They both sat too long in the loo—Rupert with the Calendar, Possum (until discovered) with a particularly splendidly illustrated Foxe's Martyrs which he had found in the library. It really turned her up, said Nurse Simmons to Phillippa, not what she would call a holy book at all. Possum was infuriated at having it taken away from him, and he revenged himself by singing very wicked words very loudly, thumping defiantly up and down the stairs, when he was supposed to be in bed.

"Bloody, bottom, stomach," he sang at me, with a purple face, as I passed him. I supplied him with blast, and he savoured it cunningly, wondering if it was sufficiently rude to be alarming. He tried it on Rupert, tilting his round, angelic face upwards to study what the effect might be.

"Chap here needs some Alka-Seltzer," said Rupert to me. "Some in my bathroom," he added, kindly, to Possum, removing him absent-mindedly from his path, his mind on the starting prices at Limerick Junction. Possum looked at him with extreme devotion. He had all the tendency of his kind to be fond only of elderly rakes, lunatics, and tramps.

"Where are you going?" he called after Rupert.

"I'm going to say good morning to your very beautiful mother."

"I'm coming too."

"Certainly not, wait till you're asked. Anthony, did you see Freddy's putting up a boy to claim on that animal he ran down the course last week? What would you say? Is it a double bluff?"

"A double double one, I daresay. Freddy's been known to outwit himself before now."

"They're so damn tricky, the lot of 'em," said Rupert irritably. "Never give you a chance to turn an honest penny."

"Blast, bloody, bottom, stomach," shrieked Possum, with a face of holy ecstasy.

He had spotted his prey on the landing, Nurse Simmons, looking harassed, with a thermometer in her hand. But Nurse Simmons had learnt wisdom. She called back to someone unseen, "I can't seem to do a thing with him this morning, and I've Mrs. Benoit's temperature to take still," and passed by the deflated Possum, leaving the field to Nanny. But Possum meant to go down fighting. "Blast, bottom, bloody, stomach," he shrieked again, and then, rising to a fine height of blasphemy, striving *pour épater* Nanny in a big way—"Bosom", he roared, like a bull. But Nanny was old and skilled in such duels. "*There's* a funny thing to say," she said, mildly, peering down at him over her spectacles. "Whatever does it mean, child?"

Possum, silenced, tried to think what, in fact, it did mean, and gave up, baffled. He tried another tactic, challengingly. "In my breakfast, I swalled my prune stones whole. On purpose. I swalled them whole, in my breakfast."

He gave Nanny a look that said, Hold that one.

"*There's* a funny thing to do," said Nanny, unmoved. "And now you shall come and help me put these nice clean sheets on your bed."

Possum, recognizing his peer, went quietly—just as Benny had quietly given up his favourite cure for 'flu (sitting in a boiling hot bath and drinking himself insensible) and Rupert had quietly given up keeping his teeth in a glass of whiskey, and Jake had quietly and very happily given up everything for ever, and was reading Beatrix Potter with tremendous incomprehension.

"I cannot wait," Gillian said to Peter, "to see *you* in thrall to all these Nannies. You're the top prize, and once you've gone under to them you'll never come up."

"Nonsense," said Peter. "They'll eat out of my hand."

"Ho, ho!—I *cannot* wait."

"There'll be absolutely nothing amusing for you to see, let me tell you. I never allow anyone within miles of me if I'm ill—and anyway, I'm never ill," he concluded loftily.

"As a matter of fact, you pompous brute, I don't think you look so good at this very moment."

We were all tucked into the front of the van, very squashed, on our way to a meet at the kennels. I squinted sideways at Peter, and saw that he did indeed look rather peaky.

"Better get a wax image of me and start sticking pins in it," he said crossly.

At the meet I said to Gillian, "If you think Peter isn't well—and I don't think he does look well—for heaven's sake don't try cherishing him and telling him to come home, or he'll stay out to the bitter end—he'll probably lash old George on to an extra draw."

"How I hate men," said Gillian.

As it happened, Peter was forced to come home at a fairly reasonable hour, because he had lamed his horse, in a fall which had left him very wet and muddy, and even crosser than he had been that morning.

"Sheer bad judgement," he said, gloomily. "I never gave the poor brute a chance."

"Oh, Peter, darling," said Gillian—we were all squashed into the van again—"you gave him all the chance in the world—I had it just on your right, and I saw it all. He just plain made a bog of it—he still nearly got there, but the edge of the ditch gave way."

"It was a beastly place, anyway," I said, but Peter refused to be comforted. He mourned on; the familiar keening note of the man who never blames his horse— "I never got him straight turning in, and then I let him rush it"—and began to shiver rather. Gillian shut the window and told me to hurry on home, as she was cold, and Peter promptly gave her his coat, which splendidly defeated her purpose.

When we arrived back, instead of going off down the mysterious, echoing and odorous stone back passages of Castle Saffron, shouting for the boy to help him off with his boots, he sank straight into a chair by the fire in the messy lair, with a huge glass of whiskey, and lay back, crossing his long legs luxuriously. After a minute steam began to rise from him.

"I know a lot of people—well, look at Dicky, for one— who got arthritis doing that," said Gillian restively, hovering.

"Silly sods," said Peter dispassionately.

After another minute I had a try, without much hope.

"You'll ruin your boots."

"Bloody bad pair," he said, squinting at them in a judicious, but far-away manner. "Worst they ever made. Can't think what took them."

I gave up, and went off to look after my own health. Gillian came up a few minutes later, and said, lowering herself into the bath, "I should think he's got a raging fever, and he's just sitting there, waiting until the horses get back, and then he's going out to look at his—pneumonia for a certainty what idiots men are—do something, darling."

"I'll turn his own Nanny on to him."

"Well, please report the whole scene to me, because I want to tease him when he's better—O, what a love he is."

"Didn't I tell you?"

I went and alerted Nanny Tom, and then I went back to the messy lair, while she was happily preparing Peter's bed, and lolled pleasurably opposite him, awaiting zero hour. He was on his second glass and, owing to his state of health, pretty drunk, as well as being rather light-headed from the fever which, I thought, Gillian had been right about being high.

"Women," he said. "Always wanting you to move somewhere else. I'm not saying a word against Gillian, mind, but she will tell me to get into bed all the time."

"Very natural," I said.

"No, no, didn't mean that at all—who'd want to if you felt like this? Even if I couldn't—could, I mean."

It seemed too complicated a question even to try to answer, and I sat quiet, waiting cosily. Presently Nanny Tom came round the door, five foot nothing, beady-eyed in black alpaca behind an apron, unconcernedly shaking down a thermometer with simple mastery, certain of victory, a monument to moral ascendancy.

"Now, dear, we'll just see, shall we?"

"Hell," said Peter in a beaten voice.

163

"Don't use those words to me. If you're ill, dear, it's only right to make sure. Keep your mouth shut, now. It's only two minutes."

Peter had capitulated without even a show of force, I noted. He lay limply back and shut his eye, while Nanny Tom looked at her watch, and told me about an interesting temperature he had had at the age of thirteen. He once made a cross noise, which meant either that he hadn't, or he didn't, and Nanny Tom said, "Hush, dear. A little patience, but you were never one for it," and presently took the thermometer and squinted at it under the light and said triumphantly, "Well, dear, you must certainly come straight up to your bed, it's all ready for you, and I daresay you won't fancy anything to eat."

Peter roused himself with a tremendous effort. "I'll jus' see Casey about th' horse," he said thickly, "I'll come strai' up then. I will, honestly," he added pathetically, meeting her eye, and cringing.

"Well, now, such nonsense I never heard—as if Mr. Casey didn't well know what to do for the horse, and better than you, dear, if the truth were known." She went to the door and called in a soft, commanding Nanny voice, "Patrick! Come and help his lordship with his boots," and came back to Peter. "Sit up a minute, dear, do. Yes, soaking wet; I thought so. Is your shirt wet, too? Never mind, we'll get that off upstairs—— Now, Patrick, his lordship has the 'flu—take this coat, and then get those boots off, quick, and you can come upstairs and take the other things."

"I c' undress myself," snarled Peter, with despairing dignity.

"Of course you can, dear. I'll just be running your bath, and Patrick can give you a hand out of those wet things," agreed Nanny Tom, bland as a diplomat.

While Patrick, bent in the curious traditional attitude,

164

was struggling with his master's boots, Peter made one half-hearted attempt at rebellion—grunting rather in the struggle, because there is no greater agony than the removal of soaking wet boots from legs that have been unwisely baked before a fire.

"Gemme some gum-boots," he said to Patrick. "An' a coat."

"Surely, my lord," said poor Patrick helplessly, in thrall to Nanny Tom's eye.

"Now dear, that's just silly, and well you know it. Patrick can bring you up word from Mr. Casey, and I daresay Mr. Kavanagh will look at the poor horse himself, if that will content you," (here, catching her glance, I found myself definitely fawning upon her) "not but what I'm sure it's not bad at all, as well you know—so don't put on that stubborn face, now, dear."

"I'll look at him, Peter," I said, basely. "And he really isn't bad and you are, and you do know all that perfectly well, so just do what you're told."

He glared at me, staggered to his feet, and stood, swaying slightly, looking angrily and muzzily from one to the other of us, like a wounded bull unable to make up his mind as to whom it would afford the most satisfaction to him to charge.

"That's it, come along, now," said Nanny Tom cosily, placidly certain of unconditional surrender.

"Have sense, now, my lord," muttered Patrick, pleadingly, practically putting out a hand to stroke him. Caught in the necessity of betraying either Mrs. Thomas or his master, there was absolutely no doubt in his mind as to which was the safer thing to do. Peter looked at his ingenuous, alarmed face, and was in turn betrayed by his own kind heart.

"Hell, c'mon, then," he said. " 'f you don't undress me, Mrs. Thomas will."

"Not that word, dear," said Nanny Tom, automatically.

"I thought you never let anyone within a mile of you when you were ill," I said, unkindly, planting a further bandillero, just as he reached the door. Nanny Tom shook her head at me and tut-tutted indulgently. He turned back uncertainly and said thickly, "You're not to tell that woman of yours one flaming word about this, see?"

"It's a question of divided loyalties," I said, smugly.

"Good night," he said, as coldly as his muzzy state allowed.

"Good-bye, now," I said, grinning. "I'll come up and tell you about the horse later."

"One day I'll do you for this," he said.

"Good-bye," I said again.

Suky pattered keenly after him, her nose in the back of his knees, but Nanny Tom still managed to get between them.

"Not that great dog, dear, not on your bed you don't have her, not after what happened last time."

I went back to Gillian. "He's being undressed now, and he's not allowed to have Suky on his bed."

"Nor his twill sheets, I daresay—O, the absolute heaven of Nannies!"

Peter, like all people who are never ill, was now very much iller than anybody else, and spent most of the next day in a state of semi-delirium. Gillian sat with him while Nanny Tom had her meals, and that evening I saw she had on her woebegone, waif-and-stray air.

"Darling, what's the matter? Are you getting this foul disease?"

"No. It's Peter."

"Don't be silly, love. I know he feels bloody now, but he'll be all right in a few days. Be your uncertain age."

But she wouldn't laugh. "It's not that," she said, sniffing. "But he's very muddled this evening, and he

166

keeps talking either to or about her. All the time. Nothing else." She sniffed again, and came over to sit on me. "I think I need your drink. . . . O, hell, there goes my mascara." She held my drink and looked sadly down into it. "You know how it is. . . . People you know, and they put up a good front and all, and if you're happy yourself it seems it must be the same, really, for them? And then, sometimes, suddenly, you see just how much it isn't? It can hit you a bit of a crack." She wiped her nose sadly on the cuff of the shirt she was wearing, which was mine.

"Don't," I said. I wasn't sure if I meant don't wipe your nose on my shirt, or don't feel things so much.

"What?" She was still looking into my drink. "But the thing was . . . but don't laugh, darling?"

"No." I remembered Phillippa telling me not to laugh, and thought what a smooth and beastly exterior I must have successfully cultivated.

"The thing was that when I went in to him he thought I was her, at first." She smeared some mascara woefully across a cheek, and I kissed her.

"Well, I hope he went on thinking so, poor old boy."

"No. That was the thing. He got a bit clearer, and then he was scared, he asked what he'd been saying, he said, "Was I making a holy show of myself? O, hell." She drank up some more of my whiskey rather quickly.

"Yes . . ." I said, "I do see." I felt rather like crying myself. "Did you pass that off all right?"

"Oh, yes, perfectly. I was pretty slick, I thought. He was quite reassured. So then he was wandering again, but Nanny T. came back, so I came away. But he does so long for her. . . . Hell!" She drank some more whiskey. "Why is it always the nicest people who get the worst hands dealt them?"

"Perhaps because they can be relied on not to cheat? God knows!"

167

"Well, I don't think He does—I think someone else must be in control of this stinking world." She sniffed some more, and took my handkerchief.

"Darling, it's not going to do Peter much good for us to get morbid. He likes jokes and gossip and getting teased. And just think what a hellish patient he'll be when he's a touch better."

"I know. But that only seems to make it worse."

"I think you'd better switch to gin."

"I think so, too."

Presently she said in an interested voice, "Do you suppose those were the tears?"

"Which?"

"The ones it was going to end in."

"I'd be very happy to think so," I said.

Chapter Eleven

Peter took to being a hellish patient very quickly and easily. He lay in a fretful, muddled heap with Suky (smuggled up by the horrified Patrick) and complained that his bed was full of crumbs and fleas— why couldn't he get out of it, as he was perfectly well?

"Such nonsense I never heard," said Nanny Tom, composedly. "You can just get up to wash, today, if you like, while I straighten your bed—such a mess I never saw, and I shall have something to say to that boy later, the cheek of him."

"And you'll probably fall down, anyway, darling, if you do get up, you look perfectly horrible," chimed in Gillian. "Do tuck down and go to sleep."

This was going too far. The hellish patient reared grimly up from his hellish bed, with his hellish pyjamas twisted round him in a fantastic fashion.

"Goodness!" said Gillian. "Aphrodite!"

"All right, all right," said the hellish patient testily. "I had a classical education, too, even if I *have* gone native."

"Put on your dressing-gown at once," said Nanny Tom very strictly. "I'm sure I don't know what her ladyship your mother would have said to you."

"Don't bother me," Peter said. "I'm ill," and staggered off.

"Well, now . . . if Mr. Kavanagh wouldn't mind just taking this great dog out . . . and if Mrs. Kavanagh would help me with the bed, then I can settle his lordship down for a sleep."

"He wants some brandy," said Gillian faintly, loyal to the last.

"The very idea!" said Nanny Tom indulgently, ruthlessly turning the bed into a cool, white hygienic square, and taking away all the pillows. "He'll feel quite different after a nice sleep."

Rupert had a plan. He divulged it to us, his eyes glinting happily, the first time he arrived for a meal downstairs. This was luncheon, and we had returned to the dining-room—obviously, Peter didn't allow anybody into his lair unless he was there too. I was sorry that that cosy régime had passed. Rupert spread grouse paste on water biscuits, and drank soda water. "I haven't been *at all* well," he said to me impressively.

"I know," I said.

"But I've got great recuperative powers."

"I know."

"Don't tutoyer me."

"I'm not."

"Yes, you are. How's his lordship today?"

"Pretty maddening, I'm glad to say."

"Better, eh?"

"Yes. He was ill enough."

"He's a nice chap, old Peter—bit lacking, of course."

I gave myself some steak and kidney pudding, listening to the audible rising of Gillian's hackles.

"Here he sits in the bog," Rupert went on, "looking after his delightful child, as noble as all get out—he's barking, the old boy, just plain barking—why doesn't he go out and dangle himself in front of an American?"

He assumed a dreamy air. "I can see it all—one of those brisk, sunny grandmommas with three slices of alimony.

Pink hair. Mauve spectacles. Oil. Bourbon. Culture. A very lovely person, deeply interested in art—he should have no trouble at all, the old boy. Happy ever after, do the place up, all in the very best lack of taste—we'd be warm for one thing."

"Don't, please, darling," said Gillian. "You know how I love you, but I love Peter more."

"That's only because he's a right trusty and right well-beloved cousin—when I come into mine you'll fancy me much the better—you've taken to disdaining commoners, that's your trouble. . . ." Rupert made a sweeping, melancholy gesture. "But listen to my plan."

We listened, patiently.

"Sachi's going to that gambling place in the desert," he said impressively, leaning right across the table and champing his water biscuits cracklingly at us.

"I thought she was making a film here, with Benny?"

"I've just sacrificed my last scrap of integrity by writing in a part for her, too," I said.

"Oh, *integrity!* . . ." Rupert gestured again, dismissing integrity. "Be your age. Where's the port, by the way?"

"We haven't got to the port stage."

"I have."

"Patrick," said Gillian.

"Yes, madam?"

"The last time we were hunting, we took a bottle of port with us."

"Yes, madam, I mind it."

"Mr. Chichester would like what's left of it now."

Rupert glared at her as Patrick left the room.

"Go on about your plan, darling," said Gillian, very sweetly.

Rupert decided to forgive her, because he was so longing to tell us. "Ever been there?" he inquired of me.

"No."

"It's respectable, y'know, very respectable place."

"Really?"

"Yes. Chum of mine was there this year. Dead respectable, he said. No tarts, no fights, just gamble, gamble, gamble, day in, day out. Old women. Schoolmarms. Middle West. Fruit machines. *Blackjack*." Rupert's voice became more heavy with disgust and sorrow upon every lowering word.

"You amaze me. I always imagined a mad whirl of wantonness," said Gillian.

"A sink of respectability."

Patrick came back with the port. He was baffled. He thought the thing out for a moment, then he placed the bottle in a coaster and set it tentatively in front of Rupert. The bottle was one quarter full. The label said Best Hunting Tawny. Rupert glared at it absently, wondering when he had ordered it, and tipped it up into the remains of his soda water. "Old boy keeps a very poor table," he said to Gillian vindictively.

"He keeps *you* for free," said Gillian, spiritedly. "No wonder he's broke."

"I am what they call a paying guest," said Rupert with dignity.

"Well, they call it quite wrong, I guess, and what's more he's always lending you money, into the bargain."

"I told you he's a bit lacking," said Rupert mildly.

It was a long time since he had discovered that it was best to ignore insults, and his technique was perfectly enamelled.

"Go on about your plan."

"Nobody plays chemmy there," said Rupert mysteriously.

"You mean there isn't a game?"

"Oh, there's a *game* all right, but nobody plays it. It's too civilized, see? They don't understand it. Blackjack.

Fruit machines. Roulette, even. Chemmy, no. This chum said there's a fortune to be picked up, turning it into a high game."

"Why didn't he pick it up, then?" inquired Gillian, coming straight to the point.

Rupert said coldly. "He had no lolly."

"But have you?"

Rupert drank his port-and-soda and hummed to himself annoyingly.

"Out with it," I said, still on the steak and kidney.

"Sachi's going to get paid some fantastic amount for twittering around there for a fortnight. Cabaret, y'know. Only got to move her lovely little limbs about, pretty unfair when you come to think of it, nobody ever offered *me* millions of dollars to expose myself. Too late, now," he said sadly, brushing crumbs off his paunch. "Who drank all that port?"

"Darling, do keep the thread," said Gillian. "How are you going to make this fortune?"

"By investing little Sachi's money, of course—delightful little creature she is, don't you agree?"

"Investing it in a chemmy game, Rupert?"

"Of course."

"But will she let you?"

"Of course. And live to thank me."

He lay happily back in his chair, leering. He really did leer.

"I take off my hat to you," I said.

"Thanks, old boy, thanks."

"But surely Louie will be there? Won't he foil your plan?"

"Oh, *Louie*. . . ." Louie was dismissed, one with integrity, one with Gillian's disdain for commoners, one with the Best Hunting Tawny.

"But how will you get there, Rupert? It costs millions, just to *get*."

"I shall travel with the little woman, naturally," he said with dignity, looking around challengingly.

"If I had a hat, I should put it on," said Gillian.

"I just rise above my circumstances," said Rupert airily. "I don't wallow. That's all. Perfectly simple. I don't allow them to get me down. I don't notice them, you might say. Is that Kümmel I see on the sideboard? My stomach needs settling."

After luncheon Gillian and I had a quiet glass of quite other port with Peter, and told him about Rupert's plan.

"He's an amusing sod, old Rupert," he said. "Bit lacking, of course."

Benny now recovered from his 'flu, and talked endlessly to Louie, who was in California. I supposed that Peter also paid for this, and I began to wonder if all these dollar-happy lodgers would really turn out to have been much help in the end. Mr. Eyeworks went about the countryside seeking what he found not, teetering on the tops of banks, crawling reluctantly over walls, and talking about camera angles, but otherwise the film-making didn't seem to be progressing very well. The tax situation, it seemed, was not as favourable as had been hoped; had, in fact, developed a new and surprising angle; and Louie was leaning once more towards the Argentine, inclined to hedge his Irish bet, and much less hypnotized by Benny now he was so much farther away.

"I get paid, anyway," I said to Gillian.

"Good," she said faintly, peering peakily out of the bed where she had finally retired with that form of the disease—particularly maddening to the girls—with which you are not dramatically ill, but merely plain, slightly fevered, and intensely desirous of death. "Darling, I feel terrible. Just go away, will you?"

I went away, and sat gloomily in the library, where rain was lashing the tall, flat windows, and mice were playing football behind the skirting boards. The gilt pelmets were crumbling, the brocade curtains were going, the calf bindings had gone, the fire had refused to go at all, and Suky had decided it would have been reckless to go out in the rain. I looked hopelessly at the previous day's *Times*, limp with damp, and discovered that nearly everyone had died; I turned to photograph albums, and found that practically nobody was left alive. There was a photograph of Maria leading in Peter at Aintree, smiling joyfully up at him, and receiving a horrible grimace in exchange, as he attempted not to look pleased with himself. The library and everything else whispered coldly to me of defeat and death. I lit a cigarette, which tasted filthy, and wandered over to the windows, and stood with my hands in my pockets and looked at the wild, grey, dripping day, at the dank bullocks huddled together beyond the sunk fence, the ragged rooks blowing haplessly about, the weedy, puddle-strewn gravel, the scowling sky; the leafless trees, and I let the black, overwhelming, panic depression sweep over me and take possession. It was almost a relief. It was like ceasing to fight against an anaesthetic. I rested in it, and hoped that my compliance would pacify the god. Something, or myself, said to myself, "This is going to be tragic. I bloody knew it before I came. Why the hell did I come?"

"Nonsense," I said. "You're getting 'flu."

"O, no," I said. "You won't get out of it as easily as that."

"Get out of what, for Christ's sake?"

"For Christ's sake," said Peter, behind me, "why didn't you ring, Anto, and get the fire made up? No need to stand around in a bloody morgue, boy." He put his thumb violently on the bell, and held it there. He was wearing an old Army mackintosh, and he looked ill and jaded and very like his library.

"You're not going out in this, are you?" I asked, hopelessly.

"Must," he said. "Your mamma rang up. Child's in a fuss. Thinks I'm dead or something."

"Well, you will be, if you go out now."

"Nonsense," he said. "I've got what they call a great constitution." He turned to Patrick, who had arrived at the door. "Build this fire up until the chimney's alight. Mr. Kavanagh's getting pneumonia."

"The way it was, my lord, it was going grand, but it died on me and I below at the silver," said Patrick, reprovingly unable to work everywhere at once.

"Well, the silver won't die, but Mr. Kavanagh will— hurry on, now."

"You'll be the one to die," I said. "Have some sense, Peter, for heaven's sake."

"I must go, you know, Anto," he said seriously. "She gets in a real fuss."

I remembered, then, suddenly and vividly, an evening shortly after we had arrived when Peter, very lame, rather drunk, and extremely stiff after hunting, had levered himself up out of his chair to go and change, and had promptly fallen down. "Lord!" he had said, staggering to his feet, clutching at Gillian for support. "High time I was sent to the kennels, ain't it?"

The child had been sitting by him, quietly and happily engaged in sorting some very tatty and tangled salmon flies. I remembered now the blanched and blazing fear in her face as she flashed to her feet, spilling the flies over the carpet, and flung her thin arms round his neck, burying her face against him, without a word, without a cry; and I remembered the sudden, moving change in his face, and the tenderness with which he had laughed her out of her fear, and left her quiet and happy again before he went off to have his bath.

Later that night he had said to me suddenly, with difficulty, unused to talking about his worries, "I sometimes wonder how right I've been—or how unfair." He had looked old. I had said, "You've been dead, damned right. Don't ever bloody well believe anything else." He had looked up sharply, amazed at my tone.

"I just happen to feel very strongly about it," I had said. "You've been right, you are right, see?"

"All right, I'm right," he had said, amiably. "No need to get excited about it. I'll play you a hand of piquet, twopenny points, suit you?"

"Suits me."

Now I said slowly, "She gets in a real fuss—of course, I remember."

"Oh, yes," he said, on his way out. "Then only one person will do. My God, I know the feeling—look, Anto, give yourself a lot of drink, and if that fire isn't bloody well blazing when I get back I'll wring everyone's blasted necks—how's your woman this morning?—don't look at those dreary albums—everyone's dead." He was gone.

It was after I had helped Patrick to set the chimney alight—and nearly ourselves, because we had used sugar and Ronsonol—that the depression returned; blacker, more formless, more threatening than ever, more full of grief and betrayal, in spite of the gay, leaping flames, and the cessation of the rain. It was not helped by the thought of what a long time Peter had been doing without the only person who would do. "My God, I know the feeling"—I kept hearing him say it, and myself, or something else, I kept hearing say, "You'll be the one to die."

The fire did no good, nor did the lot of drink. Presently I went and sought the company of Possum, but he was drawing a house or horse and bitterly resented my presence. Also, Nanny Tom was there, and gave me hell for letting Peter go out. I went and found Rupert and engaged him in poker dice, and lost ten pounds at once. "Double or quits," he said, glintingly, the moment that Patrick announced luncheon.

"All right, all right," I said, irritably, and it was, naturally, double.

"I'll buy you a drink some time," he said delightedly. "What are you so gloomy about? Mustn't let mere money worry you—I got over *that* years ago."

Chapter Twelve

The following day, still gloomy, I was hunting, having another crack on Dan's recovered horse. "You must get a hunt on him," he said kindly. "He's a great bank jumper, and he's no clown over the walls, either, when he'd look at them."

"We're in the walls today," I pointed out sadly, ordering port and brandy.

"Hit him and hold him," said Dan cheerfully. "Make him look. I'll stay behind you till he'd settle."

"Thanks very much. Very generous of you. Have some more of this filthy drink—I may as well be as blind as the horse, I suppose."

"Ah, God, he's not as bad as that—I tell you, he's great to lep." He gave me a look, and asked, "What ails you? Getting the 'flu?"

"No. I'm just plain bloody-minded."

"Happens to us all," said Dan, looking over my shoulder to where, further in the depths of the dark and smelly bar, Sarah and Benny were engaged in some very cosy chat indeed, each with an elbow on the stained counter, and leaning rather close together across their glasses.

"What's the first draw?" I asked Dan, to try to get that look off his face.

"Flynn's," he said, still looking the same way. "I wish Sarah hadn't bought that horse off Pat O'Dwyer. It's cracked. Just plain cracked, that's all."

"It seems to go through the country like a sheet of lightning."

"It puts the heart crosswise in me to watch it," said Dan. "Divil a foot have I seen it lay to anything yet."

"It must do," I said. "After all, it hasn't ever fallen. It's just a bit flighty."

"Flighty, God help us!" said Dan, pouring drink into himself. "You're very mild in your speech today, indeed. Wait till you'd see it fly a bohireen and the two walls of it, together, the very same as if 'twas the water at Liverpool. I wouldn't sit on its back across this country if you gave me gold for it."

Sarah leaned slowly back along the counter, and turned her delicious snipey face round towards us, smiling warmly, her wonderful golden eyes half closed in enjoyment, like a cat's. "I dare you, darling," she drawled caressingly, with luxurious slowness and clarity and amusement. Dan made an abrupt, uncertain movement, and met her gaze, unwillingly. Her smile widened, her curving mouth turned up at the ends and twitched slightly, insolently, and I wondered helplessly if it was really me rather than Benny who attracted these fascinating disasters.

"What's this?" I asked, in a futile attempt to alleviate the atmosphere. "The fifth form at St. Hilda's?"

Sarah let her amused, evil eyes rest on my face. "You wouldn't know, darling, would you?" she said gently. "You're civilized."

Then her gaze went back to Dan, mocking. Dan said nothing. Oh, Lord, if only he'd just slap her, or laugh, if only he didn't mind so much, I thought hopelessly. Behind the counter a filthy, merry old woman in a black shawl counted out our change aloud, and called upon St. Joseph to witness that it had her bate, the way the gintleman had ordered so quick on her, hadn't it gone out of her head entirely. Benny reached over and folded her dirt-encrusted hand tenderly over the coins, and told her to keep them. He put his arm around Sarah, and leaned across her, and said, "How's that again? A bet?" He looked immensely kind and gay and indulgent and eager to take part in any little bit of fun that might be going—not a spoil-sport like Dan, oh, no, I thought bitterly, how in God's name did I ever come to take part in this circus? It will end in tears, Gillian said in the back of my mind; but I had known that before I started, and I had come, so why blame Benny now?"

Sarah said, leaning enjoyably back against Benny, looking enjoyably at Dan, "Not a bet. A dare. Like at school, you know. Great fun for the middle-aged. Keeps us young, doesn't it, darling?" she said to Dan, very fondly.

"Gee, so what is this dare, kid? Something pretty desperate, huh?"

"I'm daring Dan to ride my horse. He's always crabbing him, and it's time he saw for himself how good he is."

"Daring him?" Benny winked at Dan in a gay, friendly fashion. "But he's the top jock around here—he don't need no daring, honey?" The unemphasized question lingered prickingly.

"If he just doesn't happen to want to play, I'll dare *you*," said Sarah to Benny. She was still looking at Dan, still smiling.

"May the saints intercede for your honour," said the old woman behind the counter to Benny.

"Thanks, kid, thanks," he said, absently, watching the situation develop nicely.

Old George put his mulberry face round the door suddenly, and said, "Stop all this damn coffee-housin'—I'm goin', I'd have you know. Put that jumpin' powder down and get forward—never saw a more disgraceful set of skirters in me life."

"And then I'll dare *you*," said Sarah to me, ignoring him. "I'll double dare you." She gave me a quite enchanting glance of sheer, bewitching bitchery; but I was not enchanted.

"I shouldn't bother," I said, meeting the glance. "I just don't happen to want to stay quite so young as all that"—and watched the bitchery change abruptly to hard, smouldering anger, and thought, poor old Dan, he certainly has got something on his plate here.

Dan had put his glass down, and turned and walked out without a word, following old George. I followed Dan. We went across the road to where the horses were being led up and down. I said lightly, looking sideways at his stony face, "It's bloody childish, chum. Take no notice."

"I'll ride the sod," he said, very low. "I hope he breaks my neck."

Old George had fulfilled his threat smartly, and was already bustling away down the dusty little road towards Flynns, surrounded by his gay, loving, enthralled bitch pack, who were relying on him absolutely to show them where a fox might be found, and looking forward to the fun immensely—which was more than I was, as I watched Dan order his man to swap the saddles over, curse him for being slow, get up, slam his heels into the startled horse's sides, and ride off in silence.

"The master seem upset, like," his man said, staring.

"No," I said. "Mrs. Nugent wants to ride the other horse. Better get that saddle on, or we'll be left."

Benny and Sarah came out of the bar, laughing together. Sarah's brows went up when she saw her horse had gone. She said nothing, and we all got up and clattered off rather too quickly to Flynn's, which was a straggly gorse covert between two large ragged fields, beneath the sloping shoulder of a stony hill. George had already put the bitches in, and was encouraging them gently. "Yoi, try," he advised them, "Tr-r-ry, then, good girls." They tried like anything, longing to please him, but there was no fox. A first season girl opened shrilly on a hare, and was severely rated by Tommy, and then spoken to sarcastically by her elders. When she had stopped squeaking George urged them, not very hopefully, to try again. They worked industriously up through the gorse. Here and there the tip of a stern, here and there an eager, busy, grinning face showed above it. But we cannot tell a lie, they said, there is honestly no fox here, hadn't you better call us out?

But George was adamant. "Yit, tra-high rouse 'm, then," he said to them.

All this was bad luck for Dan, I thought—he needed to get going quickly, while he was still angry, while the port and brandy were still nicely alive in him. Chatting to Paddy Casey, I looked round for him, and saw him walking the horse in a circle, very slumped in the saddle, his hat tipped over his eyes. Sarah always walked that horse about at the first covert, on a loose rein, dreamily, slapping his shoulder, and smiling to herself at the thought of the thrills he was going to provide for her. But now he was edgy, he was missing that feeling of freedom, of easy, shared excitement, the certainty that nothing would interfere and spoil this fascinating game of galloping and jumping that he enjoyed so much. He shook his head, experimentally, switched his tail, and jiggled sideways. Dan cursed him for a green brute, and the horse responded by raking at him vigorously. He felt, then, in Dan's hands, fear and anger, and he didn't care for it at all. He grunted, and gathered his feet under him like a cat, and moved round threateningly with his back up and his ears moving uncertainly, and presently, as the bitches worked on in silence, he clamped those ears firmly back and began to fight his bit seriously. O, Lord, I thought, trouble and more trouble. I wasn't feeling too happy myself, quite apart from the groundless depression and foreboding which still hung over me. My brother Roger, convalescent from his crucifying fall, was spending the day at Castle Saffron, entertaining Gillian, who was now on her feet, but rather fretful and wan. "Is there a chaise-longue any-where about?" she had asked Peter that morning.

"Probably. Why—do you want to receive somebody on it?"

"Of course—what would be the fun of being an in-valid otherwise?"

"Frankly," I had said, "I think that's going too far, little woman," and she had grinned foxily at me, looking extraordinarily plain, and I had realized then, with a pang, that it was no good trying to conceal from myself any longer that here was the one person who would do for me. There it was—and it was a sobering thought, because she had belonged to me on and off for ever, and had been my wife for some time, and I hadn't realized until that moment that I couldn't do without her—I hadn't, indeed, even realized before this that I myself would ever feel that overpowering need. I had thought myself to be what is known amongst Nannies as too clever by half—too ego-tistical, too disenchanted, too cold-hearted, too calculating —too everything, in fact, except this whatever it was. It was rather overwhelming, and I was hoping now that Peter hadn't produced the chaise-longue, and that Gillian wasn't at this very moment deciding that my charming drunk brother was the one who would do for her.

George now called his disappointed but still loving girls out of Flynn's. They swirled about him, declaring they had done their utmost—what more can we do? they asked, gazing hopefully and pantingly up at him. Better come along to Ballymahon, was the answer to that one, and old George moved grimly off at a jog across the fields, and Tommy had once more to rate the girl who had opened on the hare, and still felt a sneaking, ashamed interest in it, and Sarah's horse stood suddenly absolutely straight up—"As clane and clever as you or me," Paddy Casey observed admiringly to me afterwards. "Sure, the apes wouldn't be in the class with that one at all."

Dan, the old master, had reacted instantaneously, and was hunched right forward along one shoulder, his arm round its neck. For a couple of seconds they were outlined heroically against the pale sky, while the horse belted the air with his forefeet, and we wondered sickeningly if he was coming to come over; then he dropped down with an angry grunt, and jogged forward edgily with the rest of us. This was bad luck for Dan, too, that we were going to the next draw across country, because there is no more promising situation for a fresh and irritable horse to exploit, and Sarah's horse now exploited it to the full—tearing madly into trappy little gaps like an express train, or else, if Dan tried to steady him, refusing to go near them at all, and threatening to stand up again.

"Never knew him offer to do that before," said Sarah to Benny, in innocent, gleeful wonder; making me suddenly hope very much that I had not, through my stupidity, lost someone as kind as Gillian.

Old George now decided, not very hopefully, to draw some kale on the way to Ballymahon, and we all stood about twitchily and listened to them crackling and rustling through it in silence, while it got colder and colder, and our horses got crosser and crosser. And then, suddenly, electrifyingly, one of them opened, deep, like a bell, and old George encouraged her warmly, "Huic, huic, *huic* to Winsome," and some of his girls who had rather lost heart, and had been feathering idly down the edges of the kale now plunged back into it with mad, springing bounds like kangaroos as they turned to see if Winsome was right, and sure enough she was, and they confirmed it ringingly, while young horses sidled and sweated and old ones were turned into stone, with cocked ears meeting at their tips, and hearts of horse and human battered under saddle flap and waistcoat, and everyone fingered their girths and headgear and looked cagily about to see—if they were bold—how to steal a start, or—if not so bold—exactly how horrible the first obstacle might prove to be. . . .

I saw at once that if the fox broke at the north end of the field, which seemed likely with the wind as it was, the first obstacle would be intensely horrible, consisting as it did of a very high and narrow and overgrown stone-faced bank into a bohireen. My brother Roger always said that port and brandy were a great help in getting over the first "when the stones look cold to you in the morning". These stones looked unrelentingly cold, and, to make matters worse, the field dipped abruptly down to them—we would have to trot right down into the dip and take the bank almost from a standstill. There was plainly a goodish drop into the bohireen, and the obstacle out of it was anybody's guess—all that could be seen was a tangled mass of blackthorn against the threatening sky. Oh, Lord, poor Dan on that bloody animal, I thought, and then, even as I looked at the bank, the fox flitted across it and was gone, a russet phantom, had he, hadn't he?—but the bitches came out screaming, very certain, they had had a view, and flowed over it like the shaking of a black and white and tan kaleidoscope, and a general edging forward began to turn into a cavalry charge, and our field master, who knew his field only too bitterly well, and had an equally impressive command of them and of stirring language, pulled across us and stood in his stirrups and informed us that he would send the whole flipping lot of us home if we didn't flaming well give them a chance, what did we think this was, bloody Epsom, he supposed, God damn you, Poodle (his voice rose to a hoarse bawl) *come back here*, give *me* a chance, too, will you?

After what seemed to me, and I supposed to everyone else, about half-an-hour, during which even the most sober horses went mildly off their heads, he trotted down and went out over the bank, and we all bustled and bored and bumped after him, cursing, jealous, frightened, exalted, exultant—and in that moment, and during the forty-five minutes that followed, very fast, across the best of the wall country, I forgot Dan, I forgot Gillian, I forgot —tremendous relief—myself; I even forgot to wonder how much my horse really knew (it turned out he knew it all)—the true, the spine-tingling, the frightening, unfailing magic once more laid its curious, atavistic, anaesthetizing spell across my very willing heart.

In my bath that evening, coming reluctantly out of the lingering fumes of the anaesthetic, I suddenly realized that I had not seen Dan at all in that hunt, and I had not seen Benny since, and that Phillippa, when I had got back, had been quietly playing snakes and ladders with Possum; quietly and very tiredly, still beautiful, although it was her first day up, and that I, like an oaf, had told her about the hunt for almost as long—I supposed, now, ashamedly—as the hunt itself had taken.

Chapter Thirteen

Peter's child had utterly refused to do without him any longer, even though she loved my mamma and Knockmoree dearly (the place would, in fact, be her home, and my mamma her guardian, if anything happened to Peter) so he had brought her back with him that day, and Benny had some superbly dramatic moments leaving, with ostentatious unostentatiousness, any room in which it appeared likely that he might be going to be left alone with her for a minute. It seemed, I thought, unnecessary to press the point so far, because by this time he was so in love with Peter that it appeared more likely that the next pass would be at him, rather than at his child. Rupert, however, now took up the running, and decided that the correct approach should be a touch avuncular—an arm round the little shoulders here, a friendly slap on the little bottom there. Peter observed this with some amusement for a few days, and then decided that the moment had come to speak—Nanny Tom had come to him and said firmly that Mr. Chichester wasn't a gentleman who should be in the old nursery at All Hours, and on the rocking-horse, too, there was something unhealthy about it, to her way of thinking, so would you please make that quite clear to Mr. Chichester, dear?

Peter related this to us with delight, and Gillian—I was alarmed to observe—immediately rang up Roger to tell him. Peter tackled Rupert cheerfully, before luncheon, with Gillian and I and Phillippa present. He didn't take

Rupert as seriously as he had taken Benny. "Lay off," he said to him, without preamble, giving him sherry. "Just lay off, or I'll throw your teeth to the dogs, see?"

Rupert's eyes flickered once, before he decided, almost instantaneously, on dignity. "My dear old chap," he said, with a splendid touch of melancholy hauteur, "I simply fail to understand—I fail utterly, forgive me—to what you are referring." He savoured his sherry sadly; a God-fearing gentleman of the old school, upright, bayed by lesser breeds.

"If it doesn't sink in you'll have to start polishing up your Arabic," said Peter amiably.

"You speak in riddles," said Rupert, loftily, with a sad, noble stare.

"That's exactly what I do *not* do—I speak very plainly indeed, see? Lay off—or you're out."

"I thought this was supposed to be a gentleman's establishment," Rupert looked at him sternly.

"So did I," said Peter, still amiable, but returning the look with a very excellent one of his own.

Rupert tried meeting it for a moment, but he knew he had lost. "What are you trying to do?" he asked, abandoning dignity, disintegrating with delight, and coming suddenly and superbly straight out of the Satyricon. "*Train* me?"

But Peter didn't have to do a lot of training, because, to our great astonishment, Rupert's splendid plan seemed to be working out. He and Sachi and Jake were off to their gambling in the desert, and Sarah was going with them. One person I was sorry for in all this was Jake, who had quietly been having a really beautiful time at Castle Saffron, and had discovered, to his great relief and satisfaction, that he was not in the least tough, that he did not really like drinking at all, that he did like Mrs. Tiggy

Winkle and Possum, and that he wanted to be rather poor and do a little messy, inefficient farming, and not have to talk to anybody ever again for the rest of his life, except, possibly, the children whom he had never yet been allowed to have. Even Nanny relented sufficiently to say that he really seemed to be a kind man at heart, really quite old-fashioned, you might say, not hardly to be blamed at all, said Nanny, darkly, not specifying.

The other person for whom I felt sorry was Dan, who was in a desperate state of despair and nervous exhaustion, and convinced that Sarah would never come back. Peter had been over at Drumshannon, buying hay, when Dan had arrived back from his horrifying day on Sarah's horse, and I had heard from him what had happened.

"Poor old chap," he said. "Didn't at all fancy the first obstacle—I gathered it was trappy?"

"It was, very,"

"Well, Dan said—he was in an awful state—that he was too plain bloody scared stiff to take it on; he was afraid the horse would go slap through the place on the other side."

"He would have done, too. You had to go out very neat and easy, and then turn very sharp—I damned near got jumped off."

"Dan said if only he'd got a hunt straight away, he wouldn't have cared what the hell he went through, he was in such a temper, but you hung about a lot, and the horse was playing up."

"He certainly was—and Sarah was bitching about with Benny—oh, it wasn't pretty at all, I can tell you."

"No. Well, then, apparently there was a cleanish wall up at the other end of this kale you were in, and Dan took the horse up there, but he wouldn't go near it at all by that time, just kept standing up. I gathered he and the horse were both damned near off their heads by then—

Dan certainly was by the time I saw him, poor chap. He'd just hacked the horse straight back from where you found him—he looked half dead, and I should think he'd been bloody well crying most of the way—I was in the yard there when he came in—I tell you, he looked mad, I thought at first he'd been concussed or something."

"Good thing you were there."

"I dunno—I'd be inclined to clock anyone, myself, who got in my way if I was feeling like that. However—Dan threw the horse at a lad and grunted at me and walked off into the house, and I followed him—I still half thought he must have had a crack on the head, but I could see it was a bit worse than that. Well, he was sitting on a chair in the hall—hadn't got any further—head in his hands—out —completely finished. Never saw anyone so miserable in my life—don't want to again. I pushed him on a bit further, and got him a drink, and then all this came out." He paused and said, "If ever a girl needed a good, sound spanking, it's Sarah—she and your film-acting pal would make a pretty pair, I must say. Anyway, Dan would be better off shot of her, poor chap."

"He's crazy about her," I said.

"I know. And Phillippa's just as crazy about her own chap." He sighed and said, "Didn't I once hear you say that this would end in tears, boy?"

Phillippa was indeed crazy about her own chap, who seemed to be finally getting her down, depressed and dreary as she felt after her 'flu. He racketed about the countryside with Sarah, and arrived back at odd times, too tired to speak, or to do anything but lie yawning in a bath, saying he felt like hell, and refusing to allow Phillippa to comfort him. She became quieter and quieter, and spent nearly all her time with Possum, and said she didn't think she wanted to hunt after all. Finally, Peter took her off for a day, more or less by force, and luckily they had an excellent, fast morning hunt, just the thing, not too tiring for her, and Peter then carefully brought her home, and they came cheerfully bursting into the dining-room just in time to stop luncheon from being over, holding hands, very full of themselves, and as enormously irritating as people who have just had a good hunt are apt to be to those who have not. Phillippa burbled away happily about it while she ate, never drawing breath, or letting Peter get a word in, except when he quite definitely shouted her down, and she looked absolutely enchanting with mud on her nose and in the corners of her eyes, and the moment she stopped eating Peter said, "Now go and have a bath, my love." Then he met Gillian's beaming, fatuous gaze with some surprise, and went out to the horses, and Phillippa gazed fondly after him and said wistfully, "Oh, he is so kind," which seemed to me an unbearably sad thing for her to say. Gillian took her off to her bath, and came back still beaming rather madly.

"Alas, no, darling," I said.

"O, but *why not*, Anto? Don't be so beastly."

"Because, darling, if Benny was Taken This Day, as Nanny would say, Phillippa would undoubtedly marry Rupert if she married anyone—or Roger, perhaps."

"*Rupert?*"

"Yes. Phillippa's a looker-after of children, don't you see? Peter's far too grown up for her to waste herself on."

"*Grown up?* Just think what he was like when he was recovering from his 'flu."

"That's all surface stuff. He's very grown up indeed."

"I suppose he is. I suppose he's had to be, poor love." Her face softened. "He's pretty irresistible, anyway, and he doesn't know it, of course, not the least idea—makes the irresistibility absolute. Just better look out for yourself, darling, that's all." She gave me her foxy glance.

"Look," I said. "You can't have Peter *and* Benny *and* Roger—or, if you're going to, just come here a minute first."

Later she said, "All right, darling, I suppose I don't really need them." But she was still being a bit foxy, so I drew a deep breath, feeling peculiarly sick, and told her then how much I loved her. "You've gone quite pale," she said, staring at me.

"So have you." So she had.

"Do you know, you've never said anything like this to me before, not ever."

"I know. To begin with, it wouldn't have been true, and then, to end with, I was too scared. I'm sorry I've been such a fool. I'm sorry if I've lost you now because I didn't say it."

"Goodness!" she said, faintly, and burst into tears.

Rupert and Sarah, Jake and Sachi set off on their curious journey. I drove them on the first lap of it, to Shannon. Jake was morose, Sarah merry, Sachi sparkled away about the great, great fascination of Irish Life, Rupert made calculations on the back of an unpaid Tote Investor's Account, moving his lips happily, as one who repeats a magic and certain incantation. They were to get on a plane that was due to leave Shannon at 2 a.m.

At 2 p.m. the following day the telephone rang in the library at Castle Saffron and I happened to answer it. A tremendously pompous voice said could it speak to his lordship.

"Ah, there, Rupert," I said, unkindly.

"Look here, it's Peter I want," it said, less pompously, slightly aggrieved, and even a touch uncertain.

"He's hunting," I said firmly. He wasn't, but I had a feeling that it would be better for him if he was, and anyway I was determined not to miss anything.

"Since when have your dogs hunted on a Saturday?" the voice asked irritably, not missing a trick.

"He's gone to the Limerick," I said, improvising brilliantly.

"Oh," said the voice, highly suspicious, but defeated. "Can I do anything?"

The voice thought, heavily.

I said, "Extraordinarily clear line—you might be next door."

"As a matter of fact, I am."

"Next door?"

"I'm still at Shannon," it said, in an off-hand way, and hummed a bit to itself.

"Didn't the plane get off?"

"Eventually."

"Fog?"

"Yes, it got off six hours late."

"But why aren't you on it?"

"Rather a delicate matter, really. . . . Did you say the old boy had gone down to Toby?"

"Yes," I said nervously. I could hear Peter talking to Suky just outside the windows.

"Damn, that makes everything very difficult—why did he suddenly go down there?"

"For God's sake, can't he hunt where he likes?"

"It makes everything very difficult, that's all," said the voice, injured.

"Well, good-bye, Rupert."

"Don't ring off. . . . I was hoping he might use his influence. . . ."

"I don't think he has any influence at Shannon. To get you on another plane, d'ye mean?"

"Not exactly . . . matter of fact, I've got some chums here who aren't too keen to see me go—they're going the other way, you see. . . ."

"Rupert, what has happened?"

"They're going to Paris. Absolutely wasted on them, of course. Texas types. The Tour d'Argent and the Plaza-Athénée, what d'ye bet? They'll never know what the Lancaster was in the old days. . . ." The voice suddenly brightened a little. "I might go with them, I suppose, and really show them the place in a decent manner. All expenses paid. . . . That's one idea. . . ."

"But *why*, Rupert?"

"I say, I'll have to reverse the charge if you're going to go on chattering like this—hang on a moment."

Presently I said again, "Rupert, what has happened?"

"Perfectly friendly game of poker, *they* said." The voice was huffy. "Queerest bloody school *I* ever sat in on."

"You played poker for six hours with some Texas types on their way to Paris?"

"Don't shout at me. I'm not at all well. I wanted to talk to Peter. He doesn't shout. Are you sure he's gone down to Toby?"

"Absolutely certain. What do you want me to do, Rupert?"

"I must have some coffee. . ." the voice said thoughtfully, comforting itself.

"Yes, obviously, but what do you want me to *do?*"

"I may feel clearer then. . . . I've got a bit of a chill. It's not the best part of their country; can't understand it. Pity. I'd better ring this evening from Paris. . . . I'll reverse the charge. . . . He's not staying down there, is he?"

"Rupert, how much did you lose?"

"Plenty," the voice said, so wearily that I took pity on it.

"Listen, Rupert, stay there, and I'll come and fetch you."

A pause.

"Have you got one of those solid affairs . . . what do they call them . . . cheque-books? Extraordinary thing the way these types can't take a gentleman's word—they simply don't understand civilized behaviour, that's their trouble."

"We'd better arrange all that when I see you."

"Yes, we'd better arrange all that . . . I'll go and have some coffee. . . . Extraordinary of the old boy to go rushing off to Toby's dogs like that—was he trying a horse there?"

"Yes," I said wildly.

"That awful flat-catching brute of Freddy's? Much better leave it alone. Drops its shoulder. Tommy told me about it. Proper sod, he said, always trying to catch you out. Don't touch it."

"*I'm not buying it.*"

"Very sensible. Never sell a horse to a friend. Ruins 'em both."

"*I'm not selling it.*"

"Very sensible. I must go and have some coffee. I don't feel at all well. Bring some brandy for the drive back, I must have a bit of a chill—don't be long, I don't really feel well enough to go to Paris. The Hennessy X.O. Don't forget."

He rang off, still talking to himself.

"Oh, Lord," said Peter. "You mean we've got to go and bail the old basket out?"

"I've got some dollars."

"It's more'n I have."

"But, look, Peter, do you *want* him back again, quite so quickly?"

"Don't see where else he can go, do you?"

"Well, to Paris, I suppose."

"Poor old sod, he'd only get into more trouble there, and we'd have a longer way to go to get him out."

"That's true. Well, I'll be off. Shall I take the van? And I'm to bring the Hennessy X.O he says—he's got a bit of a chill."

"F—— that. We'll take some cooking stuff. I'll come with you."

"You can't. You're hunting in Limerick."

"*What? When?*"

"You're trying a horse there—that awful flat-catching brute of Freddy's."

"*Why?* I—oh, I see. Thanks, chum."

So Rupert came back, highly confused, blaming the American presidential system for everything, and with his stomach more unsettled than ever. He cross-examined Peter very strictly about his day with the Limerick, and Peter broke down and began to laugh just when I thought he had won, and Rupert said severely several times that evening that my behaviour had not been that of a gentleman, as he swallowed a mixture of Kümmel and gin that he told us was settling for his stomach.

The horrors of Christmas were now coming rapidly upon us. Possum became feverish from over-excitement, and had to be put to bed for a day.

"Wish *I* could go to bed for the whole bloody season of goodwill," said Peter, with deep gloom. Benny was rather shocked—he had strongly sentimental ideas about Christmas. He became much nicer to Phillippa, who in turn became very maternal to everyone, and went about glowing, and singing carols very charmingly, and absolutely longing—as indeed she always did, bless her—for everyone to be happy. Nanny went back to Knockmoree, and Nanny Tom had a splendid time whipping Patrick and the maids up on to the tops of step-ladders, with stars and such like.

"Oh, my God," said Peter, and decided we had better hunt six days that week. I didn't wonder he was gloomy, because, quite apart from the normal horror that the manner of the celebration inspires in those of any sensitivity of heart, he had to distribute largesse to an alarming degree. "I could just about keep my head above water, if it wasn't for this flaming goodwill," he said, sadly, working it all out with great difficulty in his lair. Every time Nanny Tom told him to do something useful with some frightful decoration or other he said he couldn't, it was too difficult to manage with his left hand, and he couldn't see properly, anyway.

"Only time I've ever heard you use *that* for an excuse, darling," said Gillian.

"I get very shameless at Christmas," he said, grinning.

"Rather sad, too, I think," Gillian said to me afterwards. "Was Maria a great one for it, do you suppose?"

She entered upon a policy of cheering Peter up by ribaldry and teasing.

I said to her one evening, speaking of an acquaintance of ours, "I thought he was having an affair with his mother."

"Oh, no, darling, you're terribly out of touch; he left her for a policeman."

"You seem to know some very curious types," said Peter.

"That's why it's so heavenly restful to know *you*, darling."

"Are you writing me off as absolutely normal?"

"I rather think so."

"Meaning dull, I suppose?"

"Meaning *fascinating*."

"All right, then. I'll make a pass at Anto, just to spite you."

"Please not, darling. He might respond—and then where would I be?"

She teased him out of working too hard—darting into his lair and flushing him out of it as one of his gun-dogs might have done, if it had occurred to them that it needed doing.

"Darling, do stop being such a gorgeous father figure, and come and have a drink—it's almost lunch, did you know? I absolutely promise you the place won't fall down in the next five minutes."

"Flip off, darling," said Peter absently, absorbed in some hideously complicated calculation about next year's seed oats. But she hovered very firmly, and presently he leant back from his desk with a sigh and put his arm round her and said, "What's your smell, my love?"

"Mr. Patou. What's yours?"

"Horse, dog, and moth."

"It's very cosy, anyway."

"Thanks very much. You're generally more critical."

"Well, you could do with a haircut," she said, kissing the top of his head.

"My God, you're an offensive woman!"

"Come on, now, darling, do, and relax."

He came.

She teased him with old press cuttings that she rooted out of a disintegrating desk in the library—"Oh, *look* what I've found now—do listen, darling—'Spurrier, a notoriously difficult horse, was beautifully handled by Lord Dungarvan, who is rapidly approaching the top rank of amateur riders.' "

"But never quite got there," said Peter, coming briefly out of the *Field*. "That was a sod of an animal, a proper sod." He went back again.

"Darling, you *did* get there, you were the very top of all one season, I quite clearly remember."

"Everyone else was in hospital. I got all their rides."

"Oh, how you do let a girl down."

"What do you want me to do?" he asked, absently, still in the *Field*, "Recite 'How we beat the favourite' or something?"

"I do so love you," said Gillian, gazing fondly at as much of him as she could see.

"Oh, *do* you, indeed?" He threw the *Field* aside suddenly, got up, picked her off the sofa, more or less by the scruff of her neck, and kissed her rather thoroughly.

I said, "Mrs. Kavanagh, a notoriously difficult woman, was beautifully handled by Lord Dungarvan, who is rapidly approaching——"

"Darling!" Gillian squeaked indistinctly, still clasped to Peter's chest. "Don't go on, for heaven's sake!"

"Me not go on, or Peter?"

"Neither of you would be best, don't you think?"

Peter grinned and dumped her gently back on to the sofa. "Now are you sorry?" he asked.

"For what?"

"For bitching me."

"Not at all sorry, darling. I *like* your beautiful handling, that horse was so right—did it win?"

"It won, and so have you won. Now you stay quiet and good for a bit, see?" He went back once more into the *Field*.

Rupert looked upon Christmas as a time at which a killing might well be made—there would be parties, and at parties people played games of chance, and got drunk, with luck, while playing them. He began to sniff the air rather, and told me he hoped soon to be able to pay back your very generous loan, dear boy.

"Good," I said, firmly.

My mamma had asked us all to spend Christmas Day at Knockmoree, and this seemed a very cosy plan.

Peter ploughed gamely off to church in the morning.
He went to church fairly regularly—looking totally unlike himself in a dark suit and a stiff collar—because, he
said, the rector was such a sad little man; which indeed he
was. He had a disheartening job, for the lot of a Protestant
healer of souls in a Roman Catholic country is apt to be
disheartening, and he got greatly bullied into the bargain
by my sister-in-law Hesther—described by Gillian as meritorious—who had once thrown him into a great state of
confused soul-searching by telling him that he must Speak
to Lord Dungarvan, who was a Foul-Mouthed man.

"And *did* he?" asked Gillian, fascinated, on hearing
this.

"Oh, yes, certainly he did. I must say, I take off my hat
to him—came up here one morning in such a state of
twitch as you never saw—took three glasses of port to
get him going at all—I couldn't think what the hell
("*Careful*, darling," said Gillian) was the matter with the
poor little sod ("My dear!")—thought at first he was
going to confess something—robbed the orphans, got
caught with a choir-boy or what have you—however, he
spoke up like a man in the end."

"And what did you say, darling?"

"I said I was very sorry, and I'd try to be a better boy,
of course."

"Bloody sorry, I *bet* you said."

"I did *not*."

Peter had asked the rector and his equally sad little
woman to dine on Christmas night. "So stay sober, boys,
see?"

"You might have told me this before," said Rupert,
bitterly, "I could have gone out."

"Where?"

"I could have gone to Dan."

"He's coming here."

"I should just like to see the guest list next time, that's all."

Peter told him where he could put the guest list when he had seen it, and Rupert said that that was hardly the way for a regular churchgoer to speak.

We had a very cosy time at my home. My mother had the art of entertaining by not entertaining at all developed to a very high degree—which meant that the boys were allowed to sit over the port and talk about where they had seen each other in the war, and to wonder what happened to that bogus chap in the Tenth for the entire afternoon, in a hideous clutter of pulled crackers and a beautiful haze; while the girls let their hair down elsewhere and told each other how they hated husbands, and Possum and Peter's child, who were intensely devoted to each other, looked at kittens, puppies, foals, dead rats, swords, the drainage system, a murder in the Sunday press, and Nanny's two hats—popping in to visit us wearing these, which rather shook us, busy as we were at the time with Anzio; a subject brought up by Benny, hopeful of some quiet heroism from Peter, and rather disappointed to find that the only thing he could remember was that he had just decided that his servant was a screaming pansy, and was wondering what to do about it when he was hit. "Never did have to do anything about it—I wonder what happened to him."

About half-past four Peter announced that he felt rather ill, and had to keep himself in form for his dinner-party, so we'd better all go for a walk. We all battled down the back avenue, stopping at intervals, and out through the curious cluster of drab buildings around a cross-roads that passes for a village in Ireland, and back up the front avenue. Peter said he felt much worse. We all went and drank an enormous quantity of tea with my mamma and shuddered at the cake. Hesther told us that port was not a healthy drink. Possum had gone to sleep in a chair, and looked so abominably divine that Benny began to wax rather sentimental over him until Possum was suddenly slightly sick, hardly bothering to wake up for it. Peter left the room. Phillippa said that perhaps it was time to take Possum home, and my mother said that the chair cover didn't matter a bit, she had always hated it.

Peter did not appear again until we were all getting into various cars.

"Lost your lunch, old boy?" Rupert bawled merrily and unreticently at him.

Peter gave him a cold, quelling stare. "Certainly not, I was looking at the foals."

"Oh, Peter," said Aunt Emmy, in honest surprise, from the top of the steps, "I never knew you wanted to —you saw them all two days ago."

Nevertheless, he battled on gamely throughout the evening; even managing to make the rector's wife speak quite a lot, which was a major victory, if not a very rewarding one; while at the same time he exercised an extremely strict control over the general tone of the conversation. It was all very wearing for him, and he did it beautifully. "Pass to Peter," I said, unkindly, at one moment. "M'Tutor's down the course." When Peter received this message he looked straight at me unsmilingly and bowed very slightly. The rector and his wife left at eleven o'clock, delighted with their evening. Peter told his child to go to bed, and he would come and tuck her up in ten minutes. "The devil's a bit sick still," said Rupert to Gillian. But she just didn't feel like laughing at Peter at that moment, and I didn't blame her. He came down from tucking up his child looking tired, and we began to play poker.

Benny seemed in unaccountably poor form. He generally played poker as virulently as he hunted, but tonight his mind seemed to be elsewhere, he got drunk very quickly, and disappeared long before the game broke up, mumbling some excuse that none of us listened to much. The cards were beginning to hang together nicely, I had just gone down in a big way to Peter, who had held higher fours, and the previous hand had been battled out between two full houses. The hands continued to be pretty spectacular, and we broke up about three o'clock —which seemed a wise move, as Rupert, who had begun to lose, had also begun to chat to himself encouragingly.

While Peter was fixing the final drinks I went outside. The stars were brilliant, the cold piercing, the bullocks' breath streamed out in pearly puffs on the icy moonlit air—it seemed highly unlikely that the Stephen's Day meet would take place. I strolled idly round towards the yard, trying to rid my thick head of too much everything, wondering if I had been right to accept half the pool against Dan on the last ace-pot—and came upon Benny, standing numbly on the frozen mud under the old, beautiful, crumbling archway, slouched, his hands in his pockets, his head lowered between his shoulders. When I spoke to him he started nervously, and turned towards me a face which, in the moonlight, looked haggard, wild, and despairing enough to frighten me.

I said, too sharply, "What the hell are you playing at?"

"Nothing," he said dully. "Nothing. I just came out. . . . It was kind of hot in there. . . ."

"Well," I said, more gently. "It's kind of cold out here. How about just coming in?"

"Sure, sure, . . ." he said obediently, lifelessly, plodding uncertainly towards me. The lightly freezing mud crackled beneath his feet, he slipped, and fell on his knees.

"You see me kneeling, kid?" he inquired, in an amazed voice.

"I see you. Get up, you fool."

But he remained in the same position. "I guess I got a load on," he said, uninterestedly.

"I guess so," I said. "And I guess you'll get pneumonia, as well, if you stay there much longer."

"What the hell," he said.

"Get up," I said, feeling suddenly very angry. "Get up, you self-pitying play-actor, you, or I'll boot you up."

"Gee!" he said with mild wonder, unmoved. "The right he-man stuff, huh?"

He got laboriously and slitheringly to his feet, and would have fallen again if he had not clutched just in time at my shoulder. "You think they were kneeling, too?" he inquired, indicating with a tired jerk of his head the moon-silvered roofs of the stabling and farm buildings beyond.

"Who?" I asked, uncomprehending.

"Hell, the cattle of course. The horses. You think they were kneeling in there? It's midnight, isn't it, for Chrissakes, kid?"

It had been three o'clock when I came out. I suddenly liked Benny a lot more than I had liked him for a long time. He was shivering violently. I wondered just how long he had been standing here—hoping that the legend was true; fearing it was not.

"Didn't you go and look?" I asked.

He gave his choking, unhappy laugh.

"Maybe they'd have got up if they heard me coming. As long as I didn't go and look they could be kneeling, huh?"

"They could be," I said.

"And if they weren't——" he said slowly, swaying,

holding on to my shoulder, "—that 'ud be just too bad, huh? Too bad. Yeah . . . too bad. . . ."

I said, "Come on in, now, Benny," and guided him with difficulty round to the front door, where he halted, uncertainly, with one foot on the first, frost-rimed lime-stone step. "Listen, kid—you don't tell anyone about this thing."

"No."

"They're all great guys, mind you," he said vaguely, conjuring up Hollywood in the Irish small hours. "Just great. All friends of mine. Helluva lotta friends."

"Sure they are," I said, not very nicely. "Just great. Just living dolls, lover. Come on in, now."

"You don't like my friends?" he inquired, sullenly aggressive.

"They're not here," I said wearily. "And I'm not fighting you. Come on in, now."

"You don't tell them," he said doggedly, and rather pathetically.

"I said I wouldn't."

I had a rather ugly vision of Benny's dearest and most charming friends having a great success at a party with the risible tale of Benny's Christmas night—or, worse, Benny himself having the success, jeering, to forestall them, at his vulnerable moment of something like truth; like innocence; like peace.

"I went out there to be sick," he said, wavering about now on the third step.

"You haven't got any guts, have you?" I asked, push-ing him on. I wanted to hurt him, to make him feel something, to admit a truth—why, I wasn't sure, unless I thought, vaguely, that it would help Phillippa.

"No," he said, simply, disarming me, and then, grin-ning, running his hand through his hair, "Don't tell 'em that either, kid, for Chrissakes."

Everyone seemed to have gone to bed, so I went too. Gillian was awake, looking bemused.

"Where on earth did you get to, darling?"

I explained.

"Did you see Peter? He's still up, I suppose he's taken Suky out. Poor love, he was feeling rotten."

"Was he? I thought he was all right after he'd looked at the foals."

"Fool. I mean he was feeling low. He went and sat in his lair after the game broke up and he thought everyone had gone to bed, and I found him there—I *meant* to find him there, mark you—and he said to me, "Come and hold my hand for a moment and don't talk." So I did just that. Then he said, "Thanks. Run along to bed now." So I did that, too—I suppose it was the best thing to do?"

"Yes."

Chapter Fourteen

Aunt Emmy began to get seriously to work on her filly, and also on me.

"My dearest Aunt, I am *not* going to take out a licence again, at my age."

"Why ever not, Anto, dear; sure you've no great age at all."

"I am far too old for practically everything, particularly for riding races."

"And she goes great for you, mind, now, she likes you, Anto, that counts a lot, you know, and don't you have great fun, now, riding her in her work?"

"Yes, I do, Aunt Emmy dear, I love it, and she's a lovely filly, but anyway I shouldn't be here long enough, even if I wasn't too old and too unfit and too everything unlike what I ought to be to ride her."

"You'd have such gas, the two of you."

"We might—or we might have a horrible accident, like the last time."

"Ah, there was nothing to that, only that you got across Conor, silly boys the two of you, you might have been killed."

"*Exactly.*"

"There'll be nothing like that going on at Peppardstown, mind you."

I visualized myself skittering madly round in a maidens at starting, and shuddered.

"Really, Aunt Emmy dear, I love you and I love the

filly, and I'm sure she'll win good races for you, but I'm too *old*."

"Ah, well, you'd never know. . . . You could change your mind, now." She smiled cosily to herself at the thought of my coming pleasure.

"Honestly, Aunt Emmy dear, you really ought to let someone else ride her in her work—don't let her get too used to me, and find her taking a dislike to her jock."

"But you *are* her jock, Anto, dear."

"*I am not*. I'm an ageing—and fast ageing, by God!—writer of useless film script."

"Ah, well, you'd never know. . . ."

"I *do* know."

"She'll be needing a little work on Tuesday."

"I've nothing against a little work on Tuesday."

"Half-past nine at Dan's."

"All right, Aunt Emmy. But don't imagine you've won."

"Won? Whatever does the boy mean, won?"

There is no more delightfully relaxed atmosphere in the world than that which obtains after a gallop in which everything has gone pleasingly to plan, and everything had gone exactly as it should on Tuesday morning. The filly had done a little serious work and done it well. It had been something of a trial, it seemed—Dan and Aunt Emmy had conferred together; Aunt Emmy had wanted to know what weight I rode at, and took me firmly on to the bathroom scales when I was vague about it; lead had been packed cagily into the pockets of a weight cloth carried by the trial horse—a good-class handicapper that Dan had bought to lead his horses in their work. The filly had gone over two miles, the first mile with her schoolmaster, ridden by Peter—the trial horse had been jumped in at the mile, and my instructions had been to ride the filly right out with him. The result seemed to

209

satisfy Aunt Emmy. She stood and listened to the filly blow, and let her smear froth over her face, and rub her sweaty ears on her once rather nice coat.

"You're not as clear as she is, Anto, dear," she said, reproachfully.

"All right. I told you I was too old."

"It's all these cigarettes and the drink—that's what will kill you, race riding, mind."

"I am *not* race riding, Aunt Emmy dear, I am script writing."

"Ah well, you'd never know. . . ."

"I do know."

Peter came jogging up to us, blowing harder than anyone, the old horse cracking his nostrils with amusement. "Lord!" he said dropping the reins, throwing a leg across the horse's neck, and sliding down. "I'm past this game." He took a couple of deep breaths and said to the lad who had ridden the other horse, "*You* wouldn't put a candle out, blast you." The lad smirked happily down his nose, his day made for him.

We pulled the saddles off, and salty, acrid steam rose from narrow, muscular backs, the saddle patches black and curly with sweat. The old horse dropped his head at once to the grass and kept it there. The other two snatched a mad mouthful, twitched, fidgeted, swung in circles, took hysterical nips at each other and then at the grass again, flung their heads up, stared wildly about looking for more excitement, found none, and gradually began to unwind themselves, and settle to their short graze, in a cloud of steam. There was a wonderful nostalgic racing smell of hot horse and crushed grass and unwashed lads and cigarette smoke and old leather; a familiar, lovely sound of tearing grazing and bits ringing, and steady, satisfying blowing, and an occasional prolonged satisfied snort.

"Fair enough, mind you," said Dan to Aunt Emmy. She nodded, beaming absently, busy lighting her cigar. All had been said between them. It was a few moments of pure, unthinking, physical happiness—but, even as I enjoyed it, I was suddenly aware that Peter was not all that happy. He was standing slightly apart from us, smoking, watching the horses, with his cap tipped over his eyes. There was nothing to suggest anything wrong, but he just wasn't feeling too good, I realized, and this was generally a time when he felt fine. Then I remembered that his man of business was coming to see him that afternoon, and that Peter was probably wondering what fresh financial mishaps were about to be sprung on him.

But it wasn't, in fact, as easy as that.

When we were driving back to Castle Saffron, after tipping his cap backwards and forwards and scratching his head several times, he said, "Look, Anto——" "Yes?" I said vaguely. "I think that's probably a pretty useful animal of Aunt Emmy's, don't you?"

"Who?—Ah, the filly. Yes. Probably. She seems to have quite a bit of foot. What was she being tried to be?"

"No idea."

He grunted, and lit another cigarette. "Look, Anto——"

"Yes? Good God!" A small boy had suddenly driven a donkey cart absolutely straight into us from out of the entirely concealed entrance of a bohireen. I swerved violently, and looked back with dread, but he hadn't, in fact, even noticed that anything at all unusual had happened. "I can't think why these roads aren't absolutely strewn with mangled corpses," I said.

"They shovel 'em up in the night. Look, Anto——"

"I must say, it's done Dan a lot of good to get rid of Sarah for a bit—he looks quite different. Pity she's coming back so soon."

"Hell, Anto," said Peter violently. "I wish you'd bloody listen to what I'm saying—God knows it's difficult enough, without you nattering on like this."

I was rather startled. "Sorry—but what are you saying? I didn't know you were saying anything."

"I was *trying* to say something."

"Go ahead, then," I said cheerfully, steering nervously between four schizoid hens, a manic-depressive pig, and a gay, abandoned tinker's toddler.

"All right," said Peter grimly. "You'll have to leave, see?"

"*What?*" I was so surprised that I stalled the car.

"Oh, for Christ's sake . . ." said Peter. "Drive on, can't you?"

I drove on, thoughtfully.

"You mean Benny's at it again?"

Peter laughed, and I was rather nastily struck by the unhappiness of his laugh.

"No. I could deal with that all right."

"Well, what's happened that you can't deal with? I thought everything was reasonably calm at the moment?"

"I'm *telling* you, aren't I?"

"No, frankly, you're not."

A lorry loaded with turf bore down on me in a friendly, but alarming manner, while its driver exchanged gossip out of his window, over his shoulder, with a tousled figure on a creamery cart. I put the heel of my palm on the horn, and held it there until he looked round, just in time to straighten up and give me a friendly salute as we brushed past each other. Peter made an irritated noise.

"I'd wait till we got home, if the place wasn't like a flaming three-ring circus."

I looked at him. Very unhappy indeed.

"Go ahead, now."

"It's going to sound so bloody silly," he said despairingly. "Look out for that chap on the bicycle, he's never been able to ride one."

I hooted cautiously. The chap looked backwards over his shoulder, in case I might be a car, lurched, and swerved ungracefully into our path, with a vaguely apologetic gesture that further unsettled him.

"I see what you mean," I crawled past him, sweating, and he grinned and waved and fell off—luckily some way behind us.

"Hell," said Peter wearily, sunk very far down in his seat with his shoulders hunched up, and the peak of his cap finally resting on his nose. "Tell you after dinner."

"No, by God, you don't leave me in suspense like this."

"All right. I'm mad for your woman, and I can't stand it," he said flatly. Then he came out from under his cap and said, "I told you it would sound bloody silly, but there it is."

There it was. I cursed myself for every sort of a fool.

"I'm sorry, Peter. It sounds bloody awkward to me. We seem to have caused you a packet of trouble, one way and another."

"No," he said, "not only that. A lot of fun as well. Couldn't have enjoyed it more—I shall miss you both like hell."

(You and Gillian give him a little fun while you're there, won't you?)

He sat up, and finally took his cap completely off, and stretched in a relieved way, and smiled tiredly. I saw then, suddenly and for the first time, how very tired he was, and how alone. He said, "I don't want to lose you, but I think you ought to go, see? She's so kind, and I——" he broke off abruptly, and said then, after a pause, "Maria was kind."

("What does Peter do for a woman?" I had asked Roger, once, idly.

"Oh—Poodle, I daresay."

"I wouldn't think so. She likes 'em richer and smoother."

"Oh, well—Rose, I suppose, or Bella, or one of the field, when he goes to England."

"But he hardly ever *does* go."

"No . . . I dunno, really . . . couldn't say.")

"I'm sorry, Peter," I said, now, again.

"My own fault," he said. "Bloody stupid of me. Ought to be able to cope with it at my age, God knows. Dunno what's the matter with me."

Fifteen years of loneliness and pain and worry, but not much else, I thought. Nothing else at all really. ("A nice chap old Peter—bit lacking, of course.") He was certainly hopelessly lacking by some standards. I felt very angry with myself, and acutely miserable.

He said with an effort, "Don't say anything to her."

"No, of course not."

"Just go bloody soon, will you?"

"Yes, of course."

"She's sweet. You're very lucky, boy. Don't go losing her."

"No, I shan't."

"I was lucky too," he said, and smiled, changing his tone, "this is just what the Nannies would call sheer greed. Does Emmy mean the filly to go at Peppardstown?"

"That's the present idea."

"With Mr. A. Kavanagh aboard?"

"Like hell."

"She's a very persuasive woman, Emmy. Better watch out for yourself, boy."

"I may be weak, but I'm not *bloody* weak."

"That's what you think."

When I told Gillian that, as the film-making seemed to have bogged down for the moment, I thought my mamma would like it if we went and stayed at home for a bit, she said, "I suppose it would be a good plan, poor darling."

"Poor darling?"

"Peter."

I said nothing

"Did you see it coming on?"

"What? No. No, I didn't. Not at all."

"So why do you now?"

I hesitated witlessly.

"All right. You needn't answer. I'm all for the solidarity of the sexes. I suppose he thinks I have absolutely no idea. . . . Did he tell you not to say anything to me? They always do. . . ."

"Look——"

"All right, I *said* you needn't answer. Poor love, I couldn't feel more beastly about it, possibly."

She brooded, and then brightened slightly, suddenly. "I suppose you wouldn't——"

"*No. I would not.*"

"All right. I was only asking . . . no need to be so snappy about it, darling."

"Snappy!—I like that!"

"Oh, dear, how we have bitched him up, one way and another, and he is the nicest in the world, bless his heart!"

"You always did say it would end in tears."

"Yes, I remember."

"How did you start knowing about this, anyway?"

"Well, because he stopped kissing me, of course."

"Oh."

Nanny was delighted to get her hands on us again. She rustled about in our suitcases, took all my shirts away, tut-tutted at our hairbrushes, and daresaid she could let us have them back before dinner if she washed them straight away—adding, loyally, that that Mrs. Thomas had all that great household to see to, and girls so self-willed these days, you couldn't hardly expect more, with his lordship so untidy, and then all those great dogs too. She then told Gillian that she looked quite washed out, and if she'd just slip into bed she could have something light that she fancied on a tray. To my immense surprise, this plan appealed to Gillian a lot. While I was dressing she sat peakily upright in the bed, with her waif-and-stray air, poised unenthusiastically above a poached egg.

"Darling, what *is* the matter?"

"It's just that I've got a perfectly horrible surprise for you," she said, looking nervous and foxy, touching the egg and recoiling from it smartly. I felt suddenly extremely and intolerably ill. Everything was much too much; empty, cold, unavoidable, unbearable, and all my own damn fool fault. The structure of the unbelievably safe and fragile world which I thought we had finally built was about to resolve itself into shrieking chaos, because the one person who would do for me had decided that the one who would do for her was my brother Roger. I knew it with as dead and icy a certainty as I knew that the impassive face that stared coldly back at me now out of the dressing table looking-glass was my own familiar, stranger's face. I went on tying my tie.

"Darling, do be interested."

"I am interested."

"Are you getting a cold?"

"No."

"You sound a bit hoarse."

"What is this horrible thing?"

To ask the question took every last reserve of vitality out of me suddenly. I had to sit down, so I went and sat on the bed. This was the end of the world, and I couldn't ever stand up again. Not that it mattered.

"I've been deceiving you, darling. You won't beat me, will you?"

"Probably not."

"You *have* got a cold, Anto."

"No. Go on."

"Well, darling, you need to grow up a bit, I know you're very clever, but that's not the same thing, and the quickest way to do that is children, so I just decided on that, without asking you, that's all. It's very dangerous at my age, let me tell you, I only hope I won't die," she added defiantly, eyeing me nervously.

Very late for dinner, I said to her: "I thought you were going to tell me you were finally off with Roger."

"You're my chap," she said.

The next morning Benny rang me up to tell me that Louie had finally decided on the film about gauchos, the thought of which had so depressed Phillippa in London some strange space and time ago.

"Good," I said heartily.

"That's a fine way to talk, kid, after all this," he said in an injured voice.

"I only hope it's all over."

"Gee, listen, sometimes I think you really are gone—right round, crazy like a hen. Honest I do, kid, you just don't make sense sometimes, did anyone ever tell you that?"

"Everyone. Often."

"Say, listen, don't you just have *any* feelings about *anything*? Not one?"

"No, none."

"Sometimes you have me puzzled, kid. I really worry

about you, you know that?" he inquired with tenderness.

"Good."

I sat in the yard at Knockmoree again, and it was a bright and gentle and steamy Irish morning, and the winner had undoubtedly taken all, sitting on the old-fashioned stone drinking trough, smoking the first, the best cigarette, highly paid for a lot of useless work that should never have been attempted, whole-hearted in love at last—sitting, in fact, as Benny might have said, in the cat-bird seat, and flourishing like the green bay tree. But the darkness, the panic, were here still; just beyond the rim of consciousness; just behind the gilt morning fresh-ness, amongst the innocent scents of earth and rainwater, horses and turf-smoke; the sense of grief and betrayal had not been exorcized; a price was still to be exacted; still something, or myself, kept saying, "You won't get out of it as easily as this."

Chapter Fifteen

Afterwards, long after, when Dan and Phillippa, just married, were staying with us for Cheltenham, Phillippa said to me, "You had a feeling, all the time, Anto, hadn't you, that something dreadful would happen?"

"Yes."

"Just that? Vague, like that? Nothing more?"

"Nothing more, no—but the nicest person always makes the best scapegoat—I suppose I should have known that much, anyway."

"He was a darling. I remember how you told me he was good. I remember thinking how dull, and Gillian saying it wasn't half as disappointing as it sounded, because you had different ideas about goodness, and I asked 'different from what?' I see now what you meant."

"He was the best in the world," I said, briefly, and she looked at me. "Do you still feel so badly about it, Anto?"

"Yes."

"It was why Benny left me, you know, isn't that strange? It wasn't Sarah at all, although she went with him—that was just something that happened. It was because of Peter he left me. He wrote to me—it was all so extraordinary, Anto, you can't imagine, it was so unlike Benny—such a simple letter, a few lines, nothing, no drama, he just said he couldn't face me any longer. Just that. Somehow I hadn't ever imagined Benny leaving me —do you remember me telling you once that I had this frightening feeling I should always go on loving him, no matter what awful things he did?"

"Yes, I remember."

"I simply never did think of *him* leaving *me*—except, of course, for shacking up from time to time." She smiled sadly. "He thought it was all his fault, you know, and I've never known him feel any responsibility for anything before, not ever—and it wasn't his fault, really, was it . . . ? that's so odd. It wasn't really anyone's fault, I suppose."

"It was mine. Don't let's talk about it any more, do you mind?"

"All right, darling, of course—but I do wish you didn't still feel like that, Peter would have hated it, he was so fond of you." She got up and put her arms round my neck, to kiss me good night, and said softly, "He'd say to you, 'Lot of bloody nonsense, boy'—only, of course, he wouldn't say nonsense, bless him." I kissed her, and asked, "Is Dan going to win on Thursday?"

"He thinks we can—he'll be dottier than Possum if we do, I'll never get either of them straightened out again, bless their hearts."

Dan did win the Gold Cup, and we all went equally dotty—but through all the shouting and the shoving, the chums and the champagne, the boxes and the bookies, the paddock and the parades, the unrelenting ghosts never left me. Here the filly might have come, this year, seeking fame in the Hurdle, and if she had come, no doubt, Peter would have been staying with us, being strictly tidied up by Gillian, perhaps even forced into a bowler, and having long telephone chats with his child, reassuring her that he was still alive.

Gillian said to me, as we reeled down from yet another box, "Anto, what's wrong, darling? You didn't utter, did you know? Rose is quite cross with you."

"Didn't I? Sorry. I keep thinking about the child."

"He's perfectly all right, he's in spanking form, what can you mean, darling?"

"Not our child, Peter's."

After a moment she said, "Willy thinks he might win the next, but they're a bit frightened of Ben's horse."

"All right."

"Don't, darling. Try not to, anyway? It doesn't help."

"I know. Sorry."

"You can get threes about him at the moment, but not for long, I'd say."

"All right."

"Get forward, then. 'Ware heel."

"All right."

But the long, heartbreaking running of the heel line went on in my mind.

Aunt Emmy had been tremendously disappointed that we really were going back to London. It seemed to her a sad form of rather mad illness; that anyone given the chance of riding her filly should take any notice of any other form of business or entertainment appeared to her a gross error of taste—as indeed, it did to me, when soft, steamy day succeeded upon soft steamy day and snowdrops appeared furtively, as frail and gallant as all get out, and I let myself sink thankfully into a mental and physical bog, and promised myself that the worst was over, and I would never do such a thing again. We had certainly bitched Peter up, one way and another, as Gillian had rightly remarked, but he had found a good deal of the process very enjoyable, and no really excessive disaster had occurred. Gillian pattered about with a vague, touching air of content, bullied by Nanny, and hindering my mamma with the flowers—disarranging them rather whenever her back was turned, and then saying hopefully that that was what the Japanese liked, really. My eldest brother Hubert and his wife—"that meritorious sister-in-law of yours"—had gone to Switzerland, and all was peace and quiet. Roger got peacefully drunk, I quietly rode out the filly, my mother contentedly knitted tiny garments, while Gillian watched her, unquietly, with unbelieving, saucer eyes, and Aunt Emmy peacefully and beamingly plotted the terrifyingly expensive matrimonial affairs of her mares. "Goodness! They do have to have such enormous dots," said Gillian. Peter and his child came over for Sunday luncheon, and Peter quietly drank too much, and my mother quietly observed him, and said afterwards to me:

"Did you have a lot of trouble there?"

"One way and another, yes."

"I think Peter seems very tired."

"Yes, I think he is."

"Well, I hope they all pay him."

"So do I."

It seemed the least that could be done.

During this week I had a couple of goodish hunts on Aunt Emmy's brilliant grey horse, and had time to observe with alarm the rapid growth of the situation between Dan, Sarah and Benny. Sarah had arrived back positively crackling with the vitality of America—she would give out sparks, like a cat, I thought, if anyone stroked her—and Dan looked more strained, diminished, and haunted every day, as he bashed on across the country, taking on every obstacle that came his way with the weary fixity of utter hopelessness—looking at him, I began to wonder if he was drugging. Benny was busily making arrangements—so Peter told me—to give Sarah a test for a part in the Argentine film, ringing up Louie most evenings to arrange it, very kindly, without exactly asking Dan's permission, or including him in on the deal. "They're all going on Wednesday," Peter had said, rather thickly, at luncheon. "Thank God. Sorry, Anto—I know it seemed a good idea at the time."

"The filly will be doing a little more work on Tuesday; you'd better come over," said Aunt Emmy, busy looking up something in the No. 11 family. "Two crosses of Teddy . . . wouldn't you say that might be perfect for my Mustang mare, now, Peter?"

"Or what about the horse Euphemia Coke's just bought —that's the best staying blood in Europe, and he's cheap at the moment—here—let me have a look. . . ."

So, in a rather unorthodox fashion, we had left them to it, hunched together over the stud book, Peter still on the port, Aunt Emmy blowing her cigar smoke about pleasurably, and I could see by Gillian's fond, backward glance that a quite different matrimonial idea had just occurred to her.

"Darling, they've known each other since they were in nappies."

"Cosy, it could be, all the same. . . ."

I rode the filly over to do her work on the Tuesday morning—a blowy, grey and blue and white, curlew-calling morning, wild and fresh, but with a lovely hint of coming warmth in it. She was close to being fully fit now, and was packed full of panache and witty little jokes; the wind made an excellent excuse for working them off on me. Aunt Emmy came along on the grey "to keep her steady on the roads". He failed signally to do any such thing, and merely helped and encouraged her no end in seeing ghosts, angels with flaming swords and lionesses whelping in the streets; hearing voices; having sudden *crises des nerfs* at the sight of a blown leaf, and generally behaving in the manner in which oat-packed horses fancy it is funny to behave in a wind—our progress was full of sideways swoops, bounds forward, backwards curtsies, and cunning attempts at the supreme jest of whipping round. "Sure, they're in great heart, the two of them," said Aunt Emmy, jogging along quite undeterred, as relaxed as a poached egg. "Mind, now, Anto, that she wouldn't have it in mind to shy out from the dog there—there's a lorry coming." She did have it in mind. I was quite relieved when we turned off on to Dan's land, and the exciting, but safe grass was under foot, and the games were over and the serious stuff ahead. Everyone had come over to the gallops that day. Even my mamma, who didn't usually take a lot of interest in the racing goings-on, had come chuggering along in the frightful little car—I suppose because it was my last day at home. It was by the mercy of God that she did come, because Peter's child was there, too—as wild and bright and enjoyable to look at as the day itself, playing with Possum a mysterious game that involved a lot of running and helpless laughter. "Hey," Peter said, watching them, his tough, battered face tender and amused, "keep out from under, now, or Dan will eat you, see?"

"Are you going to sit up?" I asked him.

"May as well lead you astray for the last time, I suppose."

"You couldn't keep off it."

"Not on a morning like this—what's Emmy going to make us do?"

"Nothing too strenuous, I hope."

If only we had gone and done our work, then and there. . . . Better not to think like that. Dan took everyone off to see some two-year-old he was pleased with, and by the time they came back Benny had been subtly at work. Dan looked tense, Sarah was in her cruelly gleeful mood. "We've got a bet on," she said to me, as I jogged up to them.

"Why?" I asked, sourly, annoyed by the changed atmosphere, the spoiling of the gay morning. "Prig!" She pulled a face at me, and rubbed the filly's muzzle, and kissed it. "Is she a difficult ride, Anto?"

"Good lord, no," I said, thoughtlessly, not connecting properly, "anyone could ride her."

"Because Benny's longing to ride her, and Dan's being fearfully nappy about it—aren't you, darling?"

Dan said suddenly, stonily, "He couldn't begin to ride a f——ing quarter of her." He then went rather red and apologized to my mamma.

"Well!" said Sarah, lightly. "That's a pretty way to speak, I must say," and smiled at Benny very provocatively.

Dan swung back towards them, and said furiously, "It's true, that's all."

It was like bear-baiting, I thought, watching—just as cruel and just as degrading . . . we haven't improved very much, we just fancy our cruelty more subtly distilled these days, God help us.

"Well," Benny drawled enjoyably. "We-e-ll, now. . . ." He smiled gently and rocked himself on his heels. "We must have this little bet," he said, very pleasantly. "Just a small one. How about that? Nothing to frighten anybody, huh?" He smiled again. Dan reacted at once to the prod. "Monkey to a fiver," he said curtly, contemptuously.

"Well, now," Benny said slowly, "that's generous. Real generous. Ain't it, kid?" He appealed to me, "When you just said yourself how anyone could ride her?"

Too late I saw the trap yawn. "Look, Benny," I said, desperately. "Anybody who was used to riding racehorses in their work could ride her. But anyone who wasn't would find her a handful—it's just completely different, that's all—it's no reflection on you. And anyway——" I thought of a better argument suddenly, "—you're too heavy." Benny looked at Aunt Emmy and half smiled, with his infinite, intimate charm. "Is that right?" he asked wistfully. "That's certainly a very disappointing thing to hear." Aunt Emmy looked vague and muddled. She hated to hurt anyone's feelings. Benny turned to Peter and said, "You're a good deal heavier than me, I guess," and I remembered suddenly that Peter had once been given the supreme joy by Aunt Emmy, who had been determined not to let him escape such a splendid treat. "I hacked her round slowly one morning," he now said repressively. I remembered it well, and how partly ashamed and partly amused I had been to see the filly drop her head and settle down with him very much quicker than she had ever done with me. "Well then," said Benny triumphantly, "*I'll* hack her round slowly. How about that?" he appealed to Aunt Emmy, with eager charm. I thought hopelessly how very much more difficult than any other form of work hacking round slowly can sometimes prove to be, and watched Aunt Emmy's ingenuous face.

"Well, now, the way it is. . . ."

"She'll hop it, Emmy," said Peter, suddenly and calmly clearing the rather ambiguous atmosphere abruptly, and Benny turned towards him savagely, his simian face stiff with rage.

"There's a lot of money on this," he said, "and I can ride."

Peter shrugged his shoulders and turned away. "Don't you think . . ." Phillippa began, nervously.

"I don't think at all, honey, I don't have to, I just win five hundred pounds," said Benny gleefully. "Ain't that so, now?" he asked Aunt Emmy wheedlingly, and Dan insolently, in the same question. "Maybe," said Dan, gloomily. He was wishing to God he had never started this, and it wasn't his money he was thinking about. "Take her very gently, now," said Aunt Emmy, giving in. "Peter can go with you, he's used to the horse."

O hell, I thought, sliding down off the filly, *hell*, why, as Peter once so rightly inquired, can't people leave other people alone? I slapped her steely, warm, satin neck and ran my hand on down her soft chest, and she blew into my ear inquiringly and pretended to nip me, taking the cloth of my coat between her teeth, rolling her gentle, mischievous eyes, flattening her little ears in simulated anger. I rubbed them, and told her what a minx she was, and she cocked them again and began to examine my pockets hopefully, then suddenly swerved away with up-flung head to observe some astonishing phenomenon three fields away, her keen veined face and blowing mane outlined, incredibly beautiful, against the sky. Angry and miserable, the gay innocent morning ruined, I thought how much more likeable horses were than humans, and how much I should miss riding her.

"No jumping off," said Dan, warningly, to Peter.

"What the hell d'ye think?" snapped Peter, furious at being involved.

"Hey, there," said Benny, unnecessarily, "I want to win my five hundred quid."

"God help me, aren't I trying to see that you do?" Dan almost shouted at him.

"You *are* edgy, darling, aren't you?" Sarah observed blandly. "I'm sure Benny would lay off, if you'd rather?"

Before Dan could answer—he had gone now rather white—Peter said furiously, "Oh, stop your bitching about, Sarah—you need someone to spank you."

"Goodness, darling, how rude!" said Sarah mildly, looking intensely angry.

"I'm a plain-spoken chap," said Peter, shortly, "and I don't like this sort of childishness."

"Really, darling?" Sarah looked absolutely straight at him, with an insolent, unflickering stare. "I'm sure you're a very good judge of childishness."

There was a moment of the most intense and appalling silence I have ever had to live through. During it, nobody looked at anybody else. I looked at the old horse, who had an itching in his left nostril, and was rubbing it snortingly against the knee of an outstretched foreleg, while his lad vainly tried to pull his head up. I heard Peter draw his breath in sharply, but when I looked up he had turned away, without speaking, towards the horse. "All right!" he said to the lad, and waited to be thrown up. Aunt Emmy's plain, sweet, crumpled face wore an expression of such unbelieving horror that under any other circumstances it would have been funny. Dan said to Sarah, between his teeth, "He's bloody right, you need spanking, and I'm going to do it!"

"You and some big man, darling?"

"Oh, Jesus," said Dan, and came over to the filly, and began to girth her up, with his hands not quite steady. Aunt Emmy came and took her head from me. Peter walked his horse away. I said to Sarah, "That was a hell of a pretty thing to say to him." She tossed her head. She really did toss it, I noticed with some surprise.

"Can't take prigs," she said carelessly, like a naughty, don't-care child, and smiled lovingly at me, indicating that I, at least, wasn't one really, at heart. I was extremely annoyed to find that even at this moment I found her not unattractive, so I said, "You'd better apologize to him, hadn't you?" She pulled another face at me and laughed delightfully and said, "I adore you when you look so disapproving!"

The filly was already working herself into a fuss, I noticed, although Aunt Emmy was there to soothe her. She was not caring at all for the electric atmosphere of worry and anger that she felt now all around her; she did not care for the feel in Dan's hands; she did not care, above all, for Aunt Emmy being upset, which was a completely novel sensation to her. She shook her lovely head irritably, and ran backwards a few steps, and tried an experimental side swipe at Dan, who cursed her, and slapped her in the ribs to make her stand up. "Gently, now, gently," Aunt Emmy said, worriedly, to them both.

"I'll put you up," I said to Benny. "Don't fuss her. Let her walk on straight away, and get yourself settled as she's moving around—don't fiddle about, don't hang on to her."

"I can ride, kid."

"Not today," I thought. "Oh Lord, what a hell of a situation, I hope to God she doesn't go and get into trouble—Peter is right, she'll hop it with him, I know she will." I said hopelessly, "She'll throw her head about when she starts cantering—don't snatch at her then, whatever you do."

"O.K., kid, O.K." He had no idea at all what I meant, I knew, but I pressed on despairingly: "Just sit still, and she'll come back to you."

"Sure, sure," he said soothingly, winking at Sarah.

Dan had gone over to talk to Peter. He stood and stroked the big horse's shoulder, and Peter leant down to him. They looked very conspiratorial. "Hey!" said Benny, restively, "what's this plotting, huh?"

It would be a plot, I knew, for Dan to lose, if possible, his five hundred pounds, but I knew it would be useless to try to explain that either. "Come on," I said to Benny. "Get up. Don't keep her hanging about any longer."

"O.K., Auntie."

It was disastrous from the start. Benny had never done any of this sort of thing before, and he was determined that there was really nothing to learn, while, in fact, there was, of course, everything in the world. He landed far too heavily in the saddle, and snatched his reins tightly up, keeping a firm grip on her mouth, regardless of what I had told him, while he arranged himself and his irons for what seemed like hours, and the filly worked herself up into a jittery rage—even going so far as to strike at Aunt Emmy, who was still trying to soothe her. Peter kept the big horse walking slowly round her in a circle, silent, slouched in his saddle, looking tired.

"We'll let them go in the small field above," Dan said to Aunt Emmy. "She's never done any fast work there."

The filly bounced angrily sideways when Aunt Emmy took her hand off the bit, shaking her lovely head. Benny's weight was much too far back on her, he was riding too long, he had too tight a hold on her, everything was wrong, and she was very, very worried. Peter brought his horse up alongside her and said, "Let her walk out on a loose rein, now."

"O.K., O.K.," said Benny, taking a tighter hold. This was drama, and the breath of life to him; he was the good guy, and he was not going to be thrown; he was the born gambler; the artist holding his own amongst crude sporting types; Hemingway grown up. Falsely dramatic to him, the situation was, to us, genuinely worrying. We were all, in fact, just about as worried as the filly.

"Don't ever do this sort of thing again, darling," Gillian said to me, reprovingly.

"Godammit, I didn't do it."

"You brought Benny here, you *encouraged* it."

The filly began to jiggle restively, switching her tail, and swinging her quarters about. "There's the pet, now, there's the girl," said Aunt Emmy, hopefully. Peter was talking to her in much the same way. We all began to walk after them, up the track, and through the stone-piered gateless entrance into the smaller field and out into the middle of it, from where we could watch them. Peter had turned away to the right as soon as they came through the gateway—he meant to start against the rise of the ground. He began jogging slowly, watching the filly, still talking to her. She skittered about in the sunlight, as sharp as the devil, gay and bright and looking for trouble, half genuinely upset, half mischievous. Peter let the horse break gently into a canter, and she threw her head all ways at once, and proceeded after him in a series of self-willed bounds.

"She's gone," said Dan gloomily. "Good enough for him. She's gone, mind you."

Two strides later she certainly had—tearing off in delight and dismay, uncertain whether she was really scared or not, but pretty hysterical all the same. Peter stood in his stirrups to pull the horse up, and found some difficulty in doing so, because the old boy was all for joining the filly's now mad career, and didn't see any fun at all in stopping. He raked very cheekily indeed at his bit, and had to be pulled off in a circle before he consented to come back and behave himself.

"Nearly went meself," Peter called to us, jogging gently back down the rise of the ground. He was going to stand in the gateway, in case the filly might take a notion, when she came round, of diving off through it for the yard and killing herself somewhere on the way. We were none of us more than worried and annoyed, God help us, because we thought that Benny could just keep her circling until she stopped, and she was fit, and unlikely to harm herself by the gallop, and anyway would probably go to her galloping companion as soon as she saw him standing there. She came round once like a streak of light, not noticing anything at all, while we all made useless soothing noises at her, and then, on her second round of the field, she saw the old horse and made straight for him, coming slightly downhill. If only Benny had let her go on straight nothing would have happened. Nothing. Nothing. She would have propped herself to a shattering halt

231

as she got to him, Benny would most likely have gone over her head. No damage would have been done. It doesn't bear thinking of, now. Benny tried to pull her off to the left as she tore down the rise of the ground, hauling at her until her muzzle was nearly touching his knee, and, thoroughly scared now, determined to get to the horse, she continued to go crabwise downwards, in a series of terrified, blind plunges—that were going to carry her, we saw suddenly, appallingly, into the left-hand stone pier of the gateway. I heard Gillian make a sobbing noise, and Aunt Emmy say, "Oh, no, . . . no."

Dan shouted despairingly, "Let go her head, you fool." Phillippa turned Possum away. The lad standing by me, said, "Jesus, they're quinched," in an unbelieving horrified whisper, and then Peter drove his horse forward and shoved him hard up against the now frantic filly's shoulder, meeting her at an angle, trying to ride her off, to turn her past the point of destruction.

He did it. Everything was so heart-breakingly nearly all right, even then. The old horse's ears were flat back against his head with irritation as the filly plunged up against him, but he was behaving beautifully; they had nudged her past the pier successfully; swung her nearly straight; the fearful, frantic seconds of danger were past: we began to breathe. She took one last sideways plunge against the horse, staggering him back, and he finally stood up himself in protest, nothing very serious. Dan shouted suddenly, hoarsely, hopelessly, "Jesus, mind the ditch there, *Peter*——" and broke off, because it had happened. There was a dry stone wall running off from the pier, and a deep, stony ditch, and they were plunging about right on the edge of it. The horse lost a hind foot down it; toppled, pawed, half-recovered himself, and went over backwards into it, and the filly, losing her balance, went sprawling down on top of him, and Peter was underneath.

When something really appalling happens suddenly, like a fatal, flashing stroke of lightning, in front of your eyes, the mental shock has very nearly the same effect as a physical concussion, with the difference that you do remember the thing itself happening—yet, as in concussion, there is inclined to be a blank between the occurrence and some point in time much later on. People will tell you, "You did this—he did that"—and you don't remember anything about it at all until perhaps days later —then the mental images, curiously isolated and horrifying, lit as brightly and unrelentingly as lantern slides, begin to filter uncertainly back into the shocked, unwilling mind. Peter lived for thirty-six hours after the accident, but it was only long after the funeral that I began to remember; that the images came back and kept me sweatingly awake night after night. Up till then I had remembered nothing between the second in time of the two horses going over into the ditch, and Peter being wheeled out of the operating theatre in Knocklong hospital; gagged and grey-faced, with blood around his mouth, an orderly walking beside him holding up the apparatus for the blood transfusion, and Paddy and the surgeon untying their masks and wiping the sweat from their tired, discouraged faces—faces which shone haggardly in the heartless fluorescent lighting. Neither of them said a word as I got up stiffly from the bench on which I had no idea how long I might have been sitting. The surgeon lit a cigarette and drew on it deeply. The shining corridor echoed around us with clattering hospital noises—the patients were having lunch, I realized, and it seemed an enormity. I didn't ask anything, but finally Paddy said heavily, "I don't know . . . just don't know," running his hand across his eyes. He looked at the surgeon, who went on smoking, and looked at nobody and said, "I never like these crush injuries—better get Moloney down, I think. I'll try him now," and walked away. Paddy said, "I want to take a look at him. Go into my office, will ye, and wait." We went down the stairs in silence, and I suddenly wondered where everybody was and how in hell I had got to the hospital. In the next corridor Paddy said, "Carry on now, and left then. Name on the door. I'll get ye a drink in a minute." He opened a door. Number 32. Behind that anonymity Peter was going to live or die. I caught a glimpse of a white coat, and the smell of ether and antiseptics came reeking out at me, and I suddenly knew I was going to be sick. There was a sluice near by, luckily, and an extremely kind old sister happened to be there, who held my head for me and was neither surprised nor shocked nor unduly sympathetic, but blessedly matter of fact; and said that she had heard that Lord Dungarvan was very bad, but, sure, weren't we all in the hands of God?

We were all pretending to eat luncheon at home the following day when Paddy rang up from the hospital. He said, "Could ye come out now? He's conscious, and he wants to talk to you—can ye bring your mother? Can she leave the child?"

"I don't know," I said.

"I'll tell ye why, 'tis her he needs, but he's afraid 'twould trouble her."

"Is he very bad, Paddy?" But I knew. The desperate hardness of his voice told me.

After a pause he said shortly, "He's bad enough."

"We'll come now," I said, and put down the receiver and went to find my mother.

Peter was lying flat, without any pillows, and he kept

weakly, restlessly, moving his head, trying to find some ease. Thin curtains were drawn across the window, and he looked greenish in the half-light. A nurse got up and went out as I came in.

"I can't bloody well see you," he said, in a slurred, hoarse voice. His eye was blackened and swollen, and his upper lip was stitched. The most inconsiderable facial injuries can appear shocking, and his were not inconsiderable. He had not got his black patch on, either, and I had never realized before how disfigured that side of his face was. He looked terrible, but it was not that that mattered. It was the unmistakable, irremediable mark of death in his face that coldly horrified me. I had seen it too often during the war not to recognize now that drained and hollow look, the fatal, final stamp. I took the hand he moved slightly, gropingly, towards me, and said inadequately, "I'm sorry, old boy," and tried not to listen to his short, painful breathing.

"Can't talk very well either," he said, running his words together. "You understand me, all right?"

"Yes, easily."

"Wanted to ask you—am I too much of a mess for the child to see?"

I said, "Yes, I think so, Peter." I tried to say it without hesitation, and my voice sounded extraordinarily hard and clear and unsympathetic in my own ears.

"Thanks," he said. "Damn cagey nurses won't say a thing." He paused, and moved his head again uneasily and caught his breath—a very slight sound in the stillness, but the sound of pain itself, more heart-breakingly eloquent than anything else could have been. He squinted up at me worriedly and asked, "Your mother mind seeing me?"

"No, of course she wouldn't mind, Peter, of course not."

His face relaxed. He even smiled, in so far as he was physically able to smile.

"Don't care for it much yourself, boy?"

"Peter," I said. "My God, I'm sorry."

"Thing is, I'm so bloody worried about my child."

"I know. Mamma's here, she came with me."

He sighed, and tried another position for his head, and found it was no good, and rolled it tiredly back again. "Am I making sense?" he asked anxiously. "I'm full of dope."

"You're making sense all right. Don't worry, old boy."

Paddy came in then, and Peter said to him, in the flat, uninflected tones of exhaustion, "Let me be, now, don't let any damn nurse in again."

"I won't, sure," said Paddy, gently, his gay, puggy face stony with sorrow. "Be easy, now."

I said, "I'll fetch my mamma, Peter."

"Won't mind, will she?"

"No, of course she won't."

He said fretfully, wearily, "It's such a bloody silly way to die."

I looked down at him, wondering how he had been able, in the short, brutal time during which he had been conscious, to think of whether my mother would mind or not, to think of asking me first. He needed his hand held very badly, but he had thought of everything but that.

When I tried to explain all this to my mother, and to tell her about his face, and how worried he was, she said only, "It's all right, darling"—and it seemed, mercifully, when she said it, that it was.

She said exactly the same to Peter, when he was strugglingly trying to think of, and put into the words that were beginning to elude him cruelly, everything that should be done for his child; "It's all right, darling," and he believed her, too, and gave up the burden gratefully, and allowed Paddy to give him morphia. Paddy did not swab his arm before he gave the injection, and the absence of that familiar gesture was icily final—my mother looked at him, and down again at Peter, who, very drowsy, suddenly remembered something else and made one last, tearing effort. "Suky." He was very nearly impossible to understand. "Don't want her hanging about for me."

"No, of course not, of course we won't let her—don't worry, darling, it's all right."

"Not a gun," he said, "Paddy?"

Paddy bent over him and said very clearly, "I'll give her something. She likes me, you know."

Peter said, "Shameless bitch," with another stiff, wavering smile; drifting into sleep; into death.

Dead people, regardless of what may be popularly accepted, do not look noble, peaceful saintly, translated, or indeed, anything at all. They look dead. That is that. "How much another thing, no more that man!" a poet once rightly said about a dead man, and anybody who has had acquaintance with death will know with what bitter correctness he observed the phenomenon. Peter had been a great man—middle-aged, red-faced, heroic. Now he was dead, and something so other from the man that was that there seemed nothing else to be said or done or suffered. "For my part——" the great Voltaire had said in his humility "—I know very little about the soul. Young priests and students know all these things perfectly, but I am a very ignorant fellow. I know not where it is, nor what it is, now whether it is." Neither did I know, and there was no comfort in the world, not even a small earthy one. I longed to be able to tell Peter about his last words, and hear his comment—it was impossibly painful to realize that I never could. When we had left him I said this to my mother. She said: "He would have loved it."

The bright, shocking lantern slides went flickering through my mind. The filly had thrashed her way up out of the ditch as Dan and I ran down to it. Dan was talking all the time he ran; an endless flow of nervous, sobbing blasphemy. I had suddenly remembered Gillian, and turned and shouted at her, in desperate anger, to stay away. She said afterwards that she had thought I was going to hit her. Aunt Emmy had put her arm round her and turned her away. Benny was sitting on the ground with his head in his hands. The filly seemed to be treading all over him as she struggled up, but he did not move. The lad caught hold of her, and then gave her to Sarah, who had run with us. The filly was black with sweat, and pointing a foreleg stiffly out sideways. Even then, my brain had registered "Shoulder".

Sarah had been there, I remembered, because I saw her suddenly, putting her arm round Dan as he crawled out of the ditch and was sick, after we had got the horse up. The horse had been cast, and struggling wildly, and Dan had gone unhesitatingly down into the ditch and wedged as much of himself as he could between the horse and Peter, and stayed there as we got the horse up; crouched; automatically and inadequately trying to protect himself by clasping his hands across the back of his head; waiting for the kicks; waiting for the horse to fall back; waiting for the familiar, sickening punishment that he dreaded more than anything else in the world.

I remember the horse snorting in a shocked way above me on the skyline, and shaking himself with a thunderous slapping of leather, as I knelt down by Peter, and Dan saying groggily, "For God's sake, don't move him. Get Paddy. Get blankets," and Sarah telling the lad to put her up on the horse, and one glimpse of her weeping as she belted him off down to the house.

I think Phillippa came and took Benny away.

Dan and I took off our coats and put them over Peter. Then for an eternity there was nothing to do, nowhere to look, except at him, and nothing to say.

We were conscious of the filly standing above and behind us, drooping, quivering, sweating, pointing her leg. The lad said hoarsely, fearfully breaking the silence. "She isn't able to move at all now—will I tell them below get Mr. O'Shaughnessy?"
"Yes," said Dan dully. "He'll need a gun."
Presently Aunt Emmy was there again, and stood by the filly and rubbed her ears, and lads came up from the house with blankets and stood nervously around, small, shocked, shuffling figures above us, until Dan snarled at them and they went away. I said to Aunt Emmy, "Where's his child?" My voice would not work properly, and I wasn't sure I had spoken, but she said, "Sophia has her."

Some time after that the ambulance came roaring and skidding through the gateway. Paddy had come out in it, and I felt then, for a moment, ridiculously, as if every-thing would now be all right—as if Paddy, by his presence, by merely being a doctor, could undo everything that had been done.

Gillian said to me, now, as we went to put a fiver on Willy's horse, "You can't go on feeling like this, darling; you can't, you mustn't. Peter could have been killed

239

hunting any day, or years ago at Liverpool, or just fallen downstairs after dinner. You know that."

"I know all the right, reasonable answers and arguments, and not one of them does any good."